SPIRE

Other books by Aaron Safronoff

Evening Breezes
Fallen Spire
Sunborn Rising: Beneath the Fall

SPIRE

BY AARON SAFRONOFF

NEOGLYPHIC ENTERTAINMENT

CALIFORNIA

To my brothers:
Jason, Mark, Jeremy, Joe, Aaron.
I hope I've made all of you proud.

~ ~ ~ ~ ~

For Brock.

FOREWORD

I published *Spire* for the first time in 2011, more than ten years after conceiving the story. Back then, the entire concept existed as a single complete scene. Not a story, not really. Joshua, his environment, the timbre of his inner voice, and the tone of the narrative were established, but that was all. To be clear, I didn't then--and I still don't--think of writing as a mechanical process. I didn't write the treatment for the novel as a character or environment study. I didn't write the treatment for a novel of any kind. I simply misremembered something that happened to me, and wrote it down.

From that first complete scene the novel developed the way all my stories do, the way I like to imagine that storytelling began: people sharing their unique perspectives of a single shared experience. I picture hunters gathered around a fire, each person telling her version of the pursuit and the takedown, trying to assemble the truth of what happened from the independent details. They argue, but inevitably reach consensus, and from that they generate a single historical record, forming one shared reality. The Story. The only difference in my authorship is that all of the hunters exist exclusively in my head. Getting them all to agree is the difficult part, but that's writing. That's how I wrote, *Spire*.

In general, I do not return to works that I've published or widely distributed because I no longer consider those works to be mine alone. The imperfections and unintended meanings are as much a part of the story as anything else. It's surreal to return to *Spire* after all this time and consider making any changes, but that's what was asked of me. I've done my best to fix items that I believe readers would have "fixed" on their own in order to make sense of a sentence. Otherwise, honoring those first readers who believed in the novel enough to spend some time in my world, I've elected not to make other edits. To all of the early fans, "The *Spire* you remember is the *Spire* that was--and remains--the conduit connecting our universes together." And to the uninitiated, "Welcome. Enjoy. Thank you."

Sincerely,

-Aaron Safronoff

SPIRE

BY AARON SAFRONOFF

Orginal cover by Joseph Garhan

Down Time

One

I liked coming down. I liked the way it solidified my sense of solidarity. I took comfort in watching the people around me, the way they were consumed entirely by the concerns of day-to-day existence. These people, they seemed to move quickly and with purpose, but when I was on my way down that impression changed. On my way down, the motivations of the world slowed and the people did too. They began to float like they were moving through water, and I floated along with them.

The street was a strong current, sucking some people up along with it while it pushed others aside. The river of traffic along the road dropped off new faces and carried others away, mixing them up. Those that were carried away were immediately replaced by new, completely satisfactory replacements.

A brief-cased-male, five-foot-nine, dark hair and suitable shoes, with matching suit and tie, hailed a taxi, got in, and disappeared completely. Next, a perfectly coifed female, standing an easy six, carrying a sleek leather-pouch-folder-thing in her left hand, raised her right to bring, was that the same taxi?, to a brief stop. She too, was sucked into the current. But sucked into the space she left behind, was another.

1

It wasn't just the young urban professionals. The drunkards and harlots were just as easily interchangeable. It didn't really matter. The fat, the handsome, the toothless, the pregnant, the strung-out, the straight-haired, the loose-legged, and the tight-assed were all so…indistinguishable when I was on my way down. I might have seen them as equally indistinct while sober, sure, but I was not an authority on that state of mind.

Where was I going…? Oh yeah, solidarity. Right. Solidarity, because I could be any one of them. Solidarity, because I was never more a part of the community than when I was sitting there on that bus stop bench, floating right along with them.

My friend, Demy, he says coming down is the hardest part. Or maybe that was a song? Something like that. Anyway, he describes the experience as completely unholy, unreasonable torture, as though his happiness is slipping away in an agonizing, slow, un-medicated, tooth-pull. He wanted to be back There.

But I didn't get it.

When I'm dosed on…well anything that's worthwhile, I'm not really There. See, that's the point of dropping chems. Your 'I' slips into this limbo-abyss nirvana-euphoria and loses all reference points. Coming down is really more like coming back, very slowly, to self-awareness. Quite honestly, I am so amazed to find my body after a trip that I get a little weepy happy. But you really don't know where you were once you're completely back, so coming down is the only time that your 'eye' really gets to enjoy anything. Coming down is when I get to see where I was while the trail is still burned against the sky. Coming back, the body is fresh, every movement fascinating, each wrinkle curious.

Anyway, I didn't know why Demy hated coming down so much. It wasn't as though he wasn't "leaving" again anytime soon. There were millions of ways to fade out. All reasonably priced, all reasonably available.

One just had to know when to be Here.

"You got a light, Jack?"

"Sure," my name wasn't Jack, but it could have been.

I pulled a Zippo out of my jacket pocket and flipped the lid. As Harley sat down beside me, he casually lifted the lighter from my offering hand and dropped his thumb quickly down the wheel. I felt the echo on my thumb as the wheel's steel teeth bit into his thumbprint. The flame slipped out with a purr, then flickered quietly. He took a long drag on a clove. The crackling sound, a quick-crushed-paper sack, was like Harley camping in the cave of my ear.

"You got some money for me?"

His question brought me around, stirred me up, put me in motion, and brought some sense of the familiar to the surface.

"Sure, sure." I reached down deep into the pockets of my jacket. I know the money will be there. It is always there.

These types of interactions, the back and forth and squaring off, were necessary to maintain a sense of broadcast-reality. The passing of money and goods between two no good hoodlums is a classic scene. It felt different though, when you were in the scene, when you were the hoodlum. But when the transaction goes smoothly, you feel like you've done the right thing.

I pinched a folded bunch of bills and extracted them calmly from my breast pocket. The denim jacket had been with me through so much that its smell and weight were as familiar as my own skin. It was a little heavy today which basically meant that I didn't trust Harley at all. I hoped I wasn't showing.

The bills were folded once, but smooth otherwise. I vaguely remembered counting out the amount obsessively, flattening each paper again and again. Of course, the last time was completely indistinguishable from all the times before it, and it occurred to me that I might be visualizing several separate instances as one event. Didn't matter.

Only one thing mattered at this point: the quality of the shit this asshole was going to pull out of his pocket. Good shit and everything would be good. Low-grade, cut-bag and I would have to play it cool while I figured out my next move. It was a fine line that I knew well enough, but knowing it didn't make it any easier to handle.

"I couldn't find what you wanted, but I got something even better. It'll go twice as far, twice as long, and it'll go for the same price. Consider it a favor."

This guy was talking too much already. Not a good sign. Changes are rarely good in this business. Paranoia being the prime side effect of the lifestyle, change invited all varieties of lengthy and expensive thoughts. And I've never met a dealer who does favors.

"Street name?" I kept it brief.

The money was out already because I had been operating on auto-pilot a few seconds ago, but I was growing more alert by the second, adrenaline kicking in. This little give-and-take was going to require my full attention, if I didn't want to get taken.

It was time to size this guy up, not chit-chat. I couldn't get caught up in the words. His eyes were a little jumpy as he sized me up, too. The dealer always thinks he's smarter than the user. But I wasn't a casual user and he knew it. So why size me up? What's he worried about?

Shit, I'm already doing loops. Talking myself in circles.

He's going to get the money one way or the other: conclusion.

"Pez. Really nice trip. Set aside a day or two though…and don't expect instant action. It takes a bit to get rollin'…"

He kept talking but I wasn't listening anymore. The sky was a crispy blue, and I was chilly. Was it March? October? It felt like spring or fall but there wasn't a tree in sight to verify one or the other.

"Pez."

I recognized the name. Some hippy punk kid called the new designer drug the Pleasure Zone, and Pez followed quickly and stuck.

My breath was condensing in the air. My skin was a little itchy and my bones were a little achy. My eyes were glassing over. Shit. I couldn't remember the chemical name for Pez. I remembered the courses, the hours reading over the material, but I couldn't remember the name of the drug.

Consideration time was up.

I nodded. Seemed appropriate. He seemed to buy it. So did I.

That was it. I gave him another nod and a perfunctory pleasantry. I traded my cash for his satchel of happiness. I got up smoothly from the bench and took my leave of that life, that scene, that event…it was already behind me. Really, so far behind me that I wasn't sure it happened at all.

My feet were heavy, but my stride was confident. I thought about the Pez in my pocket. I thought about the thirty hours of endorphins and asphyxiatic dreams that waited for me. I thought about the possibility that this shit could be my last. I should have been more careful.

I liked coming down. I liked coming down, but I hated crashing down. It was time to take another trip.

SPIRE

The Pleasure Zone

Two

Twenty minutes.

Nothing.

I needed an innocuous and mundane task to waste some time and get my mind off the anticipation. My apartment didn't have much to offer in the way of distractions though, because I didn't spend much conscious time there.

There was a hideaway bed, revealed, and unmade, taking up the bulk of the space of the room. It was a little sad looking with a pillow drooping half off the mattress and a blanket rolled and wrinkled at the foot. There was a standard Wall displaying my last search and a stream I didn't care about above a base-model Desk opposite the bed. The kitchenette in the corner served no purpose except to accumulate the unnecessary, daily sludge of living. There was a pile of junk mail in the sink and trash on the counter, neither of which was distinguishable from the other. For that matter, the kitchenette area was not really distinguishable from the rest of the studio, save the linoleum tile floor that bared itself there like a bald spot in the carpet. Cold and stained, it almost made the carpet look inviting. Finally, there was an armchair. Which I was sitting on. And me, of course.

I guess I could count the closet to the right of the apartment door as something if it contained anything at all. And then there was the bathroom to the left...

What was in that bathroom? I tried to picture it but I couldn't. It was interesting to me that I couldn't remember the contents of my own bathroom, and that was motivation enough for me to make the trip. Off to the restroom I went.

Walking to the bathroom was a vigorous exercise of sixteen steps. The sliding door to the bathroom was open as expected. It was dark, but as I crossed the threshold the luminosity adjusted to match the main room.

Luminosity. I stood there just inside the bathroom, and chewed on the word for a minute. *Luminosity.*

Lew-Min Gnaw's City. This bathroom belonged to him, to Lew-Min, the spider in the corner of the ceiling, above the sink.

"What do you want Lew?" He just stared at me with disdain, like I should have known what he was thinking.

Strangely, outside of Lew's web, the rest of the bathroom was clean. It was almost pristine compared to the clutter in the rest of the tiny apartment. There was even toilet paper available in the dispenser which I could not recall having replaced. The toilet paper, I kept that in the cabinet beneath the sink.

The cabinet.

There was something about that cabinet. I stared at it anticipating... something, I had no idea what, but I was excited. It was patiently waiting for me. It wanted to be opened. What was it about that cabinet?

Wait, wait. What was I doing in here? I blinked my eyes and rubbed my face vigorously. My heart felt stiff and hot. My skin began urgently nagging me to remove my shirt. Itchy and hot and terribly uncomfortable there in the bathroom, I decided to obey my skin's desires.

My hand shook as I slid down the smooth-zip on the front of my shirt. It parted down the middle, cleanly, and I shrugged the shirt off, allowing it to fall to the floor.

Both of my hands were shaking as I put them on the sink counter to settle myself, to steady myself. I accidentally triggered both the faucet and the Mirror. The rush of sound from the water falling into the sink fell over my mind like a curtain.

I looked up into the Mirror and the magnified image of my face stared back at me. The Mirror must have been malfunctioning because my face appeared bulbous, my cheek bones pronounced to a ridiculous degree. It was an altogether unseemly and disturbing image. I shook my head.

Whoa. Euphoria. Vertigo.

It took me a few seconds to recover and to focus, then a brief happy memory occurred to me from somewhere over my shoulder. The memory was like a lighthouse beacon calling my attention to the Pez I swallowed earlier. It cast warmth on my back and soothed my nerves. But the warmth, the light only remained diffuse for a few seconds, and then it focused and moved down. Eventually it became a beam, directed right at my tailbone.

I was warm all over but at the base of my spine, in that one spot touched by the light, the strongest feeling sat. The focused warmth moved slowly but steadily up my back. Each vertebra was excited and heated gradually.

My eyes rolled and found the back of my skull as I inhaled, filling my ribs with the progression of the light. My hands lifted from the counter as my chest expanded and the focus of light reached the base of my neck. Every hair in my head lit up like a fiber optic pincushion and I exhaled loudly in the ecstasy of the moment. My hands, were they mine?, rubbed my face and scratched my head vigorously.

The drug's effects had crept right up on me like a cat, like a thief. Pez the cat had stolen my awareness right out from in front of me and made me smile as it passed. I marveled at it, impressed.

I peered into the mirror which displayed the left half of my face only, an eye, a portion of my eyebrow, and my cheek. The view was a customized setting that I used for placing and removing contact lenses.

My pupil appeared small in the pseudo-reflection. I couldn't help but be mesmerized by it. Then, as I stared deeper into it, it began to grow. A giddy-rush filled me with expectation. The pupil was growing, swallowing up the blue, the natural blue, of my iris. It was eating it, absorbing it.

Another pleasurable flood drenched me as I realized the pupil was actually pushing through the iris, not digesting it. The blue was peeling back to accommodate a lengthening and broadening black protrusion. The blackness grew and elongated and stretched out of the mirror. I was paralyzed by the intense pleasure of anticipation, the thought of my pupil touching its own reflection.

My chest gave and I heaved forward with another rush of hot air. I held myself there, head hanging down, looking at nothing for several seconds. Then I realized the water was still running.

I touched the counter lightly and the Mirror flickered off. I touched it again, lightly again, dramatically, and the faucet dispensed with its dispensing. I smiled a ridiculous smile.

"Oh, this is good shit." I shuddered a bit happily.

The cabinet.

I turned my attention there once again. Scared, exhilarated, intensely hot, sweating, and giddy, I was drawn to touch the sliding panel that hid that space and to discover the contents of that little place. The place beneath the sink. My hands steady, I knelt down and stared at the door. Reaching up, I slid my finger along the near edge of the counter.

The door panel parted swiftly and I fell to the floor as water poured out from the cabinet driving over me and pushing me down. Staring at the ceiling, there was only one sensation, the cool flood drenching my skin. I was vaguely aware of my hands unfastening my belt buckle, unbuttoning my pants and sliding them from my body. I was relieved to have removed the fetters of my clothing.

Lew-Min made eye contact with me again. He was mocking me with an enormous smile. He was spinning a descending thread. He was floating down to the sink. He was stealthily stepping to the edge of the counter. He had an interesting glint in his eye.

He knew something I didn't know.

He was motionless for a moment as he looked for a position even closer to my head. Then his spindly legs started up again, smooth and silky, and my eyes were drawn to his movements.

Lew-Min had something for me. He slid down another thread and out of sight. I thought my eyes were closed… *when did I close them?*

I felt a heavy touch on my shoulder. My shoulder shook. Lew-Min must have grown considerably in the last few moments.

With a force of pure will I opened my eyes to take a look at the new bigger and badder Lew. A long, black, hairy arm was there hovering over my face. There was a suction cup attached to the end of it. My head was lifted toward it, and the cup was sealed around my mouth and nose.

I couldn't breathe.

I couldn't breathe.

I couldn't breathe but the ecstasy pouring through my body, the water dousing my skin in cool waves, the closeness of the best orgasm imaginable prevented me from caring anymore. Suddenly, I was seized. It was rapture so pure and undeniable, that I felt completely free. I was just rolling and flying, everywhere and nowhere at all. There was an echo of coherent thought making its way to the surface; there were hours left of this.

Pez was good.

…

"Look at this one."

"Holy shit."

11

"Is he stable?"

"Every time I clean him up he just messes himself again."

"Check out those pupils…"

"Yeah, guy's completely gone."

"Pry his lids open. Let me shine a light in there."

"Sure thing… uh, there. Shit."

"No kidding. It's like shining a light into a couple of black holes. Can you make out his eye color? I can't even see an outline of color."

"Nah. There's nothin' there."

"Well, this is definitely the guy. No Chip and his Creds match up."

"So, we're takin' this piece of shit to the Spire?"

"Yes. Put some clothes on him. Let's go."

"Sure thing, but what about the…?" A wet, plastic glove snapped, and then crumpled to the ground.

"Button him up. He can have all the fun he wants as long as it's in his pants."

The Chemist

Three

The man sat at his Desk, intently studying the chemical reactions displayed on the Wall. The bright colors of the reactions were reflected in his spectacles as he furrowed his brow at the images. He focused on one morsel of data after another, chewing up bit after bit of the complex readout.

He touched the top of his Desk with only his fingertips, tapping and sliding them along the smooth surface. The display of the reaction stopped, and the focus slid around, following the movement of his fingers. He found something of interest and gradually increased the magnification, sliding his pointer finger forward. He stared deeply and leaned even closer to the Wall.

The man's attention shifted suddenly to the hologram on his right.

The source of the hologram was a heavy-looking instrument, an elementary particle projector. The black metallic base of the instrument was a perfectly square brick, about four inches thick and about eight inches to a side. The top inch tapered toward the center, creating a truncated pyramidal shape. Out from the base, several shiny probes, lights, and knobs, protruded at various and irregular intervals.

His hands deftly adjusted several settings on the base, which adjusted the image. He turned one knob, then another. The floating globule of a hologram grew and swayed and came back into focus. A window on the Wall began scrolling text. The readout described complex chemical relationships among the viewed molecules with highlighted linkages, hue-shifted to represent attractions and energies.

He read.

Eventually, he tilted his head to the left, and then to the right. He took a deep breath and quietly sighed back into his chair. He slumped a bit. Finally, he relaxed his face, which revealed kind and round cheeks. He closed his eyes and looked down, removed his glasses with one hand, and massaged the bridge of his nose with the other. Setting his glasses down on the Desk, he rubbed his face with both hands, exhausted.

It's been a long night, the Chemist thought to himself. Tapping the Desk, he turned the microscope off and then changed the Wall with a few gentle strokes. The display became blue and liquid, rippling and shimmering; an underwater camera pointing to the sky.

The Chemist's room was a small and cluttered space. Books and papers littered the floor and several tabletops, but his Desk was clear. There was a bookshelf awkwardly placed in the center of the room, separating the kitchenette from the Desk area.

The room was mostly dark and warm. The watery Wall display was accompanied by liquid audio; the overall effect calmed and relaxed the man and nearly lulled him to sleep. The Chemist was just about to nod off when a scratching at his window startled him.

He turned around in his chair and looked in the direction of the disturbance. The window was closed and there was nothing obvious that he could see to explain the scratching sound. Peering into the distance through the window, he tried to focus on something, anything, but there was only darkness there and nothing more. Nothing obvious anyway, so he hefted himself up out of his chair and began ambling across the room.

The floor creaked under his weight. He put his face to the window and stared into the night. What little light there was in the room still managed to create some reflections in the pane, so the Chemist leaned in closer to the window, his hands cupped around his face; he touched the cool, smooth surface of the glass.

There was a casual knock at the door.

The Chemist turned his head too quickly, and his neck and back tightened in a brief spasm. He immediately began rubbing between the base of his neck and his shoulder. He listened intently for any other sound, some indication that the visitor had left or that maybe the knock was at the next door and not his?

Knock-knock, this time slightly more assertive.

The Chemist, more alert, slowly walked over to his desk. His attempt to move silently failed. The floorboards punctuated each step with a creak or groan, and he seemed much louder this time coming back across the room. He slid a finger quickly across the surface of the front of the Desk, and a drawer slid open. He lifted the gun out, uncertain, then slowly pushed the drawer closed. He tapped several buttons on the surface of the Desk and a thin red line demarcated and slightly illuminated the keys.

He walked haltingly to the door. Not sure how he should hold his gun, he awkwardly tucked it close to his side as though to obscure it from view even though the knocker could not see inside. He touched the center of the door with a single finger. The door flickered to life with the bright light of the hallway, a face, and a fist that was about to knock again.

"Oh, hey, decided to come to your door? *Finally.* Come on, open up and let me in." The man looked around as though he saw back through the door but really he was only reacting to the tiny red light on the exterior that came on when the Chemist began viewing the hall.

Vanya, whew. "I wasn't expecting you. Uh, just a minute." The color returned to his face as he walked back to his Desk and quickly placed the gun back in its drawer.

"Hey, come on! What are you doing in there, Gabe? Let me in. It's not exactly summer out here..." The man spoke into the door, urgently at first, and then trailed off to himself.

"Actually, I wasn't expecting anyone tonight." The Chemist was nervous as he opened the door just a crack.

"I wasn't expecting to be here... Gabe, I've got news. We have to talk."

Gabe was blocking the way with his body, holding the toe of his shoe against the bottom of the door. After a moment, though, he acquiesced. He stepped back and turned on the light, letting go his paranoia. Vanya wasn't exactly the trustworthy sort but he was paid well enough. "Sure, sure. Come in. Come in, Vanya."

"Thank you," the man said dryly. "Honestly, I don't know why you are so paranoid. Where do I put my...?" The man looked around for a bit then just dropped his coat on the floor.

"Yeah, just put it anywhere," Gabe grumbled to himself, then petulantly, "What are you doing here anyway? I don't have much to offer a guest. How about scotch?"

"Nah, nah," he waved both hands dramatically, "I have to keep my head on straight. There are some heavy hitters looking for you, my friend. I've been baiting the line and some nibblers have contacted me."

"Well, don't keep me in suspense," as Gabe bent down to pick up Vanya's jacket.

"First, I think you should lie down." Vanya sneered as he stepped full force into the back of Gabe's right knee and in the same motion, reached his hand around, and covered Gabe's mouth as he fell hard to the ground. There was a snapping sound inside Gabe's knee as it bore the full weight of his body. He grunted, a sound full of pain and confusion.

Vanya was kneeling partially beside and partially on top of Gabe, applying extraordinary pressure to Gabe's mouth. Gabe felt like his teeth might push right through his lips or his head through the floor. The Chemist tried to unfold his leg but was met with swift, searing pain.

"I know this suddenly seems complicated, Gabriel; but it's really pretty simple."

Gabe's eyes were glassed-over and quivering. The pain and fear made it almost impossible for him to focus, for him to understand what was happening.

"You paid me to keep an eye on inquiries into your whereabouts, investigate anything suspicious. Well, I did just that. Found some pretty impressive information."

He leaned in closer, "Do you have any idea who is looking for you?" slowly, he articulated each word with greater emphasis than the last, bemused.

Vanya waited, eyebrows raised, reading the face of his victim.

Gabriel's shaky blue eyes pled for relief from the pain, pled to be released.

"Yeah, I didn't think so. Well, Gabe, these people are pretty damn well connected." Vanya reached into his back pocket. "A couple of anonymous, but sufficiently detailed emails made their way into the right mailboxes and the next thing you know... we're here."

Vanya shrugged, "They made me a pretty impressive offer: this," he reached into his back pocket and pulled out a palm-sized piece of clear, flat, thick Glass.

"On," the Glass turned opaque and lit up.

"Recent," several icons appeared.

"Ophthalmology," the icons faded out and faded back in, rearranged alphabetically. The icon at the top-left looked like a photograph of a woman.

"Closest, Open" The photograph icon expanded and a picture of a gorgeous woman's face, half in sharp focus, the other half blurry, was at the center with the caption, "See what life has to offer." The accompanying text described why full orbital replacement was superior to intraocular lens technology, but the text was cut off by the edge of the view.

Vanya held the Glass so that he could see the image himself. "The surgery is expensive. I could probably afford it, but the military-grade occipital neuroface, and ten-times zoom, reflexive-lens implant? That isn't exactly legal. Which tags the price up with a few trailing zeros."

He held the picture so that Gabe could see it again. "I'm thinking I'll go thermographic... forgive me, I'm losing the thread here... I said this was simple and it is. I get this..." He emphasized the advertisement by giving the Glass a little shake.

"When you give me..." then a little mechanically, "Mail, From, "Sharp," Closest, Open." The crystal clear image on the Glass morphed quickly and fluidly with each command. The dizzying display stopped at a simple picture of someone's office whiteboard. Chemical symbols, numbers, and equations filled the space. And one large question mark. "This."

Gabe struggled a bit, but it only sharpened the pain and deepened his anxiety. He could not see his knee, but he imagined someone driving a screw into it with a hammer.

Vanya removed his hand from Gabe's mouth. Gabe raised his head a couple of inches on impulse, sensing escape and relief. Vanya slapped him, still holding the Glass steadily in his left hand. He leaned deeper with his knee, and shoved his hand back into Gabe's face in a flash, slamming his head back down to the floor. A dull thud. A moan.

"Focus." Vanya stared deeply into the blue eyes. The eyes finally focused and stared intently back at him.

"There," Vanya spoke calmly, directly, "There's no escaping this, fat boy. You're going to give me what I came here to get. You know I'm not leaving until I get it. Take another look." Vanya shook the Glass and motioned to it with his eyes and a tilt of his head before staring back at Gabe.

"Don't just look at it; read it."

A kind of calm blanketed Gabe as he squinted to read the formulas on the whiteboard in the picture. Vanya held the Glass closer to Gabe to help him see. The pain and the situation fell into the background as Gabe worked on the numbers and pictograms. He thought it odd to have everything written out by hand, or to even use a whiteboard, but it was familiar to him nonetheless.

"There. Now, put your mind to work. In fact, I'm going to help you out." Vanya eased up, removing some pressure. "I think you know you can't run with that leg..." He removed his hand from Gabe's mouth slowly. There was some blood on his lips and in his nose, and a splotchy red patch on his cheek.

"Let's make that leg more comfortable, too. Whaddya say?" Vanya took his weight completely off of Gabe and slowly, gingerly, unfolded the twisted leg.

Gabe moaned, "Fuck," through his clenched teeth.

"Better?" Vanya patted the side of the injured knee, drawing another wince and groan from the wounded Chemist. "Now, I need you to fill in that blank. And don't think you're going to fool me with some random symbols or something like that. I'll be checking your work with my client."

Vanya slid his Glass into the back pocket of his jeans.

"What makes you think..." a pause, a wince, "... that I even understand it?"

"I'm not going to kill you, Gabe."

Vanya waits for the words to sink in.

"I'm not." He shrugged nonchalantly. "I'm not afraid of you Gabe. You have nothing. You're not calling the local arm of the Collective that's for sure. What's that on your Desk? No way does that equipment belong to you."

Gabe knew each object in his apartment, each piece of lab equipment, each book. He knew which ones were stolen, which ones were illegal to have, and which ones were both. He was obsessed.

"But, I really don't understand it, not all of it anyway."

"Look Gabe, I'm not going to kill you, but I will finish this job. I'm telling you so you don't waste my time, our time. Let's not play games. You understand. I know that you do."

Gabe propped himself up on his elbows and looked down at his leg. "I don't believe this is happening... "

"Believe it."

Nervously, "Well, I understand some of it," a shrug, "I mean, that's what I've been working on, but I'm still working on it. I could never have predicted the effects I've seen... the virtually inert compounds inexplicably change and become reactive... "

Vanya placed his hand gently on the swelling knee.

Gabe, nonplussed, defensively blurts out, "What?! What do you want? I'm explain–"

A slight squeeze, "I'm not here for a science lesson. You have a sample. A sample of brain tissue. You will give me that sample. You have a full recording of the reaction. You will give me that recording. You can answer the question mark in the picture, and you will."

"The sample? You can have it," Gabe smiled hysterically, "Take it. The recording, too... neither will do you any good. You can't synthesize the missing piece." He began laughing, a slight nervous twitter. "I can't anyway. That question mark? Yeah, even with all the information, there is no explanation."

Vanya sized up his captive. He leaned deeply into the Chemist's personal space. Gabe tried to shrink away. His body shriveled and collapsed, and his nose inexplicably closer to the ground, pushed through his face. A bead of sweat formed on his forehead. Vanya and Gabe were close enough to feel the heat of each other's skin.

After a moment, Vanya sat up. He looked toward the red lines illuminating the Desk. "Unlock the Desk. I'll take everything you've got."

20

Vanya positioned himself behind Gabe, who was now up on his elbows, grimacing. "Ready?" he asked, and without waiting for a reply, he looped his arms around Gabe's chest and hauled him across the floor. He stepped behind the desk chair, holding Gabe out in front of him, and deposited the unbalanced Chemist in it, not completely without care.

Gabe steadied himself with the arms of the chair. He took a deep breath, and felt his aching knee with both hands, evaluating the injury.

"Here, allow me." Vanya grabbed the back of the chair and turned the Chemist to face his Desk, sliding him into position.

"Whoa! Whoa. Okay."

Gabe's hands were shaking and hot. Each stroke on the Desk left an ephemeral, foggy ghost print as he entered the password. The red outline disappeared, and the Desk keys illuminated softly.

"Drop everything on this." Vanya placed his Glass on the Desk, eliciting a quick light scan. The Wall flickered to life. A new window appeared, and then rapidly faded away, an acknowledgement of the newly connected device. Vanya executed an elaborate set of strokes on the face of the Glass.

Gabe located his spectacles, and put them on. And though he was tense, he went to work locating and transferring files. His fingers were light and fast as they danced across the surface. Never needing to look down at his hands, he just stared into the display.

Scratch, another sound at the window. Scratching, like an animal trying to get in or like someone trying to get everyone's attention.

Vanya and Gabe turned to look simultaneously at the window.

"I thought you said you weren't expecting anyone tonight?"

"I'm not... uh, I heard it before," he shrugged, "I mean, earlier, before you... I'm sure it's nothing."

Vanya looked down at Gabe, whose hands were still at the ready, poised above the keys. It was quiet again. The room was motionless.

Scratch. Vanya's head snapped back to the window, focusing intently. The scratch was unmistakably deliberate.

Let me in.

Let me out.

Over here.

Not a branch. Not the wind.

Still, there was no obvious source.

Vanya looked back at Gabe, the window, and Gabe again. Gabe shrugged slowly. Vanya looked back to the darkness beyond the window. He took some tentative steps toward it before he looked back at Gabe.

"Back to work, Gabe."

Gabe busied himself once again with the transfer of files to Vanya's Glass.

At the window, Vanya discovered nothing out of the ordinary. He put his face up to the pane and tried to look into the corners of the night. Far below and several yards away, a single streetlight was still working, casting a halo over an aging car and an overturned reclamation can. There was also a tree, its leaves rustling from a gentle breeze. The ledge beneath the window couldn't possibly support more than a squirrel or a pigeon. While still looking out, Vanya moved his hands around the interior border of the window.

Vanya looked back at Gabe, who was focused on the Wall, hands masterfully busy at the keys.

"How do you open this?"

Without turning, Gabe responded, "It's old, manual. You just lift from the bottom."

Attention back on the window, Vanya inspected the bottom and found a place to fit his fingers. He pulled lightly at first, but there was no give. He pulled harder, and harder still until finally he put his whole body into it and the window shot up, slamming wood on wood at the top.

Cool, fresh, night air filled the room. Sticking his head out, Vanya braced himself in the sill. He looked down, then up and around. No scratching sound, and no possible source; no explanation for it.

"I'm done." The Chemist's voice seemed to come from another world. Vanya took a last glance, and then came back into the room.

"Good. I'm getting the creeps," he said as he crossed the room, "I just wanna get this done and get out of here."

He stopped beside the chair, grabbed his Glass, and immediately began issuing commands with his fingers, inspecting the transferred files. The Desk responded to the Glass having been removed, but Vanya only noticed that peripherally.

"This is everything?" he asked without looking up, continuing to scan.

Gabe did not reply.

"Ah, this is the recording obviously...," he found something and paused to watch. "... and the sample?"

Gabe did not reply.

Looking up from the Glass, Vanya spied the microscope on the other side of Gabe. He was almost looking through Gabe before he noticed him. Gabe's eyes were wide and frightened.

Realization suddenly caught Vanya. It began in his heart. A slow, dull thud. His chest was open, but there was no air in his lungs. His skin cooled and the blood rushed from his hands and face, going nowhere. His eyes opened wide with betrayal and disbelief.

He didn't ever actually see the gun, but he knew it was there. He had read it plainly in Gabe's frightened, quivering eyes. He had recognized that fear. It was the fear of knowing that you had just decided someone's fate; that you were capable, that you'd made the choice.

Vanya didn't hear the shot. He didn't see the flash.

Gabe sat for a moment and experienced nothing. It was impossible for him to know how long he stayed that way, but it wasn't long enough for anyone to come to investigate the sound of the gun shot.

Hand and forearm quivering, Gabe came to his senses.

Vanya's body was several feet from where Gabe was sitting. The mass projectile had hit him square in the chest, caving it in and splitting his back open around his spine. The force pushed him back into the bookshelf, knocking it over. There was blood dripping down through the books of the fallen shelf. Vanya's upper body was draped over the shelf in a backbend. His waist was twisted strongly to one side, and his legs were twisted, resting on the floor.

Turning back around and setting the gun on the Desk, Gabe stared blankly at the Wall. The scan light passed over the gun. Within moments, the monitor began displaying information about the capacity, power, and development of the Class 5, High-Density Mass Accelerator. The information window startled the Chemist into action. He wanted to leave and he had to clean the Desk before he could go.

He navigated the menus clumsily, going in circles. Prompts appeared for passwords that he had rarely ever used, eliciting several attempts before he succeeded. He finally paused and considered the warning displayed. "... permanently deleted. Are you sure you wish to continue?"

He tapped a final key.

He pushed himself away from the Desk, tried to stand, and was reminded, painfully of his injured knee. He sat back down, hard. He thought for a moment, then wheeled himself over to a closet under the power of his good leg. He opened the door and looked inside. Moving a couple of boxes out of the way, he found an old, cane-like umbrella at the back of the closet. He tested it, and was almost erect before it snapped and broke under his weight. Grabbing for the chair, he managed to slow his fall to the ground, but hit his head hard on the seat.

Eyeing the closet, he spotted a broom that he'd rarely ever used. He leaned forward and after a brief struggle it fell toward him. He quickly unscrewed the head from the handle and pulled himself up with the aid of both the chair and his newly fashioned walking stick.

Looking around the room, flustered, he shuffled through the inventory of the apartment and tried to figure out what he really needed. His attention back on the closet, he reached for a jacket. Blood rushed from his head and he experienced a moment of vertigo as the broom handle bottom briefly slid along the floor, before stopping against the jamb of the closet door. Gabe steadied himself, reached in again, and grabbed a jacket and a scarf. He leaned the broom handle against the wall and hurriedly armed himself against the cold.

One last item.

Gabe placed the bottom of the broom handle against the floor molding with each step as he made his way toward the microscope. When he finally arrived at his desk, he placed the full weight of his body on his good leg, in order to free both hands. He manipulated a couple of knobs at the base of the microscope. Armatures and wiring were exposed as the base opened up like a four-petaled flower in bloom. He flipped a small lever. A pressurized sound accompanied the formation of a small liquid bubble, which originated from an almost imperceptible needle within the center of the base. When the bubble was the size of a small marble, a red fluid was injected into its center, and then the needle retracted. The red-dyed fluid swirled within, but did not mix with the surrounding material. The swirling motion slowed and stopped. The sample suspended within the tiny, crystal-clear ball was preserved and protected. The Chemist flipped another lever which ejected the ball. He picked it, like a berry, and took a moment to inspect it. Then he swallowed it.

He fumbled with the broomstick again. Positioning it carefully, he made his way to the door. Gabe tested his injured leg gingerly as he opened the door. There was pain, sharp but not unmanageable... not yet anyway.

Gabe turned to look at the apartment one last time. The Desk was off. The window was open. Standing in the entrance with the door wide, a breeze carried the smell of burnt hair to his nostrils. He stared at Vanya's misshapen body, held by some inexplicable emotion. Finally, he shook himself free, knowing that he had to leave.

Tapping the side of the Wall, Gabe turned the lights off and left.

The sound of the auto-lock engaging was the only disturbance in the room for several seconds, and then a small amount of light coming in through the window flickered, bent, and snapped back.

Again, the light flickered and bent. It looked like a cylinder of glass moving in front of the window and into the room, only not as smooth and regular. The world was bent and distorted, casting light and shadow into unexpected locations. Suddenly, the activity stopped and there was nothing to see, no strange optical illusions, no aberrant reflections or refractions.

Several minutes passed, then as before, the wall by the window took on odd proportions. It began to move more quickly, and as it moved the outline of a familiar shape became clear. It was the silhouette of a woman.

The figure moved without a sound across the room, hovered over the Desk for a moment and disturbed nothing. She bent closer to the microscope then straightened and surveyed the rest of the room. Stepping quickly and silently around Vanya's corpse, the slender body knelt down. The Glass was lifted into the air, becoming an inscrutable visual distortion as it was inspected and flipped over by the intruder. Finally, it was absorbed completely by the silhouette.

The figure stood and took a few steps closer to Vanya. A protrusion, long and slender, extended from her chest. A bright flash lit up Vanya, flooded the room, and caused an epileptic display of colors to emanate over the entire surface of the figure. Despite the confusing array, the effect gave depth and shape to the intruder. She was slender and tall, and if she was wearing clothing, it was skin tight.

A few more snaps and tricks of light, and she became amorphous again. She floated to the front door, turned on the viewer, and found no one in the hall. The first, distant alarms of the Collective could finally be heard coming from the open window.

She unlocked the door and opened it quickly. For a moment, there was a golden aura outlining her lithe body, then an electrical snap-pop, and the hallway light died. She didn't bother closing the door behind her.

SPIRE

The Circuit

Four

"I don't really remember..."

It was all so confusing. Standing in the club, trying to describe the last several days to Demy, it sounded even more confusing than it felt.

"So you were tripping out of your mind and things got fucked up. Sounds about right to me," Demy yells over the booming bass. He looks past me, scouting out the dance floor.

"But it was more than that," I mutter, mostly below the sound of the music. I was abducted. Arrested. Something. There were people in my apartment. "Sure I was dosed but... I was on the floor of my bathroom, and there were people, guys in my apartment..." I spoke beneath the music, not sure if I believed the words myself.

Staring out at the rolling waves of dancing, undulating bodies, I thought I'd like to be out there with them, drowning in that howling sea of hormone-driven insanity.

It's frustrating, trying to get my thoughts together, to get my friend to believe me, to even hear me out at all. Demy and I had been through a lot. Maybe too many nights of altered states had condemned our relationship to this; this automatic dismissal of the night before.

Damn it, Demy! It wasn't the drugs! The thought is a screaming thermal rush to the skin of my face.

I grab Demy and pull him close, "They. Were. Real. Demy, these guys, they were suits. They... I don't know, they tested me for something. Something genetic, some chemical..."

I can hear the strangeness in my own voice, coarse with desperation. I can smell the starvation on my breath, sour and sweet. There is fear in Demy's eyes, like he doesn't recognize me. I don't recognize myself. Startled, I release my grip.

"Hey man, I get it. I do." Demy's face is full of concern and sympathy. He places his hand, heavy and calm, on my shoulder to emphasize his compassion for me. "Something happened, something that really fucked with your shit." He paused, familiar eyes reading mine. "You drinking tonight?" a smile, "You should be." He downs the rest of his beer, turns back to the bar, and tries to flag down the tender.

A random guy bumps into me, sweat and heat pouring off his body. He gives a distracted apology, never turning his attention from the crowd, and jumps back in. The club space is getting tight and I am getting anxious to leave.

Demy turns back around from the bar, empty-handed. "Fuck it." He hops down off the stool and puts his hand on my shoulder again. "Let's get out of here." He speaks directly to me, his radar off.

I feel so much relief. Looking into his confident smile, I couldn't imagine him leading me wrong. Turning around, I begin swimming through the tidal force of the crowd. As I push my way toward the exit, I see an opening as the waves of bodies part, and jump into it.

A woman stumbles into me, *I'm magnetic tonight.*

"Joshua!?" The wide, brown eyes are daring and excited. I open my mouth to speak, but before I can utter a word, "DEMY!" She jumps up and wraps her arms around Demy's neck, only her toes touching the ground.

"Rivva! What's going on? " Demy beams her his best lighthouse smile.

"I'm soooo, so good!" She's got the drug drawl on her tongue as she paws at Demy's shirt, sliding down his chest. Her voice is tremulous, her body undulating.

There is some back and forth between the two that I can't make out because of a tidal wave of laughter that rises up from crowd. I don't need to hear any of Demy's and Rivva's conversation, though... I know what's going on. Demy would be delighted to show her the way to the shore tonight.

He glances up from Rivva to look to me for approval.

I nod and fake a smile.

Demy knows I'm disappointed, but we both know that won't change a thing. I turn my back to them and flounder my way out, alone.

The outside air is cool, much cooler than inside the club. A recent rainfall has covered everything with a mercuric sheen, and left a thick fog hanging in the air. There were a few lights above the lot, projecting through the mist, creating golden halos and spheres.

Behind me, the old manual door swung closed, slowly. It was heavy and thick, and a deep thud reverberated through the jamb as it sealed shut. The door dampened the music and screaming dancers, and made them seem far away, but I could still feel the booming bass.

The parking lot is the opposite of the club. Other than a few giggling late arrivals, it is calm and motionless. There is nothing more for me here tonight.

But there is nothing for me anywhere tonight. I'm in the middle of the parking lot when I realize I don't really have a place to go. I don't want to go home. Just thinking of it creeps me to the core and I shiver it away. And Demy's place is no longer an option, certainly off limits with Rivva in the picture. Weighing my options, I turn to face the club again. *Fuck it. If I go back in there at least I can score something to make me more comfortable for a while...*

Contemplating but not yet taking a step back toward the club, I see a woman approaching the entrance. She walks the ramp and stops a few body lengths from the door. She is outside of the white light cast by the fixture above the door, standing in shadow but still strongly visible.

She is dressed for sex, a clear outline of curves drawn against the wall of the club. The building, it must have been a warehouse at some point, is a throbbing blurry background to her rigid, self-possessed posture. She takes a long drag on her cigarette, and the cherry brightens like a lone Christmas light, capturing my mind for a moment. Staring at her, I can taste the tobacco on my lips and smell the smoke in her hair. She ends the long drag and the glow fades. Nonchalantly, she pushes the lit end into the wall of the club, snuffing the life from it.

In that moment of contact, she is transformed. The cigarette conducts the throbbing blur from the building to her fingertips, and eventually to her entire body. She vibrates independently for a few seconds but ultimately she harmonizes. She fades from the fore to the background and I lose sight of her.

On second thought, I don't have the energy to go back in there again tonight. A woman like that would just tear me up tonight even if I could find her in the crowd. She's gone and I should be going. Somewhere. Not here.

"Oh shit, oh shit, oh shit!" The harsh whisper comes from farther out in the parking lot, away from the club. It's a distant, diffuse sound, making it difficult to pinpoint. Something about the quality of the voice refuses to be ignored. I can't walk away from it, like walking away from this call-for-help would weaken my character. Tonight is not the night for me to question karma, so I wander toward the whisper.

Walking up and down between the rows of cars, I stop at intervals to look under and look around, but I can't hear or see anything. I notice my breath hanging in the air and finally catch the message from my cold-sweaty arms that I'm getting chilled. I stare at the goose-pimples on my forearms, wishing for my jacket, when I hear the rustling of someone near me.

I stop and look under another car, and I can clearly make out two someones on the other side. Someone is hunched down and someone is sitting, back to me, leaned against the car. Standing up, I walk around the front of the car. There's a young guy there, holding his knees, rock-stepping in front of a woman whose limp body is propped up against the side of the vehicle. Her legs are straight and flat out in front of her, hands palm-up at her sides, resting on the asphalt of the lot. Her eyes are open, staring blindly, and are oddly dark, even in the poor lighting. The man doesn't seem to notice my arrival any more than the woman does, neither of whom makes any sound or motion toward me. Neither could be more than twenty-three.

Finally, I say something. "Hey... uh..." The guy stands up faster than I would have thought possible for someone who appeared practically catatonic. He doesn't take a glance in my direction, he just runs. He slips along the way, but catches himself on a truck. He turns down through a row of cars and out of sight.

I stare into the darkness for several seconds, where I saw him last, and listen to his footsteps, fast, regular, and fading. When I can no longer tell if I'm imagining the footfalls or still hearing them, I look down.

Is she alive?

She hasn't budged or blinked. Getting closer and leaning down for a better look, I try to see into her eyes, to see what she is seeing, but I can't find a hint or the slightest insight into her state of mind. The whites of her eyes have turned dark, not black, but in the low light of the parking lot, the color is difficult to discern.

"Hey." I'm only a foot or so from her face. "Hey, snap out of it." My voice is nervous and afraid. I don't expect that of myself, which tightens my strings and strangles the words.

I've seen ODs... a guy takes too much, he's shaking and convulsing on the ground, drool running out of his half-smiling, half-lunatic face, while another is beating his head bloody against a concrete wall... and nothing unnerved me as much as this stone-calm woman.

"Hey!" It's a harsh whisper. No response.

33

I snap my fingers by her face a couple of times but I can't even elicit a twitch from the corners of her lids. Her eyes seem deeper, turned inward so strongly that they can only see within. I clap my hands hard between her face and mine. Again, no reaction.

I still can't make out the color in her eyes. Each orb has a dark fog, obscuring the iris, surrounded by wet, thick, blue? Green? Red? My heart is heavy in my chest. I finally notice that I'm holding my breath and let out a plume of frosty exhaust followed by a quick, cold inhale. It's so cold. I shift closer to the woman and hunker down even deeper into my bent legs.

Looking into the foggy irises, I think there's some kind of movement. The pupils are slightly adjusting, widening. There is movement in the fog around the pupils, the dark holes breathing, the fog spinning inward. I take a deep breath, pulling the harsh cold into my chest again.

I let out the air, long and deliberate, and through my breath, I can see her foggy eyes sucking it in. Her eyes plump up for a moment, filling with the breath.

I'm mesmerized. I take another pull of the chill night air. Her beautiful orbs shrivel slightly, the fog swirls, stormy and angry, as the breath leaves her eyes for my mouth and nose.

My chest is so cold. I wrap my arms around my legs and pull them closer. I let out the breath, sending it deliberately into the voids of her eyes. The mouth of each fogged iris grows, hungry for more.

Breathe in, breathe out.

I rock back and forth to warm myself up just a bit.

Breathe in, breathe out.

She's looking right at me.

"Oh shit." She can see me. She can see me staring into her. She can see me violating her. I'm too close. I'm looking too deeply. I'm in her…

She's looking right at me. This woman, this woman recognizes me.

"Oh shit, oh shit." She knows me. My past. All the choices I've made. I'm violating her just being here, just sharing this space with her. I exist in her now because she sees me...

She's looking at me... and she's smiling. It's a smirk of plump and pouty lips, of full and laughing eyes, sanguine surrounding charcoal gray.

But... *I just wanted to help.*

Her mouth quivers and the smile slips from her lips. As her nostrils shakily flare, her lips part, revealing decayed, rotting teeth, smeared with patches of blood-red lipstick. The skin of her face sucks to her bones and her eyes sink into their sockets.

I'm not afraid. She just needs comfort and rest. My hand, not entirely of its own will, reaches out to caress her sunken cheek.

Her skin is so cold that my heart skips and I gasp for air. I pull my hand away with a preternatural quickness. Losing my balance, I fall hard onto my tailbone. I brush up along the side of her leg and a cold surge hits me again. I search for purchase, trying to haul myself back to my feet. Scrambling and sliding on the pavement, sharp pebbles digging into the palms of my hands, I finally get a grip and stand.

I look around to see if anyone is looking back at me.

Nothing.

No one.

The place suddenly feels like a graveyard instead of a parking lot. There's an icy mist floating from the woman, like dry-ice sublimating. She isn't moving. Her eyes closed at some point, or maybe they were always closed. Standing here, staring at her, I'm not sure of anything. I... *miss her?*

Shaking my head vigorously, I run my fingers through my hair and try to figure out what to do next. The thought of touching her again is frightening. Flashback or no, I can't will my feet to take a step closer to her, much less touch her. Still, I can't really leave either. I swallow hard and look around the parking lot again. Someone has to come out soon, and where did that guy go anyway? I'd almost completely forgotten about him.

Visually examining the woman, it slowly dawns on me that she is not breathing. Her chest is sunken and static. No breath escapes her nostrils or lips. A moment ago, those lips were so full, but now they seem pale and overly relaxed. She is not the siren or the monster from moments ago. An involuntary shudder challenges my next breath.

I don't know how long I stood there just breathing and staring. I remember hearing laughter in the distance.

A woman entertaining another woman. Their footsteps approaching in a stumbling arrhythmia. The abrupt change when the red-haired woman shudders, but does not scream, when she sees the corpse. The brunette asks me something, touching me firmly, trying to get my attention. The feeling of my mouth forming an answer. The periscopic view of the brunette taking the pulse of the corpse.

She tells Red to calm down, something cliché to inspire confidence. Everything will be alright. She's holding a Glass to her ear, giving an address, describing the parking lot and the situation. When she stands and puts her arm around her date, when she is fully occupied with the Glass and the body, I leave.

I disappeared successfully. I'm not even sure if they looked for me or remembered that I was there. Hands in my pockets, headstrong against the cold, I eventually heard the distant siren of an ambulance coming down the avenue. Stopping and turning, I realize it is coming from the opposite direction. I wait until the siren is killed before moving on. I never even saw the lights.

Cold Pizza

Five

I'm not sure what to say next, if I should say anything at all. There was a long silence between us when I finished explaining what happened when I left the club.

I didn't expect to remember so many details, or to just go on like that. As I told Demy the story, the words ran out of my mouth like they were escaping prison, going in several different directions at once, too fast to track, too confused to know where to go next. Demy is a bloodhound, though, so he picked up the trail without too much trouble. He understood me, even if I didn't understand myself. On the other hand, I don't think he believed my story was anything more than a delusion, a hallucination.

Demy's apartment is pretty comfortable, much more accommodating than mine. There is a full-size couch holding me; even with my body sprawled out length-wise, there is room for one more. The living room is spare, other than the couch and the coffee table; not many adornments, open and clean.

The Wall is tuned to the news, but I'm not interested anymore. I turned it on looking for some report of the ambulance from the other night, but I hadn't found anything.

"I remember seeing the ambulance as Rivva and I left," Demy calls out from the kitchen, "The Circuit was still running hot so there were only a few spectators. The scene was pretty quiet." Demy recounts the last part of the story from his perspective, staring in the general direction of the couch. He is looking out from over the bar that divides the kitchen from the living area, "I couldn't see anything... I blew it off, you know? One of those things that happens at clubs, especially the ones I like. I went to Rivva's place..."

There is silence before I expect it, and it lasts so long that I actually look up from my position, mostly buried in the cushions. I don't put much energy into it but enough to peer over the arm of the couch to see Demy directly.

He's struggling a bit with a twist top.

"... I hadn't even... thought about it again," some effort from the exertion on the bottle, "until your insane story." Demy holds the bottle into his shirt. Fffttt, the top twists off and he flips the lid to the counter in the same motion. The sound of the metal on the counter echoes Demy's nonchalance, the way he treats everything.

I bury my face in the pillow that held my head moments before. "I just don't think you're taking this seriously," I mumble muffled. Maybe it is crazy. It all certainly felt real enough when it was happening and I wasn't on anything. But, who knows, maybe I am finally losing it.

Demy walks over to the couch. "Shove over, buddy," he pushes at me with one hand while he speaks. He takes a swig from his bottle, gives up trying to move me out of his way, and just sits his ass down.

I squirm out from beneath him, and sit half upright. Demy is leaning over the coffee table, sliding and tapping at the surface. He's searching for something on the news and he finally settles on something. It's a feed from the ambulance.

From inside the open double doors of the ambulance, the parking lot of The Circuit is clear, despite the misty night. No reporters are on the scene, so the coverage doesn't extend beyond the tunnel view from the back of the ambulance. Text is appearing over the scene, describing the date, time, and nature of the call.

Paramedics are on the ground with the body of the woman. They are moving quickly, but without urgency. More text appears, accompanied by a fade-in of a young man's voice, "... arrival. Paramedics did not attempt resuscitation. The rigor of the body clearly indicated that death had occurred much earlier in the evening... "

I'm entranced by the video. After some moments, the paramedics lift the bagged body on a stretcher and confidently deposit it in the back of the vehicle. The voice-over details the use of various materials, expenses, and durations with regard to the efficiency of the deployment of rescue units and their relative success rates.

The text writing on the Wall describes statistics relating fatalities in the area of The Circuit night club to various increments of time, fatalities during the same times of day, in similar location-types, like dance clubs and a couple of counterpoint locations, places that break the trend. A graph is drawn and as each line of text appears, a new corresponding line is added to the graph. The dead woman, Early Sandoval, according to the display is represented by what looks like her identity card photo. A red marker in the graph shows where her death falls into the statistics.

"... cause of death was not determined onsite. Assumed drug involvement with contributing factors of malnourishment, exhaustion, and..."

"She was dead long before you got to her," Demy says without looking from the Wall.

"I don't know... I saw something. And there was that other guy, too. He wasn't just hanging out with a dead body." Running my fingers through my hair, I look away from the video. "D, listen... listen to me. The woman, Early, she was clinging onto life. She didn't want to hurt me, but when she reached out to me, to help her, it was like icy fingertips clawing inside me... at my soul." I stare at the side of Demy's face wondering if any of this makes sense, if any of it is real.

39

Demy stares back, his face poker-blank, completely unreadable.

He curls up his lip and furrows his brow sarcastically low, "Icy fingertips? Your soul? *Really*?" Then he relaxes, invites me to relax with him, "You know that I've always enjoyed your, uh, emotional sensibilities but you have to admit, this sounds awfully familiar… like Cocktail, right?"

Fuck. I was never going to live that down. It was my first time combining so many different chems, really experimenting on myself. I swore for days that I'd touched other people's souls. My friends, Demy among them, remembered it a little differently. Apparently, I'd become obsessed with the word 'Cocktail,' describing the mixture I'd made and taken, but then I took my clothes off and supplied visuals of the various different meanings. I *touched* people all right, but it wasn't with my soul.

As that day had faded into a dreamy memory, I'd laughed at myself, too.

This was different.

"Fuck, Demy," I was exhausted. "That was like ten years ago. I haven't confused my soul with my *self*," I gestured rudely, "since."

Back on topic, "I came to see you last night so I could talk about being kidnapped. I was freaked out. I wasn't on anything for days. I was cold-sober when I hooked up with you."

Demy stands tall and straight and looks hard down at me, then he wags his finger, "No hallucinations." It was a poor mock-Vader, but it makes me sort of chuckle and I guess it shows, because he smiles back at me. "Joshua, you and I have been through a whole lot together, so believe me when I say this is the craziest you've ever been." He hands me the beer. "I think it might just be time to slow down, go more conventional."

I drink from the bottle, easily more than my share, and hand it back. "What about being kidna…"

"You were fucked out of your mind then," Demy says firmly, cutting me off. He downs the rest of the bottle at a single pull. "And let's be honest friend, you've been operating at full-burn for a long time…

40

maybe you finally burned away the barrier between reality and fantasy?"

He waits patiently for his words to hit me. Real doubt sneaks into me for the first time.

An earnest look on his face, an empty bottle pointed at mine, "Turns out, that barrier is pretty useful. Bet you wish you had one now." The last is somewhat patronizing, but what can I say? I'm the wreck that needs his couch and comfort.

He must have realized he was rubbing me the wrong way a bit, "I know, I know, you and I never saw it the same way. You partied like you were chasing after something inside of you that you just couldn't reach, and I... well, I partied for the women."

Demy's demeanor softens and he sets his bottle down. "I'm sorry you've had a rough time of it, you know, since your brother and all," he hesitated, "But you've got to slow down. You gotta rebuild that barrier. Bury at least one of your remaining brain cells in reality."

"I don't know, I always thought I was getting somewhere. Close to unlocking my potential, some secret that... fuck, I always thought that someday I'd stay on the other side of that barrier forever." I sound defeated and disappointed, but I manage a soft smile anyway.

"There's nothing on the other side... except your delusions, laser brain."

"Yeah," the tension melts away. It isn't that I believe Demy, but what's the use in arguing? I feel safe here and Demy is just looking out for me, so I let it go.

I feel clear for the first time since the Pez. Early evening is filtering the sunlight that's coming in through the apartment windows, bathing the furniture and walls in the odd waning-yellow of sunset. I feel like I'm at the end of a long trip, my body exhausted, my spirit tired.

"Do me a favor, Joshua, stay here tonight. Relax. I've got several meds from the lab, nothing experimental, just solid stuff that will calm you down and put everything in perspective. You can help yourself."

41

There was Demy, solid as ever, my voice of reason, squashing my fantastic notion of the weekend's events and setting my mind at ease. I could let the whole thing go, for tonight at least, and look on everything with fresh eyes in the morning.

We'd gone to school together for a few semesters, but Demy finished his degree, while I dropped out. We were both pursuing biochemistry degrees, but like everything else, our views of university life were pretty different. I thought it was a great place to feed my addiction to pushing my limits. Demy saw school as a way to get laid on his way to some legitimate currency and a worthwhile career. Turns out it we were both right. The end result of his version, though, was considerably more stable and lucrative than mine.

Well, my version never really ended, so the results aren't in yet. I almost laugh out loud at the thought.

My mood is considerably improved, "No chems tonight, but I might take you up on staying here. Just need to shake the boogeymen from my brain." The relief, realizing that I am not going back to my apartment tonight, is swift and pure. Thinking about the bathroom gave me the shivers – a little thrill, but mostly the shivers.

"Well, hey, if it helps you relax," Demy turns his attention to the table again and with a few strokes, brings up his research materials on the Wall, "you can take a look at my work and tell me if you see anything interesting. You were always better at this than me. Less motivated, but better. On the other hand," he taps once, "there is always porn." Breasts, beautiful and ripe, dance up and down on the Wall.

"You know me too well," I can't help but smile now. Staring at the naked woman, I can imagine her skin on mine and the thought softens the sharp edges of my nerves with pink curtains and elegant perfume.

"What, not holo-capable?" I draw it out sarcastically, knowing that Demy has some embarrassing moments of his own. In particular, an evening with a hologram projection table that left us all scarred. He'd grown up a lot since then, risen in the ranks of BioGen, and become an adult more or less. Meant very little to me though, as I lie there grinning at him, reminding him that it wasn't always this way.

Demy punched me hard in the thigh, "Fucker."

"Asshole."

Smiling, Demy had his last say, "Listen, don't dirty the couch, okay? Use the bathroom, put down some sheets... whatever. Try to control yourself. And Jesus, at least wait until I go to bed. I don't want to know what sounds you make."

"Why not? I doubt you've ever heard another person genuinely orgasm... it might be inspiring for you."

"Nice."

Demy walks into the kitchen again and makes some noise putting dishes away, cleaning up, and arranging the place for his morning rituals. I sit up fully and reset the Wall to the research. The complexity of Demy's work is somewhat beyond me. Being out of school for five years and working random jobs instead of continuing my education has left me pretty rusty. Selling drugs rather than manufacturing them had its benefits, but thinking critically wasn't one of them. Still, I was interested. Whether it was nostalgia or envy, I enjoyed looking over Demy's work.

"Mind if I order some pizza?" I yell distractedly.

"Knock yourself out," the answer came from the back bedroom, "Just don't make a mess."

"Anything for you?"

"Nah. You know I can't eat that shit. I invest all of my indulgence in alcohol. I already run every morning for forty minutes... I'm not interested in making it an hour."

It's reassuring to hear Demy's voice, to chat about concrete interests like work, sex, and food. Demy was always worried about how he looked. His complaints about weight-gain were annoying when we lived in the dorms, but out in the world, in the surreal wake of the weekend, they're welcome.

"I'm going to bed. I know it's early, but you know Rivva," Demy says softly, "No sleeping allowed." He's padded up to a position behind the couch.

I look back over my shoulder, dividing my attention between the table, where I'm placing the pizza order, and Demy. He's dressed in lightweight bedclothes, standing in the last bright-orange flare of the day. He looks like a model for the modern male. Educated, strong and lean, well-groomed, and well-dressed even for bed, Demy was the ideal most of us were trying to achieve. I must look like a sack of shit to him, burned-out on his couch, ordering pizza with one hand on the table console, the other on the back of the couch. He smiles at me just the same.

"Okay. I'll try to keep my screaming volume down for the evening."

"Thanks," Sardonically.

"No problem. Night."

"Night."

I can't hear the footsteps in the carpeted apartment but I hear the door close and I know I have some privacy. I hit the console and go back to the chemical analysis of Demy's latest trial pharmaceutical and stare at it blankly for a few seconds.

There's something else I really want to see.

After another minute, I give in. I pull up the stream from the ambulance, and watch the entirety of the vid several times over. There isn't anything abnormal about it. I pick over the details, but really, it reads like any other article. The coverage is unbiased, unemotional, and unremarkable, according to the stats.

An interrupt appears on the Wall, the vid pausing and audio fading out, calling my attention to someone ringing up from the entrance to the complex. I acknowledge the interrupt and a small window opens up on the Wall and takes focus.

"Hey hey, pizza man," I say to the teenage girl holding my pie.

"Large Supremo for Demetrius Cohen?"

"Yep yep. Bring it up. Thank you." I open the entrance from
the table console and the window closes. The ambulance video
automatically cycles back a few seconds and resumes playing, the
audio increases to the previous volume, and I watch again.

My chest is nervous, and my breath broken, as I notice that some
of the text has changed. The letters are a scramble at first, causing
me to blink repeatedly and try to regain my vision. My eyes feel
like they're focused at the wrong distance, staring at a chain-linked
fence. Each time I try to refocus, the image slides apart, but I'm still
looking through it.

Instead of text and graphs displaying statistical data, the images
are closer to something from Demy's research that I was looking at
earlier. I rub my eyes and look again in disbelief. I didn't accidentally
go back to his research folder, did I? No, I didn't. And I'm not
looking at an overlay with both video and research displayed at
once... it's just the video.

The paramedic's voice morphs into Demy's voice, "... yes... he's in
my apartment right now... yes... yes, he is showing signs, probably
two significant events... "

I tense up and my mind erupts with paranoid thoughts. Demy's
voice continues, recounting details of what I'd told him earlier. I
cannot make out everything being said, and the voice on the other
end is totally unintelligible.

An interrupt window appears and blocks everything else out. I snap
to attention and stand bolt upright.

I don't even think about it. I walk quickly to the entrance, grab my
jacket from the nearby hook, and open the door abruptly. The young
lady is attractive even with the pizza hat and uniform, and the
gaudy advertisements flicking around her obnoxiously.

"Your Supre... "

I don't stop to chat or explain. I just smile like a madman and
walk hurriedly by her. The elevator door is down the hall, and I
catch it before it's been called elsewhere. The doors are half-closed
and as they open back up for me, I can hear the pizzaman saying

something about assholes and yelling into Demy's apartment, looking for someone to accept the delivery so she can get paid. As the doors finally begin to close again, I see her leaving the pizza on the floor.

She stands and turns around in time to see the doors closing, "Hey! Hold the door!" But I'm stabbing the "close door" button about as fast as I can.

She describes a few uncomfortable positions, in which she would like to see me and my mother, including a few adjectives for my genitalia that are pretty unrealistic. The doors pinch the last of her words, and I breathe a sigh of relief.

The lift's inertial controls are high-quality, so I hit the bottom floor without even realizing it. The doors can't open fast enough for me. I surprise a young couple waiting for the lift in the lobby by squeezing through the opening, awkwardly, as soon as I fit through. Making a dash for the entrance, I glance over my shoulder, but no one follows, and the couple is already aboard the elevator and forgetting me. I slam open the double doors, feel the rush of cool air, and step out onto the sidewalk. Looking right and left, I'm not sure which way to go. Either way, in the city, there were plenty of places to disappear. I just need to pick a direction and go.

"Hey! Joshua, where are you going, man? The pizza just got here... not cool leaving it on the floor like that..." Demy's voice is a creepy ghost on the com to my left.

I take a long look into the camera, or where I imagine it to be, and decide that even if my brain has finally turned to a fried egg, it's time to go. A little ashamed for thinking anything bad about Demy, I cast my eyes at my feet, pull my sweatshirt hood over my head, shove my hands deep in my jean pockets, and turn to the street.

"Whoa, seriously, where..." I lose his voice as I cross through the thick traffic.

Some headlights are on, as twilight shifts the world to a warm autumn orange. The avenue is six lanes across and I can feel the drivers and passengers tracking me as I pass between vehicles. I hit the opposite curb, turn sharply to the right, and walk with absolute resolve and purpose toward nothing in particular.

SPIRE

Halo

Six

It must have been midnight by the time I calmed down. My mind was filled with paranoid butterflies, their wings whispering hints of words I wish I hadn't heard. I kept seeing the face of the dead woman, Early, wondering if it was all my imagination. I thought of Demy. He said I might have finally burned out my last sane cell.

Maybe he's right?

But how would I know?

I stepped under a street light and looked around to see where I'd ended up. Noticing my hood again for the first time since I left Demy's, I pulled it back to my shoulders. I hadn't realized how hot I'd become just from walking, I'd been so consumed with organizing my thoughts. My whole body heaved a sigh of relief as I exposed the skin of my neck to the cool night air.

Foot traffic was sparse and meandering. Several cars roamed the streets but they moved along, unfettered by the congestion or frequent lights of the earlier hours of the day. The pedestrians were a mix of professionals, students, and tourists. I fit in well with this crowd, anonymous in the diversity of ages and occupations.

I saw a street sign: 25th and Sandstone. I must have been here at this exact corner a hundred times before, but it felt unfamiliar tonight. It'd been awhile since I'd been back to my old stomping ground. Some of the bars and restaurants had changed owners and facades. It was reassuring, actually, to see the changes. It increased my confidence that I would see no one who knew me.

My legs were tired and the skin of my thighs was scratchy from exertion. There was a bright marquee overhead for a bar that looked like a promising place to hole up for a bit. There were no windows, just a large wooden door with a vertical barbell handle. I pulled the heavy door open and stepped in.

The place was busier than I expected from the look of the exterior. The music was loud but not over-powering. There were naked men and women displayed on low glass tables around the main part of the room. Each table was lit from beneath by a bright ring of white light, casting interesting shadows across the contours of the beautiful people. There were some booths as well, some curtained and some not, around the perimeter of the main floor.

Several spectators, mostly clothed, sat around the tables. Drinks and lovers, hands and mouths, exchanged roles casually. The din of conversation and laughter, the clatter of drinks, the easy nature of the place, all helped settle me down. I spotted the bar at the far end of the room and made my way over.

The tender was a pierced woman. Her right eyebrow twice, her nose, lower lip, nipples, belly button, and ears were decorated with delicate silver bars and hoops. Her skin was a healthy, blushing pink. She had a tattoo beginning beneath her navel, a green vine that hooked around the soft curve of her belly, continued up, weaving back and forth, sprouting a leaf here and there, and finally flowered a purple lily as though it was her right breast. Her chocolate hair was pulled back loosely, a few wavy rivulets spilling around her face and ears, and down the nape of her neck.

She was alert, washing glasses under the bar with swift and confident motions while observing the needs of the drinks and patrons in her view. She threw a smile and some kind words at a regular then turned to me. Her eyes were bright, wide, and violet.

A well-practiced, flirtatious smirk greeted me with an upward nod, "What can I get for you?" Her voice strong and clear, her eyes sober and beautiful, she was mesmerizing. A subtle flash crossed her indigo irises, and I recognize it as the moment of evaluation. She was deciding how much attention to spend on me.

Perve? No.

Drunk? No.

Money? Not much, but I'll get some out of him.

I stared into her eyes, stared but could not utter a word.

"You stoned another one, Lily!" a laughing, liquor-thick, comment from the other side of the bar.

This enchantress of a tender had obviously tongue-tied more than her fair share of patrons. I stretched for the words, realizing I should say something, order something, but I couldn't think of the name of a single drink. Lily was the only word that came to mind, and I was pretty sure ordering a "Lily Drink" would have achieved a level of embarrassment previously undiscovered. Keeping my mouth shut, I remained dumb, hoping for 'stoic.'

I noticed the bar for the first time, looking for some hint of a drink I could order. The bar was a glass ring, lit from within and from the bottom. It was a larger interpretation of the display tables I passed when I crossed the main room.

The laughing voice, the one that called me out for my dumbstruck look, belonged to a pretty woman on the opposite side of the ring from me. Lily followed my eyes to the woman and turned her head in that direction. "Knock it off, Keira." Back to me, with a flirtatious toss of her hair, Lily gave me a wink then rolled her eyes, poking fun at Keira. The gesture was light-hearted enough and made me feel more at ease, bailed out of the red-faced situation. It wasn't hard to imagine that Lily did quite well for herself as a tender.

"When you decide what you need, cutie, just holler." She placed a napkin on the bar in front of me, bending closer to me than she needed to, in a carefully calculated and elegantly executed tease.

She had all of my attention in that moment and she knew it, which drew me in even more.

She tapped the napkin then leaned back, vacating the edge of my personal space. I felt suddenly and inexplicably lonely.

"I'm Lily." – "...{Sara}." Her voice echoed and stretched as she said her name. Her lips moved as though they simultaneously said both "Lily" and "Sara." "Sara" came from someplace quieter, privately whispered directly to me. My spine chilled from tail to tip. There at the tip, the base of my skull responded with an electric shiver.

The blood rushed from my face. A cold sweat covered my forehead.

Voices? Am I losing it?

Lily, adept at reading body language as an occupational prerequisite, saw the fear as it washed over me. She looked concerned, serious for a split second, but without an immediate explanation for her customer to go ghostly, she blew off whatever her instincts were telling her to do. "Just, uh, call for me..." Then she turned her back to me. Her attention back on Keira, Sara put her game face on, and stepped away.

My stomach twisted, and a dizzy-spin caused the world around the bar to bend and pull away from me. Luckily, a seat at the bar finally opened up and I sat down. I put my hands firmly on the countertop to steady myself.

I noticed my fingernails, the details unusually sharp. They seemed alien with vertical lines running from cuticle to tip. The closer I looked at them the farther they were from my body. My arms were longer than they could possibly be and my awareness was floating somewhere near the ceiling.

I squeezed my eyes shut, tighter and tighter until I could feel a rush of blood through my sinuses into my ears. For a moment the world was quiet, far away, and stable. I took a deep breath and opened my eyes again. And another deep breath, gaining strength, I looked up and around.

It's the same old world.

The people around me at the bar were trying to hook up, some attractive and some attracted. The enthralling, and sometimes spasmodic, dancing on the tables elicited urgent looks from all around. I saw through a drape to a private booth. A spine was arched away from another in a description of exaltation, a writhing shiver, and a pair of hands appeared that belonged to neither body that I could see. Things were normal. Beer and lust, liquor and sex, all were on tap this evening. But the itching behind my eyes and in my mind wouldn't subside.

I enjoyed challenging my reality, I did, but a line of ten tabs had never really made me feel like this. The altered state, whenever I achieved it, was never close enough to sober life to be confused with it. No. This felt like life. The voices sounded real. The visual artifacts and memories were my own. This was the karmic bill for all those nights of lucid dreaming, living beyond the body I was given.

Honestly, the debt was probably way past due, principal plus interest. The inexplicable memories of intruders and captivity, images of the undead woman, confusing Demy for my enemy, were just the first payments against a hefty bill, the expense of my experimentation.

They were going to have to wipe me clean. The Collective would have to be called. It was only a matter of time. The hallucinations, aural and visual, would eventually compromise my judgment... have already compromised me.

Genetic causes, environmental, or self-imposed, the Collective treats all of the maladaptive sort the same way; plug and scrub. "It's the only sane solution for society." Approved before I was born, it was the cure for all mental dysfunction—and the financial hemorrhaging that resulted from all other forms of treatment. A 'plug and scrub' began with a chemical soup served up to diminish both your discomfort and the integrity of the proteins you use to make new memories, and re-imagine old ones. They plug into your Chip, if you have one, and start playing stimulus pulses, electrical discharges, across the prefrontal cortex. That part goes on for hours. Eventually the bad behavioral pathways of the brain are cleared out... along with most of your memories. During the time it takes to complete the process, the generated voice of your biological mother recites keywords to evoke images of each important developmental stage of your life. Specific memories are eradicated if a relationship is found between a subject's undesirable behavior patterns and the memory. If you aren't equipped with a Chip, the process is a little more random. The results of a chipless plug-n-scrub can be pretty frightening.

I'm chipless. I missed the window. The technology was approved for the general population after I was past the cut-off age. They still won't chip a child after three; too many complications and inexplicable rejections to make it a good practice. I never thought I'd be wishing for my brain to be caught in a web of spidery silicon mesh, but right now that's all I want.

I shook off the paranoia and stared across the bar. My eyes were drawn immediately to Lily's surprisingly expressive back. The divine 'S' of her silhouette echoed internally by her spine. The lift of her left hip pulled up at the left side of my lips, and I imagined a better place I could be.

"I don't think she noticed."

"Huh? Wha..." I turned and noticed a woman sitting at the bar beside me.

"I don't think her Gauge flagged the inhibitor in your system. The one that's blocking her read." The woman didn't look at me when she talked. Instead, she simply stared down into the bottom of her glass. "It's far too subtle for any Engagement System she could possibly afford. Believe me, I engineered it myself." At the last, she nodded her head, and I made out a wry smile subtly forming on her face.

"Inhibitor? Look, I think you've confused me with someone else. We've never met. As crazy as this night has been—damn, the last several nights—I'm sure I don't know you." I spoke as assertively and naturally as I could. Imagining the Collective showing up because this woman has mistaken me for a bad date twisted me around in knots. I could almost hear her throwing out accusations of elicit GEaR and drugs, so I wanted to distance myself from her immediately.

"We haven't met, but…" she faced me. Two fantastic eyes fixed on mine. Each was a wide and translucent, thick-liquid, grass-green orb. A sharp black dot was visible deep within each. "I've been looking for you."

She closed her lids softly, and slowly opened them again. This time, an average set of eyes appeared; common, white, opaque humors with pupils and hazel irises. Again, she smiled at me. This time, there was a smug certainty on her face that she directed my full attention.

There is GEaR, legal and illegal, then there is *GEaR*. This woman was sporting the more fantastic sort, the kind of myth or military. No way was she an average Officer of the Collective.

"I, uh… look, you have mistaken me for someone else." I actually feel fairly confident despite the nervousness in my voice. A few possession charges would never attract this kind of attention.

Despite manufacturing my own stuff from time to time, I'd never been characterized as anything more than a small-time user in the eyes of the Collective. In fact, back at the University, the Collective had done a sweep of the campus for something–I can never remember what–and when they found my makeshift lab they practically laughed at me. They confiscated my equipment of course, but I was never even charged. Consequently, my "coursework" hours in the "lab" went way, way up for the rest of the semester, but no one seemed to notice.

"Oh Joshua, you're cute when you're scared," the woman spoke with an openly contrived flirtatious slant. Then to the tender, "Lily! Bring my boy here a vodka tonic!"

A distant sound, an orgasm at one of the tables, provoked some imagery in my mind and some regret in my stomach. *What the hell am I doing here?* I half-looked back out to the main area of the bar, I was curious for a glance. I felt like it might be my last opportunity to see something splendid. There was nothing out there though, except a twisted mess of foreign shapes and sounds. I couldn't place the source of the sound and the moment was lost.

"Okay, I give up. What's this all about? Who are you?"

"Eve."

Seconds passed. We simply stared at each other. I put on my best annoyed-out-of-my-mind face, and she responded with a sly look that I could only interpret as savoring-the-moment.

I couldn't decide if I was being arrested or picked up. A drink was placed at the bar for me. Eve waved her inner wrist over the bar and a half-inch, rectangular red light blinked twice from beneath the bar then turned blue. With a tap and a slide, she tipped the tender and closed out her tab. "Drink up," she said to me, almost apologetically.

"If it's all the same to you, I'd rather know what the fuck is going on." The rising edge of my words was uncomfortable for me. I'd completely lost my cool. The last few days had taken their toll placing my voice into a volatile register.

Lily heard the confrontational language and glanced in my direction to see if there would be trouble, but she didn't miss a beat with her current customer who was chatting her up for more than a drink.

Eve stood and leaned into me. Her movements were deceptively quick, deft and elegant, feline. She placed a finger on my lips, quieting whatever words she thought I might say. "Shhh. It's okay. I got this one."

She put her lips to my right ear, "They're coming for you, Joshua. They had you once already, but they didn't know it. You remember some of that, I'm sure. The inhibitor I made for you retarded the process and diffused some of their scans. It prevented them from seeing the fullness of your reaction and they let you go. That inhibitor, though, it's breaking down in your system right now, and then we'll see if I'm right about you."

Eve leaned back a bit so that I could see her face, so that she could see mine. "It cannot be stopped, the change that has already begun. No one understands how it works," she shrugged nonchalantly, "But I saw a pattern they didn't and I found you first."

She grinned knowingly and softened a bit, "You're not going insane, Joshua." Then more seriously, "I know it feels that way, but that's what it has been like for all of the subjects... you've seen the results already, in Miss Sandoval."

I was stunned into silence. I grasped at words, but they dissolved as I tried to put them together to form a thought. "Look, Eve, slow down. 'They had me once...?' What the hell does that mean?" *I was actually kidnapped?*

"You'll be able to answer that for yourself soon enough." She reached toward the bar without looking away from me and retrieved her drink. She swirled the contents around and the ice tinkled against the glass. Tilting her head back, she downed the remains.

"Now, I've given you a head start, my precious pinkie... let's not squander it. I want to see if you're really worth all the fuss." She took a step away from the bar then looked back, "Goodnight, Joshua."

I couldn't move. I couldn't even call out to her. I hated the idea of being bait, food for some waiting snake. *What the hell did she mean?*

Eve walked toward the entrance, like a shadow moving across the floor. No one seemed to notice her. I slowly realized that I couldn't really follow her either, even though I was looking right at her. With each step, she became more a part of the background noise, her confident and deliberate movements altered and faded into the overall movement of the scene. I tried to focus, to pick out some feature that I could hold onto and I noticed her hair. It was short, spiky, and brown... I think auburn, but as she passed in and out of the shadows and colored lights, I wasn't sure.

I needed to follow her. I finally snapped out of my stupor, and realized that although she hadn't said much, she'd said enough. Crazy or not, coincidence or not, her references to the madness of the last few days warranted a longer conversation.

Suddenly, my legs were infused with energy. I jumped up from the stool and dashed across the main room. I quickly edged around tables and the involved and distracted patrons sitting around them.

Trying to get through to the entrance, I tried to keep her in my view.

"Hey! Cool down, fella... givin' me a mad downer!" I had bumped into a man who had been deep into his fantasy, or looked that way at least.

"Sorry, I..." I slowed down just long enough to apologize directly, but in passing. The gentleman's attitude, however, had already clearly turned from aggravation to interest.

"You could join me? And I'd feel better about the whole thing," he drew out the last two syllables and his voice rose as I took a few shuffling steps toward the entrance.

"No, I... no, I'm with... sorry." I turned away and picked up the pace. I could hear the man getting back to his endeavors. He said something like 'good luck' but I wasn't sure.

Eve opened the door and stepped outside. Seconds later, before the door returned completely to a closed position, I shoved it open with my body in full stride, and stepped out into the night.

Black Out

Seven

A wash of cold, damp air hit my face. My breath was visible and audible. Looking across the street, to the left and to the right, I saw no one. My pulse pounded in my ears. I strained to see into shadows, to look around corners, but the street was deserted. Headlights turned slowly onto the street followed by the whir of an engine and the chewing sound of rubber on asphalt.

As the car passed me, I stared at it, attempted to stare into it, but there was nothing to see through the tinted glass. The brake lights burned red trails into my eyes as it stopped at the intersection. A moment—it felt like hours—passed and the car turned on to the cross-street and out of sight.

I took a few steps down the sidewalk then I felt a prick at my cheek. I'd had a static shock from a kiss before, and it felt just like that, soft, wet, and spiky at the same time. I spun around and scanned the scene.

A dizzy wave washed over me, my stomach flipped, and my eyes floated like I was drunk. It was like Inertial Dampening Sickness, or at least more like that than drugs or drunkenness. But it only lasted a couple of seconds. When the feeling subsided, I shook my head and checked my cheek, but there was nothing remarkable.

No Eve.

I was alone.

I was in a portrait; a single man on a poorly lit section of sidewalk, standing against an empty night. A nearby sign yells at me in neon red that it's late and the world is closed to me. It was a lonely picture even if it was a little melodramatic. Friends and family? Nope, just me and an empty street.

I took a deep breath then sighed it out through full cheeks. My brother and I used to hang out around here whenever he visited me at the university. We talked about his work in quantum communication and about my lack of work towards my degree. I don't think he was ever disappointed in me, instead, I think he was sorta proud. He never said it, but he had a particular look whenever I mentioned my adventures with illicit chems. His smile and posture would be sarcastically condemning, but his eyes would light up with curiosity. The truth is that he probably mistook my reckless behavior for courage. But who knows? It's not like I can ask him now.

Looking around again, I couldn't even find the bar we used to frequent. I felt silly, lost, tired, and even more confused.

I returned to the heavy bar door, shook my head, and shut my eyes hard until they were stinging from the pressure. I tried to compose something of myself, to look normal, but I was haggard and I'm sure it showed. *Oh well.* I opened the door and went back inside.

Inside, the bright white overhead lights were on, the tables and bar lights were off, and the booths were all open, curtains tied back. The furnishings looked right, but where did everyone go? Disoriented, I looked around to see if I'd somehow come into the wrong place. Even if I missed the repeated light-ring décor in the tables, chairs, and the bar, there were displays on the walls and above the bar that read, "Halo." This was definitely the same bar I'd left moments ago.

"Sorry, we're closed." A strong male voice echoed from somewhere I could not see.

A head popped out from inside one of the booths, nodded to me, "Sir? Yes, you. Service is closed for the night."

"Wha...," my voice broke as I noticed Lily notice me. She was cleaning glasses and resetting the bar for the next shift.

"Heya, cutie," she pitched her voice across the room to me. Then to the man, "Don't give him a hard time, Ronny. You're the one who's too lazy to lock up."

"Whatever you say," Ronny responded, more disinterested than grumpy. He returned to his tasks in the booth.

My legs warbled as I crossed the main room. The structure seemed the same, but the bright lights and the absence of the music caused my brain to slide around uncomfortably in my skull. "I was just in here... with a woman... I mean, I wasn't with her, but..." I was grasping for the words, trying to put together a question to ask Lily.

"Yeah, I remember," Lily was still preoccupied with her closing responsibilities but she glanced up as she spoke. She was wearing a loose-fitting purple shirt now, beneath a pair of well-used overalls. "Tongue-tied then as you are now."

She stopped for a moment, took a sip from a drink she'd made for herself, and then she raised her eyebrows to me. "Here. You look like you need this a lot more than I do... maybe loosen you up a bit." She slid the low-ball over to me, and I was glad for it.

I downed the contents of the glass at a single pass. Lily, momentarily back at work, looked up, saw the empty glass, and smiled and nodded at me. She stood fully upright again, and her hands swiftly went about the automatic task of remaking the drink while she beamed at me, "So, why'd you come back in here, tonight?"

"I, uh... how long was I out?" the sound of my voice echoed around inside my head and my ears, the same as when Lily {Sara} first introduced herself. I wasn't sure if I meant, 'out' like a blackout or like 'away' from the bar.

My discomfort must have been plain on my face, because I could tell I'd thrown Lily off. She assumed I came back for some kind of after-hours tryst of which she approved, but now I was basically insulting her, not going for her the way she expected.

She frowned, "I don't know, you came in... quarter past midnight? Left maybe ten, maybe twenty minutes later? I'm not sure." She leaned over the bar a bit, squared herself up to me. "I keep getting mixed signals from you... I gotta ask... what the fuck? My Gauge shows you as completely safe, but then you get this look on your face like, I don't know what, then my read glitches out and you aren't even there. No body temp, no rap sheet, nothing." She backed up, and waited, more than a little impatiently for my response.

"I don't know...," embarrassed, I started looking at anything except Lily.

Then, without warning, the whole story pours out of me, "I started the weekend with some nasty drugs; hallucinated a kidnapping, mine, by the way; a dead woman spoke to me; I stumbled on a Stream about my best friend running tests on me while I was ordering a pizza; and then a figment of my blackout, she was sitting right there, told me all of it was real and then simply disappeared." I caught my breath, "And then... then I inexplicably lose a couple of hours." I shook my head and then shrugged.

Some amount of sympathy must have existed in the tired tender, because she tilted her head a little and seemed almost intrigued by my story. "You ordered pizza?" she smiled.

So surprised by her question, I actually needed several seconds to catch on. Then I couldn't help the thick-exhale-chuckle that shook me with relief. "Yeah, yep," I nodded and had the courage to look at Lily again, "I ordered a pizza. Supreme."

"Supreme? I'm a margarita-madam myself. But I like to switch it up... go for all meat sometimes even." She seemed to have forgiven the strangeness, and the glitches, in our interactions. It might be that I've met another seriously experienced drug-user in this Lily.

As if to answer my thoughts she continued, "I've had a few hard trips, too." She turned away from me and busied herself with the last of her labors. "Really though, it's what we're always pushing for, right? It's just not the same if you can tell what is reality and what isn't." She looked up again at me for a moment, "I'm almost finished here, just sit tight. I know an all-nighter where we can get some food and talk… see where we end up in the morning." She smiled. Her lips and eyes dared me to decline.

If today started with an intimate knowledge of Lily's tattoo, I think every insane moment this weekend would be completely worth it. Under other circumstances, I probably would never have met her, much less talked to her.

Renewed a bit, I stood tall and anted-up. "I'm game." She turned her attention back to clean-up detail.

A calmness set in, the kind that usually arrives with the sun, the morning after a horrible nightmare. Of course she was right… just a bad trip. Demy had said the same thing. So, maybe it all makes sense?

Doesn't it?

There was really nothing special about any of the events of the evening. The Pez must have still been working through me when I was at Demy's, still putting the voodoo on my perception. The effects might still be working on me now, even, but this moment felt fine and good. Even in the surreal environment of a brightly lit bar going through its closing routine, I felt normal. I liked this Lily… or Sara?

"Hey, I just remembered one of the trippy moments…" Lily knelt down to operate a cleaner. A fan with a soft whir kicked on, but I thought I heard her say something affirming, so I continued, "Right, so along with ordering a pizza, I also heard you say your name was Sara. It was like dual streams mapped to the same window, but through my eyes and ears. Your lips moved, and your voice spoke, 'Lily' and 'Sara,' and it freaked me out, like my senses were overwhelmed with too mu…"

Lily stood up and moved aggressively over to me. The bar was the only thing between us.

63

"I don't know what this is about but you're going to have to leave," her voice was harsh, direct, and implacable. "Ronny!" she yelled to the front of the main area. Ronny had moved to the last booth, the one closest to the entrance.

"But," I was flustered, trying to find firm ground again, "But, what did I say... I don't..."

"You need to leave." She annunciated each word clearly but I wouldn't be dissuaded.

This rollercoaster had to end. I wanted off. I reached over the bar, "Wait, Lily, wait, what did I...?" and it hit me all at once, "That was real?!"

"Why the act? Why try to pick me up? Get your kicks fucking with your marks? I knew there was something wrong with you... something just off... kept glitching out my read. How did you find me?" She was venomous, 180 degrees from the vixen I knew a moment before.

"Look, whatever you're thinking about me, you're wrong," I leaned farther over the bar, "I don't know anything about you! It's gotta be a coincidence...," but I lose the conviction of my words as I realized the fear in her eyes.

She was cornered, and I was apparently the aggressor, the threat. Before I had the chance to convince her otherwise, Lily-Sara-Whatever tapped the bar. A light flashed up around me and I was slammed with a high-voltage shock.

I didn't really feel my body as it flew back and hit the table. Or maybe I landed on the ground? I was only peripherally aware of the distance and impact. I heard another commanding call to Ronny. Lily sounded as though she was talking into an aluminum can.

I tried to pick up my head but it felt impossibly heavy, like I was trying to lift a bowling ball with my nose. *I guess, I guess I'll just stay right here for a while.*

Evening

Eight

The sun burned a hole through the surface of the ocean, and spilled sanguine over the sky. The red welling up from the wound bled into the blue and gave birth to a mixture of orange and green. Close to the horizon, wisps of low clouds were cutting white ribbons into the twilight sky.

The view from the 127th floor of the Spire was breathtaking. The monolithic, formerly military, installation was erected over 100 years ago on an island, little more than a mile and a half away from the City. It rose up from the grave of a once-proud national monument. This new monument, though, was made for a different purpose and from materials that would never fall victim to the same fate as its predecessor.

The dark green, almost black, obelisk was seamless and polished to a glassy finish. After the End War, the Collective established Spire as one of its homes, a base of operations for the eastern portion of the continent. The military didn't so much dissolve after the war as much as it was folded into the Collective, becoming an unnamed authority, assigned to police the police.

The public face of this cloaked branch, spent a large portion of its resources on "inSpiring" the population. The propaganda machine occasionally leaked details of its activities to satisfy the conspiracy theorists, and to give everyone else something tangible to criticize. These carefully contrived tidbits of supposedly insider-information served to obfuscate the true objectives of the organization and kept would-be investigators looking in the wrong directions.

Consequently, few individuals had clear visibility into the darkest faction of the Collective, its inner-workings and motivations. On the 127th floor though, one could begin to understand…

Looking deep into the Wall, Eve watched as ships of air and water marked the sky and sea. They were so small.

"Eve." The man's voice was a deep bass, the kind of voice you felt in your chest more than you heard with your ears.

She hesitated, and then leaned closer to the Wall. She was close enough to touch it, to put her face to the cool surface, and to pretend it was a window, a way out. But she didn't touch it. She stared deeper into the sunset and thought about how that sun would rise for some tomorrow, but probably not for her.

"Eve. You know how much I like the view. Don't make me turn it off to get your attention." The large man sat behind his desk, staring at Eve's back. He was well-dressed, the expensive suit clean and pressed. He projected the calm and confidence of someone who had crushed his enemies both with skill and with might. He was a man in control.

Several holograms populated the length of the man's crescent-shaped Desk. Text and pictures streamed across the holograms, each rapidly and constantly updated. The room was large and unadorned otherwise.

Eve imagined a safe and uncomplicated place—a place that she could go where courage and destiny were fables, a place where she would not have to face this man, a place where she would not have to explain her actions or accept the consequences of her choices. Eve closed her eyes and took a deep breath. She held her hope invisibly, showing no signs of weakness, and turned to face the man.

"Leader," Eve acknowledged him with a nod, slightly tilted to the left, and a delicate smile.

Leader 127 pushed back into his chair, placed his elbows onto the arm rests, formed a fist with his right hand, and covered it loosely with his left in front of his chest. His biceps stressed the fabric of his suit jacket, and promised to tear at full flex.

He looked at Eve without blinking, attempting to discern her thoughts. His face was a mask that revealed nothing of his emotions. The severity of jaw was dramatized by a perfectly trimmed, raven black beard. He had a full head of equally kept hair, thick and strong.

His controlled expression and hidden intentions inspired fear. It silently planted seeds of doubt in whomever he interrogated. Often, all he had to do was stare that cold dark stare at his subject and wait for him or her to crack.

Most people who were subjected to the full weight of the man's gaze gave up any secrets immediately, recognizing the futility of attempting to keep anything from him, hoping for forgiveness through honesty. Eve was cagier than most, though, which was a trait the Leader respected and admired. Unsuccessful in his initial attempt to obtain an explanation, he shrugged his eyebrows, softened his eyes, and returned the nod.

"Desk, all, horizontal display only." The holograms faded out of the air and into the Desk surface, leaving nothing between the two reticent occupants of the room.

The twilight was turning quickly to dusk. The ambient light of the room was turning purple, even though some of the overhead lights were already brightening in response to the darkness.

Eve, wearing the requisite close-fitting amber-colored linen dress, looked like an angel against the Wall, the setting sun burning the edges of her silhouette.

"Your continual feed has come under investigation, Eve," the Leader leaned slightly forward, glanced downward, and nodded his head a few times. "Hacking a live stream isn't easy when no one is looking... while being observed, almost impossible. I'm impressed," he spoke as he glanced back up to Eve and returned to his more reclined posture.

Eve placed her hands behind her back in an antiquated militaristic stance. It's about as at-ease as she can be, enduring interrogation by the man who controls her fate.

"You knew it wasn't perfect?" the Leader only barely phrased the sentence as question. "Of course you knew. So, I can only imagine that you wanted to tell me something...?"

The overhead lights were now responsible for the majority of the illumination in the room. The landscape Wall was gradually fading and darkening, blending in with the room's walls more and more with each passing moment. Behind her back, Eve's hands began to sweat. Anticipation and anxiety shivered down her spine and quivered in her stomach.

A minute, full, counted, and longer than any she had ever known, passed.

"Eve, this project will not suffer your reluctance to move it forward any longer." The Leader's voice was fatally serious. He reached forward just enough to tap a few sequences into the Desk. A single hologram appeared, and the Leader executed a quick clockwise circle with his pointer finger, flipping the image to face Eve's position on the other side of the Desk.

"Gabriel M. Beaumont... you were supposed to collect him but according to your feed he wasn't there when you arrived at his apartment," the Leader tapped a few more times and the image changed.

"Early Sandoval... surreptitiously given a dose of the compound by you," he placed additional emphasis on the last word as he stared through the hologram at Eve. "She wasn't on our list, and your response to the inquiry regarding your independent administration of the test was what? Mistaken identity?"

He looked at Eve admonishingly, his spoiled child. "We weren't able to run any tests on the body by the time we recovered it. And you haven't even bothered to explain why her initial position wasn't reported for collection. That's curious."

"Joshua Falken...," he paused longer than his previous introductory statements and evaluated Eve's response to the name. "Now he, he was on the list. Administration of the compound was clean and we brought him in. He tested poorly and we dumped him."

Eve stood calmly, unwilling to take the bait. The Leader was toying with her now.

He must have been evaluating her feed personally. Her circumvention was only clever enough to avoid cursory inspection and nothing more. The Watchers weren't likely to notice the inconsistencies or the patterns in her behaviors. Anyone scrutinizing the data more closely than that though—anyone looking for something to be wrong—would certainly have found problems. The way she would circle an area, then circle another, forming a loose figure eight, and then appear to spend quite a bit of time in the same area might seem odd, but would not have warranted investigation.

A second glance might reveal some static in the feed. The interpolation she implemented wasn't perfect. The data was never perfect either though, so even that flaw might not draw attention on its own.

Someone noticing both oddities, however—the behavior and the pattern of missing bits—would not have to go far before running the red flag up the pole. If she had known of the Leader's special interest in her, Eve would probably have been more careful. The Leader was good. He'd probably marked each and every time Eve's feed was bullshit for as far back as Eve's archive went.

Eve's stomach was cold.

"Joshua... your acquisition of Joshua was seamless." The last words were spoken with strong pauses between each. "I expect that it went perfectly because of all of the extra observation and attention you were giving him." The Leader waited again. Eve breathed evenly and calmly, and did not speak a word.

"Judging by the proximity and frequency of your unmonitored excursions, I'd say you were hunting Joshua before we were, before his name had been revealed." His eyebrows raised ever so slightly, wrinkles deepening in his forehead, before he spoke again, "I cannot explain that last bit, Eve, and I require an explanation."

The office was shaded in the amber of the overhead lights. The colors of the single vertical display showing the report on Joshua Falken were the only other colors in the room. The Leader looked like a demon with the mixed colors and the shadows both above and below the contours of his strong face. He waited, admiring Eve's will to resist, giving nothing away. Nevertheless, she would be broken.

"I'm impressed, but also disappointed. We can obtain no greater detail, with regard to your off-the-Watch activities, from what we have collected which only leaves some unpleasant, and likely damaging, neuroscopic interrogation methods." The threat was empty, not because he wouldn't have her cut and sampled a thousand times over to get what he wanted, but because her fate was already decided. There was no tolerance for insubordination at her level, and Eve had been operating on her own for too long to be reconditioned.

He scrutinized her a little longer and decided that she knew that her life was forfeit. He had hoped to gain some information from the woman, to reconcile the betrayal, before ending her.

Finally, the Leader stood. His enormous size and strength imposed his will into every corner of the room. "You're very good. I never even suspected you. In fact, you underestimated yourself. You're on the top of my list, the Elite. You are one of the few in which I have personal interest because your talents go beyond your training. You're so good that I use your choices and techniques to inform future training," he smiled. Eve really hadn't known. He could see it plainly on her face. If she hadn't been of the highest caliber, he would never have been observing her directly, not even occasionally.

"Take her."

Four forms behind the Leader moved forward. The light bent and collided through their shapes for a disorienting moment, but it only lasted a few seconds. They were soldiers, armored and armed, and they approached Eve from each side of the Desk.

"You're wrong," Eve interrupted the Leader calmly.

Two more Light-Benders moved from positions near the Wall behind Eve. The Leader seemed to grow in size, adopting an animalistic attack posture. He addressed his prey coldly, "Wrong about you, maybe."

"You're wrong about how this will end."

As the four soldiers from the front closed in on Eve, she stepped back, her arms and legs tensing with muscular vigor. The distance between her and the two immediately behind her was only just beyond arm's reach.

She slowly inhaled through her nose, quietly building strength from her diaphragm. Blood charged into her toes and fingers as her chest opened but remained deeply connected to her torso. Her focus expanded, her augments kicked on, her adrenaline spiked, and her serotonin receptors went into full bloom.

There she was again, in the center of the moment as it was unwrapped. As the layers peeled away Eve could see new pieces of the world, vibrant and clear. She waited there quietly, in that elastic time, for the moment to open completely.

Time is a fictional notion here in the quiet before the storm. It is nothing but a story of linear progression, contrived by the single-threaded minds of a concrete society so that they can function without fear. It is protection from the truth that reality is flexible, unknown, and ever-changing and that each one of us is vulnerable and ephemeral.

Eve had been there before, in the eye of combat, and she recognized her thoughts as delusions. She had been trained to believe such thoughts were a side effect of her ego as her GEaRS made her capable of absorbing and assimilating huge amounts of information from all of her senses.

I'm only here, right now, because I believe they are wrong.

The training agreed with reality, regardless. Delusional or not, combatants that believed they were invincible were victorious more often than those full of doubts. Besides, cutting to the core of it, all of that extra information, high volume and high speed, was good information even if it came with a taint of egomania.

The moment was full and open.

Eve's hands came to life, fingers long and relaxed. She swept her arms up, one after the other, in front of her and then over her head. Her fingertips traced sharp arcs through the air and her linen dress trailed after, slower than her body and the material stretched to catch up, creating gossamer sails at her sides.

With incredible agility, she slipped between the two soldiers that were behind her. She hooked each of the soldiers in passing, her augmented fingernails penetrating their armor. Pulling them off balance, she pulled them together in front of her, cracking their armor together in a thunderous crash. The impact from the collision knocked them both unconscious and they crumpled to the floor like rag dolls.

Stepping back explosively, she crossed her arms, hugging herself. Then she grabbed the opposite shoulders of her dress and tore it from her body, casting the cloth in front of her like a net. Activating her own cloak, she folded into herself. She was completely invisible even before her shredded clothes touched down on the incapacitated soldiers.

"Sir... that's not standard issue..." Celeste, one of the remaining four soldiers, said aloud. Her voice revealed curiosity more than concern.

The Leader's personal guards were well-equipped with countermeasures for all known cloaking technology. Standard stealth devices were deactivated upon entry. It should have been impossible for Eve to enter the presence of a Leader with an engaged stealth system. Celeste was being over-communicative, and the Leader made a mental note of it.

The conscious soldiers methodically and quickly scanned the area, pointing their weapons into every inch of the room.

The Leader blinked his eyes, revealing a pair of dark agate Mantis orbs, similar to Eve's grass-green versions. As he scanned the room, his eyelids were peeled open to an absurdly large aperture. He leaned slightly forward and walked his fingertips along his Desk. The front arc of his Desk turned into a combat display but the only entities outlined in the room were the Leader's staff.

"Been doing some offline manufacturing? Full of surprises, my Eve. Thank you for the demonstra—"

A soldier inexplicably and suddenly fell to the ground. The remaining three turned in unison, focusing instantly on the movement and sound. They were too late though, as Eve had already taken up a new position behind Celeste. She mimicked Celeste's every movement, using Celeste's body to block the Leader's probing gaze. Eve didn't know if the Leader could see her or not, but she wasn't taking any chances.

Eve hadn't really been sure that the dermal cloak was going to work at all. She'd been in the office since the implant and it had always gone undetected, but she had never activated it in the Spire. However, Leader 127 should not be underestimated. He probably had some off-the-record GEaR of his own.

The Leader sniffed the air, sampled it. He turned his head slowly, left and right, small and abrupt inhales in each direction. An image of the room began to form in his mind; more than vision, it was made of scents, sounds, and heat.

He looked hard at Celeste. "She's behind you."

Celeste spun around with precision and quickness, but Eve was faster. Circling Celeste as she turned, Eve crouched then sprung up and through the backs of her knees. The young soldier was lifted and flipped into the air. There was a loud crunching sound—armor or spine or both—as Celeste's body folded over itself, her head pinned and pinched between her chest and the floor.

Her body convulsing, Celeste's finger twitched and squeezed the trigger of her rifle. A single, high-energy round tore a column from barrel to ceiling. The air burned as the bullet passed, leaving an ephemeral but vivid trail. The impact resulted in a spectacular blue electrical discharge.

Seeing the shot as a momentary distraction, confident that he knew Eve's position, 127 made a move to end the game. He brought his Intra-Ocular Display into focus, finding the distance with practiced precision. Responding to his eyes, the IOD became more opaque. He focused on an element of the display and it turned red, then he swiped his hand through the air as though he were hitting someone with the back of his hand.

A radiant blast erupted out from around his Desk, blasting the room with a rippling concussion of air. The compression revealed the Leader's personal shield, making it visible for an instant. He remained untouched, unmoved by the passing wave. His conscious soldiers were not as well-protected. The blast hit all of them, and each in turn hit the far wall and dropped motionless to the floor.

The Leader scanned the room as the dust settled, but he could not find Eve. There was no sign of her, conscious or not, in the room. But she was there, she had to be there. The room was locked down already, 127 having taken the appropriate precautions.

Finally, he smiled and looked up. Eve's naked body was beautifully limned against the ceiling. It must have taken an enormous amount of physical strength to hold herself like that to the ceiling with her fingernails alone, augmentations or not. He wondered if she had sensed his play, if he'd given it away, or if she had already planned to crawl up there when he blasted the room. Either way, she'd improved her situation considerably, though he felt he still had the edge.

Then he heard his own voice calling down to him.

"Door open," the audio was perfect and the far door, the only way out of the office, opened on the command. "Override, grant access, Eve 85927. Lockout local commands."

Eve dropped to the floor onto all fours. The Leader made no move against her, but stood intrigued and curious. "You might make it out of here tonight, Eve, but you'll never be able to stay ahead of me."

"If I'm right, I won't need to."

She ran.

The Leader remained behind his Desk, standing motionless and thoughtful for several minutes. Finally, he sat and tapped out a few commands.

Within a short time, a man appeared at the entrance to the office and waited there silently. The Leader nodded and the man entered the dimly lit room. Sitting calmly at his Desk, 127 was a goliath compared to the slight stature of the man waiting attentively.

The Leader sat staring, miles away, through the Wall into the night. The silence between them was comfortable and well worn. Eventually, the Leader addressed the man.

"Jacobs, I'll need my access restored from SENTRy. I've locked myself out, uh, so to speak." He addressed the man without looking from the view. "Also, get Medical in here for my personal guard. There's been a bit of an accident, as you can see."

Jacobs whispered instructions quickly and quietly into his Glass. At the same time, he also used his Glass to scan the room.

"I'll need to requisition a tech team to analyze the last several minutes of activity in this room. Have records of all of Eve's movements in the Spire reviewed, everything from the last eight weeks... up to, and with particular attention to, the next half hour."

The Leader was sure that Eve would avoid identifying transactions as much as possible, but she could not possibly avoid them all. She knew she would never be able to return to the Spire once she left, so she might risk being seen to get supplies. Her choices, her actions, would speak where her voice failed.

"And Jacobs..."

"Yes, sir?"

"Put together an extraction team for Joshua Falken."

SPIRE

Wake

Nine

It felt like needles were being driven directly into my retina each time I opened my eyes. I tried to listen carefully but the sounds were all muddy and distant.

Voices?

Maybe?

My head exploded with pain as I lifted it and a wave of nausea passed through me. The muscles in my legs and arms ached as though I'd been working out but I couldn't remember the last time I was in a gym. *Did I pass out?*

Wincing back the pain, I opened my eyes wider and looked around. At first, there was nothing in focus and my perspective was messed up. It was as though my eyes were crossed and I couldn't uncross them.

I squeezed my lids shut and open, shut and open again, and the image slowly resolved to an unfamiliar, tiled ceiling.

"... waking up... "

A woman's face appeared a foot from mine and my memory-lag cleared up like a stretched rubber band suddenly released. The snap back was a whip cracking me into the here and now.

"What the fuck!?" I said with as much angry energy as I could muster. I tried to push myself away but my hands and arms are not only throbbing, they're bound. Squirming away from her, I spit words at Lily, "What the hell? What did I do to you?"

Lily stared at me strangely, "Who sent you?"

"Sent me? I don't have any clue what you're talking about," I kept backing away from her until I hit the wall.

A strong sense of claustrophobia squeezed my chest and suffocated my brain. I shut my lids hard against another wave of nausea and head-throbbing pain. A cold sweat started to bead up on my arms and face.

I opened my eyes and focused directly on hers, "Whoever you are or were… I don't care. I've been following trip-phantoms around for days, so my grip has loosened some, but," I tried to wrench my wrists free, but the motion made the ties bite into my skin, "… but, whatever your 'intrigue,' I don't know anything about it and I don't want to know anything about it."

I wondered for a moment if I could somehow reverse the pain in me and project it outward to pierce this woman's bullshit balloon… or at least hurt her a little and get her to give up whatever crazed notion she had that inspired taking me captive.

Lily was kneeling, looking at me and looking away alternatively. She seemed almost nervous, jittery. She was scared… almost as scared of keeping me tied up as of cutting me loose, but not quite.

Seeing the fear on her face changed my perspective on the situation. My frustration and anger faded some. Lily might be crazy, but what if she wasn't? What if she really had something to fear?

A calm feeling washed over my skin. The tension in my body released and I found I could relax even though I was bound. I felt good, healthy and strong. My senses were uncharacteristically vivid, rich with texture. Even the clothing I wore etched great detail into my skin.

My head swelled and my eyes floated. The room—the size and shape, the contents—were somehow available to my touch, even from a distance. I saw a box and felt the papery, dry cardboard of it. The walls were rough and tasted dusty and dirty. There were rows of kegs, metallic, round, and smooth. I touched everything... without really touching anything at all. It felt like I was filling up the empty spaces of the place with my skin.

I saw Lily. Her face was turned away from me.

I was free, observing her body with the razor's edge of my new senses. She was beautiful and fragile.

My arms and legs grew longer and talons erupted from my hands and feet. I slowly reached out to her with my devilish claws. Placing the fingers of my claws around her exposed shoulders, I touched her with one finger at a time, eerily arrhythmically. The tip of each black barb was pushing against her skin without piercing it, like a razor blade in a fingerprint.

If she moved, she would shred herself to ribbons against me.

I was not satisfied. I needed to surround her completely not just cage her shoulders. I wanted more. So much more.

Against the wall, I felt two large boney knobs push out from my back. The knobs grew and the pressure shoved me out from the wall. I breathed in deeply, my chest expanded and a pair of wing-like limbs broke out of the growths on my back. As they unfurled, it was clear they were more obsidian than feather, composed of jagged, layered scales and veins of agate. Flexing them fully open from my back I flattened my chest and grew broader.

Wrapping myself around Lily, I entombed her with my lethal body. I pulled myself closer to her effortlessly, my arms hugging her in a threatening embrace. With one hand, I held the entirety of her back, and with the other I held her skull. I pulled myself even closer to her.

I was salivating and my lips were quivering as they peeled back from my rigid teeth. My jaw was ripping at my face to open wider and I felt my own hot breath reflected back from Lily's cheek.

She turned her attention and her face toward me again. Her fear-filled indigoes shimmered with uncertainty. Lily was struggling with what to do next. I could see that she wanted to trust me, to let me go. But she didn't know how. Even if she was wrong about me initially, she thought that I'd certainly want to hurt her now.

"You're doing that creepy thing again, jamming up my read. And what's wrong with your..." Lily knelt closer to me, reached out with the softest hands I can ever remember touching my face, cupped my cheek and pulled back my lid so that she could see in, "... your eyes are..."

A deep, quick involuntary inhale yanked air into my chest. It was as though I'd just barely made it back to the surface in time after being beneath the water way too long. I blinked several times rapidly, coming to, waking up.

I was going to kill her, hold her, save her, fuck her, love her? What was that? My head hurt like I was coming down with the flu. And, I felt uncomfortable with myself. I had no problem allowing my emotions to run wild, for my thoughts to go down any path uninhibited. They were just thoughts and emotions, I owned them and they weren't *real.* They were just in my head, *weren't they?*

But it hadn't felt like that. I could have hurt her. I'd felt it, so palpable, so vivid. I could have ripped her apart. I didn't want that. I didn't really want her to suffer. It was a fleeting emotion, I felt for only a second. I mean I should have been angry. I was teased, mistaken for I-don't-know-who, shocked, and bound.

I was confused, and she was definitely frightened. The raw emotional turmoil of the anger and lust faded as I saw through to her, and realized she'd just made a mistake that she didn't know how to unmake.

Then curiosity stole her attention, "What is wrong with your eyes?" Her voice was concerned. She had, at least for the moment, forgotten her fear and anxiety.

I was becoming a little delirious, overwhelmed with overlapping memories. Every second since I had been nabbed was held in front of me, a crawling collage of time that offered no distinction between my dreams and consciousness. I could only sit and stare back at her dumbly.

"Your pupils are throbbing... and your eyes...? They're thick and the colors are richer than they were. They're almost completely opaque, but... there're swirls, almost like marbles?"

As she peered closer, I realized that she had seen nothing of my fangs and talons, felt nothing of my aggressive intentions. She was straining to get a better look at my eyes and she pushed back my eyelids. She pulled one up a little too hard and I felt a sharp needling flash of pain. Shaking my head away from her prying fingers, tears welled up and I rapidly blinked them away. Trying to wash away the sharp burn, I stretch and contort my cheek and brow, and wrinkle and unwrinkle my nose.

"Lily, I know you're scared of me, but honestly, I don't know why," although those claws might have been a reason if they had been real, if she'd known they were there. "What are you mixed up in? Do you generally expect bad people to come looking for you?"

Lily inspected me closely again, "Your eyes are... almost human again. Is that some kind of new... I don't know, reptilian thing?"

The memory collisions subsided and my head became somewhat less foggy. I still felt the pre-flu grogginess, but I felt better having the confusing overlapping images out of my head.

Lily's curiosity about my eyes was disarming. She seemed like a tech brat to me in that moment—the offspring of wealth, feeding her boredom with expensive toys—or maybe she just seemed like a genuine Gearhead. I suppose the latter fit her better but I wasn't expecting to find out one way or the other. The odds of after-glow, pillow-talk and back-story, and morning coffee had diminished considerably since I called Lily 'Sara.' Sadly, I guessed that part of my night was just a dream.

"I'm chipless. Zero GEaRS." I kept my answer short, because I wanted to get back on topic, "Who exactly were you expecting? Or hoping never to run into?"

"Laterali," she shrugged more to herself than to me.

Being that I wasn't a child anymore, I reacted with more than a little skepticism. The Laterali, a group of death-for-hire assassins, had appeared in my lifetime in more than their fair share of fiction, and not at all otherwise. The 'boogeymen' might actually be coming for Lily, but I doubted it.

"Well, clearly, by the ease with which you captured me, I'm no assassin." My voice was condescending.

She reached into the front pocket of her overalls and pulled out a box-cutter. Then, moving quickly enough to make me nervous, she positioned herself behind me. Two snaps and tugs later, and my hands and legs were freed.

I sat myself up against the wall and rubbed my wrists and hands, attempting to return circulation to my fingers.

"I kept getting this strange feeling that I knew you, and when you came back to the bar? I thought you wanted to party, you know? And then you mentioned that whole name thing and... I... I'm sorry."

Lily moved to a standing position in front of me, looking at the walls while she absent-mindedly retracted the blade of the box cutter and dropped it in the breast pouch of her overalls. I would have mistaken the move as flirtatious, a come-and-get-it gesture earlier in the evening, but now I knew better. She exuded sexuality in everything that she did, and not always consciously. Mixed with paranoia and volatility...

"Your tattoo should be a fly-trap instead of a lily, you know that? Would have been a nice foreshadow," I responded flatly. Then, not without compassion, I offered an apology, "I'm sorry, too."

Whether she deserved an apology from me or not I wanted her to feel better. If didn't matter if the Laterali were fact or fiction, Lily was certainly scared of someone or something and it can't be easy living life in constant fear. For her, every shadow might be hiding another kind of shadow that has been hired to kill her.

Lily read my apology as a little patronizing or maybe somewhat sarcastic, "Look, it doesn't matter whether you believe they exist or not, I don't take chances. I have my reasons."

She stared into the middle distance and stood motionless. Her face became serious, hardened against an unpleasant image. After a couple of moments, she braced herself against the memory, "I don't care what name you put to them, there are people looking for me and I prefer not to be found."

Looking down at me, wearing a wan smile on her face, "Anyway, I agree that you're not one of them." She gave me a half smile and a turned-up eyebrow, "But you aren't exactly normal either..."

She extended her hands to help me up. I hesitated for a moment, and then declined her offer by simply helping myself up. Although I felt somewhat compelled to know more about her, I wasn't interested in going on some wild tangent from my own. I needed to get away from here, find somewhere safe to sleep, and get myself sorted.

Where had Eve gone?

I couldn't remember what she told me exactly, but returning to my apartment seemed like it would be a mistake. People were after me and they'd already lifted me once from my apartment.

Laughing at myself, I realized Lily and I were both probably running from our imaginations. But the moment of relief passed as quickly as it came. I remembered Early Sandoval and that could not have been a coincidence.

I tuned back into Lily. I'd left off paying attention to her and she'd been filling in the silence.

"... more than I should have spent, but it saved my butt more than once. The customers that come in here are pretty tame and they can find better than me at the consoles or in the booths, so I don't often even get harassed. Mostly, our patrons are the kind that an ordinary bouncer can handle. Heck, even Ronny can handle most of... shit."

Her animated face twisted with doubt, "I asked him not to call the cops, you know? To let me deal with you," she took a moment, presumably to imagine Ronny in the situation, "He is the overly protective, older brother type. The kind who doesn't listen, as well as he means."

I stood there staring blankly. This was some nasty coincidence that I happened to step in and get all over myself. I had to get myself straight, find out if Eve is a reality, if anything she said was true. I wanted to tell Demy I was okay, but I wasn't sure if I'd be lying… wasn't sure I could trust him. And before any of that, it sounded like I might have to run from a C.O. or two.

It was time to leave.

"Am I losing you?"

Focusing on Lily, I realized that I'd better pick up my part of the conversation.

"No, I uh… look, I was telling you, you know, before you electro-shocked me out? That I'd been into something pretty bad lately. I'm confused and I want to figure out what happened to me. And…" Looking at her, I wanted to offer something better than 'I'm more interested in my shit, right now,' but I didn't have the energy.

"You don't have to say anything else." She read my mind, "I don't want to explain any of this to the Collective either." She looked around and then, "Let's get outta here. I know just the place."

Shades

Ten

He woke in a cold sweat, his heart pounding. His surroundings were unfamiliar and it took him a moment to place himself as his mind stumbled forward from the blackness. Not just unconsciousness, but blackness.

Gabriel had had to make several stops last night. Finding a place to stay when all you had, ill-forged false-financials notwithstanding, were a few hundred dollars, a broomstick cane, and a smile, was a difficult task.

He had cut his Credentials out of his arm with a scalpel and dumped them as soon as he was out of view of his old apartment. He'd butchered his skin in the process, but it had to be done. Vanya probably hadn't given any information to his client—because he was still looking to get paid—but that did not make Gabe feel any better about walking around as the man Vanya thought he was. Gabe wasn't an artist of counterfeiting but given some time, and some tools, he would be able to obtain a new set of passable Creds.

While he made his way looking for a vacancy, he stopped off at random convenience stores and had palmed a few boxes of painkillers before the night was done. He was spotted once, but the attendant had looked the other way. Looking back, he realized how pathetic he must have appeared for the clerk to basically give him a pass on stealing.

It didn't matter. He was glad to have the drugs. He might not have made it to this motel without them. The pain in his leg had been screaming for him to stop before his first dose of relief, and he'd almost succumbed to it.

He shivered beneath the worn-thin covers of the motel bed and remembered the black shapes from his nightmare. The feverish dreams of the evening had been filled with frightening portents. The memories shook him again and pain came swiftly in response to the movement.

Squeezing his thigh gingerly, just above the knee, he felt the marbled stiffness of the muscle beneath his skin. The whole leg throbbed with a steady ache. He reached for another dose of pain relievers from the container he'd left on the nightstand, but his hands failed him and he just ended up knocking the open container to the floor. The contents spilled out and Gabe, only able to suspend himself for that one moment, gave up and allowed himself to sigh back into the mattress. Quiet for only a breath or two, the dream images came rushing back to the broken Chemist.

They were forms, lightless vacuums reaching for him, surrounding him, attempting to extinguish him. They were memory wraiths. Peering into the spectres, they sucked the breath from him, suffocating him. He tried to look away, but each direction held a new horror, another incomprehensible shadow of something familiar, yet unknown. There was no escape from the blackness.

Gabe squeezed his eyes against the nightmare, squeezed them hard enough to shut out the thoughts. Opening and closing his hands he warmed them up a bit and rolled himself over onto his good leg. He reached down while clutching the bed for support and grabbed for the blue gelatins. The little pills slid and rolled around on the floor, but he managed to gather a few.

Pulling himself back onto the bed into a seated position, he took one pill after another, biting each one open so the liquid would run smooth and viscous over his tongue. Relief washed over his body as the fluid dissolved.

The chemicals synthesized for the drug were not altogether unlike the kind that Gabe worked on—more stable perhaps, but not really that different. But then again, these drugs were legal. He wondered for a moment why he hadn't just gone with convention, why he hadn't chosen a more upstanding occupation, but the thought faded quickly, usurped by the lingering terror of the dream.

There was a knock. Like a knock at the door, but he wasn't inside. He was out in the open, under a big, burning-orange, twilight sky. He stood alone in a street, mirrored-glass high rises obscuring the distance, but he did not feel closed in. Then the knock came again. Louder, more insistent, but the sound had no discernable source. Shadows grew long, stretching from sidewalk to sidewalk, crossing the vacant street. There was no one, save Gabe, and yet the knock came again, louder, harder. The world quaked in response, but the sound did not change shape, it was still just a knock at the door. He took a couple of steps toward nothing in particular, lost and confused, stumbling for sure footing, struggling for an answer to the knocker.

Buildings shadowed buildings, creating alleys of nightfall around the intersection at acute angles to the streets and avenues. The darkness was spiraling and growing and Gabe was roughly at the nexus of the convergence.

Again the knock came, shaking the world, pounding his skull. It was as though his head was held tightly against a door, held with more pressure than he could have applied under his own strength, and the knock delivered a vibration directly to his brain. The sound, the echoes and trails of the sound, were shaking from inside his bones.

Gabe rubbed his face and his forehead. The memory was thick and sticky. He was caught in the knock, stuttering through the experience of both recent nightmares, real and dreamed. Vanya, blackness, Vanya, floor, thud, knock, thud. His head just kept hitting the floor, over and over again. The loop began with a sad, "Why?" and ended with the unforgettable sound of his brain hitting the inner wall of his skull and his head bouncing off the hardwood.

Gabe moaned at the memory.

The rush, the first push of the PainFree, softly ended the cycling of the two nightmares. In the calm of the medication, he thought about the last time he'd slept in a nice bed without anxiety, without fear. He tried to focus on a pleasant time in his life. He thought about the ocean, about the summer sun of his childhood. But like a hanging tooth, he couldn't stay away from the dream. He wanted to remember it, as though remembering it might help it go away forever.

In the dream, the darkness drew in around him, held him motionless. The shadows along the ground no longer matched the objects that cast them. They were somehow darker and their edges dulled, growing in different directions.

When Gabe looked closer, he saw that there were distinct shapes moving within the shadows, areas of blackness and emptiness within the darkness. The blackness moved with sentience, as though it was hunting, skulking. The shadows stalked the landscape, moving with stealth and precision until prey was found. Then hunger-quick, they pounced.

The Shades devoured brick and mortar, asphalt and concrete, anything and everything that was human in the dreamscape. Gabe's nightmare-self stood still, trapped by the Shades, afraid of being spotted.

The shadows were almost cast directly on him. He peered down, down deep into the one closest to him and the knock came again, angry this time, urgently demanding to be answered.

He fell to his knees, and his leg cried out full of pain, screaming blood through his ears. Gabe fell over to his side to relieve his knee and caught himself with his hands. His face was inches from the asphalt, completely shadowed.

His eyes watered as he peered into darkness and saw the Shades see him. Their movement ceased, they became statues, waiting. Then, cautiously, they began their approach. Through Gabe's watery-eyed vision, distorted and afraid, the ground turned into a swirling mess of cold, empty blackness. A movement–close, powerful, and quick–blew hot breath onto his face.

Gabe noticed that his hands were shaking, clammy and sweaty. Maybe it was remembering the dream, maybe it was a side-effect of the PainFree, or maybe it was his body struggling to repair his injury. No matter the cause, his heart was beating faster than it should for a man sitting motionless in bed.

He felt sweat beading up on his brow, and heat in the skin of his face. He clutched the edge of the mattress again, put his weight on his good leg, and levered himself down to the floor. He sucked up two more capsules into his mouth. The half-filled container in one hand, the mattress in the other, he knuckled himself back up onto the bed.

Parts of the nightmare were fading. Were the Shades wraiths, cats, humans in dark cloaks? He lost the ability to tell the difference because he was re-writing the dream by remembering it.

The knock, that was clear. The hot breathing in his face as the Shade pounced on him and grabbed him? That, too, was frighteningly clear. The Shade gnawed at him in the dream and in his mind, as he struggled to remember the details. The wraith, man, thing, was there and it finally spoke to him. The voice scratched at his ears...

The heat from the exhausted breath blew over him. Hugged by darkness, a shrouded face met his like a shadowy reflection come to life, and this hooded, indistinguishable face spoke without lips, without movement. Another hot breath moved every hair on Gabe's body, and a voice pushed into his mind.

It was the sound of a metal claw scraping down a chalkboard. The claw was the Shade's voice and the chalkboard was every bone in Gabe's body and the words were the shivering feeling down his spine to his tailbone.

"Let..."

"us..."

"in..."

Knock-knock. The door to his motel room made a soft request, "Anyone in there?" or, "May I please come in?"

Gabe had begun nodding back to sleep while remembering his nightmare.

"House keeping," a male voice quietly informed from the other side of the door. A soft rustling sound followed and then the door lock released with a satisfying metallic click-thunk.

"NO!" the Chemist finally came around to his senses but his voice was choked, "No, please! I mean, I'm in here, please come back later!" He didn't want to deal with anyone, didn't want to see anyone.

A muffled and slightly annoyed, "Sorry," came from the other side of the door. Gabe shook his head to himself, wondering how he had ended up here. As the floating giddiness of the PainFree moved counter to his motion, he became pleasantly dizzy. He sucked in a deep breath, his chest opening up without effort. The meds were working.

Gabe's fear of staying at the motel for another night, and his fear of falling asleep into another nightmare were strong, but the comfort of the PainFree was doubly strong as was his exhaustion. He lost the urge to move on. He eased himself down onto the bed. Struggling with the blankets a bit, he finally managed to cover himself somewhat. Like a child holding a stuffed animal, he clutched the container of meds to his chest with both hands and fell asleep.

Fast Breaks

Eleven

"Wow...," the look on Lily's face was difficult to read. I felt like I should offer some clarification, but if I opened my mouth I was afraid I would just confuse matters more. My explanation of the last several days had gone on for way too long.

She was a good listener, offering reassuring nods here and there, mumbling encouragements to continue, and she even helped me back to the thread of the story when I lost my way. It was nice to articulate the events, to manifest them in a way that made them all seem less dreamy and paranoid, less delusional. Maybe I was completely out of my mind but at least I didn't feel as badly about it talking to her.

When Lily and I left her bar earlier that morning, she had led the way. I wouldn't have recognized the streets we'd taken. Even without the throbbing distraction of my back and head, I would have been completely lost. She had taken a shortcut through an alleyway at some point that completely turned me around, and I never recovered. It was probably for the best. Being lost could make me harder to find. After all, I'm not going to any of my usual places. I'd never even seen this part of the city. Still, who was looking for me? What resources did they have? I didn't know.

The "All Niter" was a diner with room to serve maybe thirty people at once if those thirty people didn't mind being a little cramped. The small restaurant didn't have to worry about crowding this early in the morning, as there were only two other occupied tables. I felt myself drawn to each of the other patrons. Maybe I just wanted a distraction from the story I was telling, or maybe Lily's sensual energy was intimidating, either way, my consciousness strayed to those other tables.

A young man, a university student by his manner, ordered coffee after coffee, barely looking up from his display. I couldn't make out exactly what he was working on but I could tell that his Glass was sporting some expensive accessories. It was displaying a three-dimensional workspace and a projected key-space so he wasn't limited by the surface of his Glass for inputs. He was pretty savvy with his equipment too, because he moved fluidly without ever checking his position with his eyes, which wasn't an easy task without tactile feedback. He was a machine, or as much of one as a human can be. He was plugged in, attached to his work, detached from the world.

The other early-morning patron was a wintering man, his age evident from the light dusting of snow throughout his hair and in the day-old scruff on his jaw. But he wasn't so old that his black whiskers were faded, rather, the white bristles stood strongly among dark ones, like ghosts standing among the living.

I glanced over at the wintering man again and again, marveling at what a clever crafter his experience had been, chiseling deep character into his face. But there was even more to him than that. His body was sculpted too but it was more than a simple stoic expression of the events of his life; it was an instrument of change.

But the man was quiet right now; maybe age had slowed him down? Or maybe, like an old-world viper coiled up in a zoo, long-fanged and split-tongued, he was a predator resting out of reach, harmless. I could look at him, but I was scared to even consider touching the glass.

Sitting at the booth in the diner, I realized I was picturing a python where there was only an old man. My version of him didn't make any sense. I hadn't seen him do anything at all really, except occasionally offering a thank you to the waiter for refilling his water. He simply sat and stared, while I made up absurd stories about him.

Lily sipped at whatever beverage she was nursing. I hadn't even noticed that she'd ordered it. I felt strangely safe in the diner, reassured by how normal everything appeared to be, and how well-lit it was.

"So, do you really feel like you can't trust, um...," she paused to look inside herself and quickly returned, "Demy, right?"

"Yeah, I don't know. I mean, yes, his name is Demy. And no, I don't know if I can trust him or not... we've been friends for a long time, but we're not as close as we used to be."

I thought it over for a bit then continued, "Mostly, I hit him up for food and drinks once in a while and we reminisce. And the thing is that I can't imagine him purposefully doing something to harm me. We had our disagreements like any good friends but never anything serious."

"Well, who knows, right?" Lily fiddled with her mug, "Who knows what state your brain was in—the things you are describing, the detail, the memory after the fact—it's so clear. It's not a faded dream like most trips, you know?"

She stared into the distance for a minute, trying to capture some elusive memory or maybe the just right words, then her eyes sparked, "Like most times, I'm left feeling exhausted with a strong impression of... I don't know, something...? Like, just a vague set of images and impressions, of anticipation and pleasure."

As she tried to articulate the feeling, she lost it. I knew exactly what she meant, though, and trying to explain it always had a way of washing it away.

Lily came back into focus, "Of course, *some* of it is vivid, too, but not all of it, and definitely not like what you're describing. Whatever you were on was powerful."

"So, what are you saying then? That it was all a bad trip? But a trip on something so spectacular that I can't tell the difference between that and reality?"

She took another sip. She'd heard the anxiety in my voice and realized that taking a pause would probably help me calm down. I took the queue. Needed the break. I took a deep breath and let it out slowly.

A serene moment passed. She stared into her cup and gently pushed the steam away with pursed lips and a controlled exhale. Another sip. Another breath.

"I wouldn't go that far," Lily returned her cup to the table and her attention to the conversation, "I wouldn't say it was all hallucinations and a puff of smoke... I'm just suggesting you had no way then to interpret what was happening, and looking back at it probably isn't helping. I'm saying, I don't know, give Demy a call, get something fresh in your head. See what he has to say." She shrugged, "It couldn't possibly hurt, right?"

My turn. I chose a pause over a response. I took a break from considering my next move. I regretted not having a cup-of-anything to distract myself, so I reached across the table, picked up Lily's mug, ignored her challenging look of disbelief, noted the fiery flirtation in her defiant eyes, and stole a sip. Couldn't possibly hurt, right?

I almost spit it out. Revulsion filled my belly at the taste. It was something rancid and fishy and it was filling up my mouth and nostrils.

"What the hell is this?" I swallowed hard and shook off the momentary nausea.

Lily couldn't contain herself. She started laughing, bodily. Her shoulders shuffled up and down as she tried to stifle her joy at my discomfort.

"Jesus, that's horrible!" I stared into the cup, looking for some explanation, as if it had personally offended me. If Lily mentioned her penchant for fetid, fishery run-off at some point, I hadn't caught it.

"It's like I just licked something that washed up on the beach... that's been dead for days."

With my tongue hanging loosely out of my mouth, I flagged down the waiter and gestured dramatically that I needed some water.

When Lily's laughter finally subsided, she spoke through her tears, "The look on your face...," a last gasped chuckle, "... absolutely priceless."

Eventually, she composed herself. I just sat, feeling like a clown while I tried to focus on something other than the rancid flavor on my tongue. Her smile made it easier, but it still tasted like shit to me.

"Well, whenever you need a good laugh, feel free to take a piss in my mouth."

I was just going for a joke, but it occurred to me immediately after I said it that I didn't know her all that well. I was rolling the dice. How would she take it? The expression on my face was still contorted in protest of the lingering taste in my mouth.

"I only piss on people I really like, and you have to be pretty special to get it in the mouth," she didn't miss a beat. Maybe luck was finally on my side.

She reached across the table, taking her drink back defiantly, "Next time, don't take what isn't yours, Joshua..."

I couldn't tell if she was teasing me to try, or laying down some non-negotiable ground rules.

Her tone became a mockery of seriousness, but with an undercurrent of genuine intent, "... then maybe you won't be punished."

She grabbed a fistful of my attention and gave no indication that she ever had to let it go. Lily was a practiced flirt, established. What made her a pro was that despite knowing it, I kept falling for it.

After the stress of re-counting the last few days, her playfulness was disarming and welcome.

But I decided not to return the innuendo.

My nerves were too frayed to act on it. It was nice just feeling normal again. How could I explain that to her without being insulting? Without ruining a future chance?

So I sat there, silently hoping the wan expression on my face was explanation enough, the words eluding me.

She shrugged and smiled, looked down at the table for a moment. She must have understood my silence, because she changed the subject, "Call Demy. Just... call him."

She was right. I should call him.

"You're right." I reached into my pocket, pulled out my Glass, and touched the surface.

I pushed and pulled some of the items around on the screen in order to locate my Demy connect. Eventually, I found the little looped-video icon of him flipping me off. That's right. What was I thinking? Demy was too much of an ass to be orchestrating some kind of conspiracy against me.

I was too much of an ass to be *involved* in a conspiracy. It was time to wake up from this insanity and talk to Demy about it.

Tapping the icon, I activated the connection and Demy's living room appeared. I had half-expected to see his, "I'm *two* busy video," which involved a couple of his ex-girlfriends doing things to inspire jealousy. It was something he had put together just for me, but instead, all I got was the open-connect to his apartment.

It was dark and his living room was empty, so there wasn't much to see. I knew it was too early for him to be awake but I guess I was hoping to be wrong, that maybe he was waiting up for me. I decided to leave him a message.

"Heya, Demy... I, uh, I'm sorry about last night," then I noticed the open pizza box was a few slices shy of a whole pie, "I see you ate some of *my* pizza. Typical. Anyway, rattle me when you get up.

I'll try to explain. *Actually*, I'm kinda hoping you can explain some things to me, too. Later."

I washed the screen away with a brush of my hand and my Glass turned opaque. In my head, I'd already started the conversation with Demy. I imagined the two of us in his apartment sussing out the details. But before I could pass that happy idea on to Lily, a creepy tingling sensation shook my spine. It began just like the Pez. Then at the center of my neck, just below the hairline, the creep turned cold and wet and splashed me like I was dunking my head backward into a bucket of water.

I closed my eyes, more reaction than thought, and felt the air become thick and slow. Watery figments were leaving trails down my scalp and my forehead, down my face.

My mind was clear and broad, and I had that feeling again from the bar storage room, that feeling of total exposure. I was touching and seeing everything near me. I was exposed to every surface in the diner with every inch of my skin: the windows, the cushions of the chairs, and the texture of the paint on the walls. The feeling was even more vivid than when Lily had me tied up, and that had already been extreme. It was like I was being flipped inside out so that I was connected internally to the diner. The diner was inside me.

My chest was stretched to the limit. I didn't notice that I was holding my breath at first, but when I did, I let it out. Calm and controlled, I opened my eyes.

Lily was staring at me, her face a mix of fear and concern. She was pushing back from the table, but the motion was languorous and thick.

She was beautiful. So damn gorgeous. I could smell her hair, an oddly seductive mix of the bar, smoke, conditioner, and feminine warmth.

I became curious about her fear. I didn't want her to be afraid anymore. Smiling deeply into her, I snuck my cheekbones impossibly close to hers and slipped my arms supportively around her back. I lost my fingers in her hair, gently holding her head.

Lily's lips were moving, mouthing words into mine. There was the sound of her voice, too, but it was distant and dampened. I didn't know the words, but I understood what she needed me to understand. *Something was wrong with my eyes* and she was scared of me, but also *for* me. I couldn't say anything. I wanted to hold her and comfort her, to protect her from whatever frightened her, but I couldn't articulate the rawness of those feelings.

And then, Lily let go of her fear. I could almost see it leaving her body as each muscle eased away from the tension of holding her guard up. She held me, too. She wrapped her arms around me. I don't know how long the embrace lasted, but I enjoyed it forever.

Then, as in a lucid dream, I came to consciousness without waking up. I realized that I had not left my chair. Simultaneously, I was displaced, confused, and aware, like the peculiar feelings were all expected and normal. I recognized it from meeting Early and from wanting to be untied when Lily had me zip-tied in the storage room.

This time, there was no one and nothing to shock me from the feeling. I was compelled to be there, to be *that* connected and *that* present. I wanted to stay enveloped in the moment. There was a hunter in the diner that I needed to find.

The hairs on my arms tickled and I held them up slowly to see what was happening. Small, delicate, smoky wings were lifting up from the skin of my arms and hands. They were shadowy creatures, small, with great wings like butterflies. They were fascinating and wonderful, but I felt pressure to move them, to persuade them to fly. I gently turned my arms over, facing my palms to the ceiling, and the smoky images took flight and fluttered around the diner.

There were five butterflies in all and they headed off in different directions, leaving trails of ash behind them. As they flew, I felt part of me go with them, taking in all that they sensed.

The university boy sipped his coffee.

The waiter was absentmindedly wiping down the surface of the front counter.

The cook was snapping a towel at a potato that he had cut so that it would sit up on its end.

They were within themselves, preoccupied, and unthreatening.

They were vulnerable.

... I needed more. More information, more quickly.

The butterflies descended and the moment one touched a surface, it turned into a downward rush of ashen dust as though extinguished by a ghostly, white breath. Then a spectral fog billowed up around the impact, like the base of a lit rocket before it overcomes gravity. One butterfly after another landed and the diner filled with ash.

I saw movement, silhouettes of activity. The dusty fog was displaced by the impressions of people who had passed through the place. The negative space created by the wake of those people was subtle and fading but I knew it was there. I could not see faces in any of the forms, and most were too vague to even guess at height or weight. They were loosely human shapes. Then, the last wispy butterfly landed.

It landed on Sara's head and her body lit up in a soft glow, curly ringlets forming in the smoke around her. She was vivid, strongly limned against the background of grey, but there was also an illusory quality to her... her image.

She had questions... many questions. She was scared, a little intrigued, and very cautious. She was curious about what was happening to me. All of her distractions manifested as tendrils of light that reached out to me shyly. The end of each tendril curled, like a vine growing in a time-lapse film, and danced in front of me. They were coaxing me for answers, but careful not to touch me the wrong way, afraid of what I might do. I reached out to touch one, to reach back to her, to quiet her anxiety, even though I was capable of explaining nothing.

The others in the "All-Niter"—not the displaced impressions, but the few who were actually in the diner that night—radiated similarly to

Sara, though not as brightly. It was as if some intangible aspect of each person was recognizing my presence for the first time. They reminded me of children, their genuine surprise and joy at being really seen and engaged by an adult.

I was startled by the sudden realization that the wintering man had vanished completely. Not only was he gone, it was as though he was never there. He left no impression, no trail, no sign of his ever having existed. There was no remnant of his time here... none that I could see. Mr. Winter wasn't there, but there was something else...

The diner was suddenly full of sinister movement. Inside and outside, enemies were circling and closing in on us. There were cloaked Collective Officers of a class I did not understand who were cautiously approaching the diner. Although I could not see them, I felt the echoes of their objectives bouncing off of each other. They were working together, strongly connected to one another. There was also some pressure on them from somewhere else to succeed.

There was a man, almost incorporeal, a shadow moving stealthily along the wall. He moved without disturbing the diner in anyway. There was no sound to his footsteps, no smell to his skin. He didn't even displace my butterfly dust... much. He didn't know that I could see him. His energy was dramatically concentrated inside of him. Though not necessarily dark, the light he emitted was flat and cold. He positioned himself behind Sara. The shadow-man was lethal. He was trying to decide when.

I decided for him.

inSpire

Twelve

"Show me Cal, timestamp 21 minutes 11 seconds," the Leader's voice was deep and powerful, commanding. He was staring hard into the stream from the morning's extraction attempt.

The Leader's office was empty at this early hour of the morning. His personal guards were available in the corridor, but within the confines of the room, he was alone. Like all of those in his position, his home was an apartment adjacent to his office, so he was quick to respond when SENTRy reported the failed extraction attempt. It had only taken him a few minutes to get up and begin his review of the streams.

Success had been the expected outcome. It was the most common result for him in his career, so failure was considerably more interesting and worth waking up for. His curiosity needed to be satisfied. He considered such challenges as rare opportunities to improve his skills.

The Leader's record in the military, his expertise in the field as an Individual Concealed Emplacement, had secured him his position within the Collective. During the End War, ICE units were given orders that included no exit strategies, no communication, and no fallbacks. They were fire-and-forget, they were unrestricted, and they remained emplaced until their targets were annihilated.

101

Targets were not just removed or subverted, as that would have been left to standard covert ops teams. Instead, ICE units were employed when total destruction was the executive order. Most never returned from their assignments. Those who did were awarded the highest commendations and released from service. Leader 127 had completed twelve operations before his Commanding Officer refused to issue him another. It was the only time that superstition had ever been cited in an official report. The commander wrote, "... two operations executed by the same soldier is unexpected, three rare, and four without precedent. Thirteen is an unreasonable and ominous number to request and will not be forwarded..."

When the military was rolled into the Collective, 127's special talents were recognized. His ability to pass those skills on to others earned him the title, "Leader." Since then, regardless of the vast resources available to him, he invariably used small teams for his operations. He kept his units close to him so that he would know them, how they performed, how they thought, how they reacted. He required a level of intimacy that he could only cultivate if the number in his circle of trust was few. By virtue of his small teamsize, 127 only knew a few outside his circle, and even fewer knew him; even in the darkest corners of this unnamed division of the Collective, he was considered a shadow, a legend.

The Leader's objectives often matched his expertise, requiring high levels of precision and low visibility. He trained all of his units personally, and imparted what he could of his experience and knowledge to each one, individually. Eve's recent defection and now this–his team's inability to secure Joshua–had aroused a sense of challenge in the Leader that he'd not felt in a long time.

His Desk projected three displays inscribed within its outer arc. The left viewport displayed debriefing information from his team after they were retrieved by a different division's clean-up team. The right had information about Joshua Falken, beginning with his birth certificate and ending with the current length of his middle toe. The center viewport, the Leader's primary focus, was a paused stream from one of the extraction team operatives.

"What is this object?" he drew a small circle into the projection with his finger. The words, "Indeterminate," appeared in response. A list of objects appeared near the area the Leader indicated. The suggestions came with a variety of details, such as compositions, manufacturers, combustion rates, and coordinates relative to the source. Object names like "Chair," "Table," and "Floor" appeared. The objects were highlighted in the frame and lines were drawn to their information windows.

The Leader casually placed his thumb and pinky finger into the image, tapping the diner chair in the foreground and a picture hanging on the wall in the background. All of the previously displayed information was wiped from the screen and replaced by the selected objects. He held his hand there for a moment longer, and a connecting line between the two objects appeared. Using his middle finger, the Leader dragged a point along the line and coordinates updated, following his movement.

"List objects near position," the Leader looked on calmly, and was not surprised to see a similar list to what he saw previously. Although this time, "Sara Watanabe" was included, with a link to her family of origin. But the Leader already had that information displayed in another vertical projection to his left, so he ignored her. Other than that, SENTRy did not identify the object he was pursuing.

He leaned in and stroked his chin, contemplative.

With his left pointer finger, the Leader executed a counter-clockwise circular motion on the smooth surface of his desk. The stream played seamlessly in reverse at a speed relative to his motion, small fractions of a second ticking down in the upper-left corner of the image. Then he stopped.

"Locate Joshua Falken."

Joshua, sitting with his back to the camera perspective, was outlined and a line was drawn to his details in the viewport at the Leader's right. A synopsis of his current health was also displayed, with links to enhance the information to any amount of desired detail. A medical file also appeared with an animated anatomical representation showing current heartrate, temperature, and numerous other readings.

The Leader, at an excruciatingly slow pace, circled his finger clockwise, his eyes going back and forth between the stream and the details about Joshua. Joshua's temperature rose and his heartrate slowed as the time progressed forward. Both effects were happening at an alarmingly fast speed. Then suddenly all of the details went to zero. The area that previously displayed Joshua's position changed to "Out of Range for all selected operatives."

Leaning back, the Leader placed all five fingers of his right hand on the desk. He slid them forward and flicked them up in a single motion. Cal's stream shrunk and four other streams flew into view from somewhere off the display. They were arranged in an arc and their times were synchronized. The Leader examined each in turn. The details displayed remained unchanged.

Again, the Leader jogged the stream forward. Even though SENTRy insisted there was nothing there, Joshua or otherwise, there was definitely something, a visual anomaly. A billowing and rippling distortion of light, like vertical heat gradients or like a lens melting was right there, where Joshua used to be. His clothes hung in the air and held his shape for a moment before wrinkling and narrowing, and falling toward his chair. As the stream progressed, the distortion moved from Joshua's chair to a position behind Sara and unfurled around her. The distortion then enveloped Sara from behind and formed into a vaguely human shape. With tremendous strength and speed, the arms and body of the thing pulled Sara up and out of her chair, hugging her into itself. Her chair fell through the distortion unhindered, although it was kicked around a bit by Sara's feet as she tried to find the ground. The distortion extended back, reaching away from Sara and then swiftly swept forward in a propelling motion around to Sara's front. Both moved back together a couple of meters from the table.

Jogging forward even more slowly now, the Leader peered into the stream, taking in all of the information. He read and he digested. His tactical and analytical prowess, were brought fully to the task. He counted six apparent appendages extending from the distortion.

Two wrapped around Sara's torso, two around her legs, and two–although they were dissipating quickly–retracted from the forward-sweeping, propelling motion.

As the stream crept forward, the creature became more human, more tangible and opaque. Then, nearer to the table than to Sara, the sword of an assassin cut through the air and into the chair where she had been sitting seconds before. The Leader showed no interest or surprise.

The ways of the Laterali were not unknown to him. Furthermore, he had already confirmed that the Collective liaison to the Laterali had traded Sara Watanabe to them. Sara had thrown a flag when she was tagged during the fine-grain review of Eve's transmissions. 127 had overseen the details himself.

The assassin was uncharacteristically slow to react. It might have been his first mark or maybe in the moment that Sara had been swept from her chair, the world had taken on an inexplicable and indefinite form; the Leader could only guess. Either way, the assassin did not move immediately for a second attack, instead, he looked around as though Sara was no longer in the diner.

The assassin's organic cloak, a thin skin of genetically enhanced chromatophores and thermal dampers, was working to hide him from the world again, but it was too late. He had already registered on the extraction team's radar and been tagged. He would be eliminated moments later.

The Leader reflected for a moment on the value of such a witness, but the Laterali were anonymous, even to him, as dictated by their arrangement with the Collective. Clearance to vary from that arrangement was above even 127's head. It wouldn't have mattered if the extraction team had held their fire; a failed assassin was a dead one. The Laterali would have seen to it if his team had not.

Collective field operatives have a standing KOS for the Laterali at the assassin guild's request. The Laterali had less tolerance for failure than the Collective in that way. It worked out well for public relations, promoting such events as continued efforts to reduce organized crime.

He refocused himself on the stream. Sara was about two meters from where she had been sitting in her chair. The rippling form holding her became even more defined and more human. Eventually, the extraneous appendages disappeared completely and the naked body of Joshua was clear. He was intact, holding Sara in his arms, hugging her tightly to his chest.

The Leader paused there a moment to look closely at their faces. Joshua's pupils were gone. He had only blue, marbly irises with sharply broken black fissures through the middle. Otherwise, his expression was oddly serene and in control. Sara was nervous, but not screaming and she didn't look shocked or even scared. In a different context, the Leader would have guessed she was listening to someone soothingly calm her down.

In one of the streams, one of the extraction operatives began to track the assassin at that point, and with a couple of motions that stream was eliminated from the Leader's review. He picked three from the four that remained and tossed them to each of his projected displays. The fourth operative would eventually be asked to help flank the assassin as was written in the report and the intervening time was not of interest.

A couple of taps and the display sizes increased, creating a panoramic display at the outer edge of his desk. He rolled the streams forward again. The three shown sources were from the closest agents. They were just outside the diner and moving into position to intercept Joshua as he and Sara quickly shuffle-stepped together then separated to more or less run for the exit. The Leader jogged the time forward to the frame just before Joshua arrived at the door then he let it play on at slightly reduced speed.

Joshua hit the exit and the door exploded off its hinges. It flew straight into the middle operative, hitting him squarely in the chest, knocking him back several feet and out. All of the Collective Officers were cloaked. Joshua seemed to have no external technology and according to his file, he was GEaRless. How Joshua was aware of his team was not readily apparent to the Leader.

"Locate Joshua Falken," there was a detectable up-swing in his voice as he gave the command, genuinely curious. SENTRy finally came through and a small version of the full details appeared as an icon at the center of the display. It only sat there for a moment as the video continued to run, before the Leader quickly exchanged it with the vacant stream of the unconscious officer.

127 watched as Joshua stepped through the opening into the parking lot of the diner, opened his arms wide, and pressed his hands intensely toward the earth. His muscles were rippling and his body was vibrating from the exertion, veins thick and pulsing. At the speed of the playback, Joshua seemed like he was growing, that he would just keep growing and become a giant. But the growth eventually stopped; he was only breathing.

The Leader noted that Joshua made eye contact with neither of the officers. He hadn't even made a motion in either direction. Sara, on the other hand, looked straight through and around both officers, looking for a direction to run. Her expressions were made more dramatic by the slow speed of the playback, or at least more obvious. She settled on Joshua, expectantly, not knowing what she should do next, but again her anxiety was assuaged by some unseen accomplice and she moved to a position behind his naked body.

The order to fire non-lethal suppression into both targets appeared in the officers' readout displays. Joshua's arms moved as though the stream had suddenly been put into fast-forward. His hands crossed in front of his chest, palms in. Then his palms turned out and his fingers tore through the air as his arms swung open. The world suddenly turned to liquid on both monitors. Rivulets of changing densities bent and warped the background. The Leader thought to himself that it was mostly like staring into the bottom of a clear, perfectly still puddle of water, and then tapping the surface.

The streams finished, one following closely after the other into the dark.

The Leader was perfectly still for several minutes, staring through the displays. He made up his mind to interview each member of the team personally although he suspected little more information would be uncovered.

"Record," the Leader spoke, "Joshua Falken has displayed at least partial manifestation approximately sixty-one hours, twenty-seven minutes after initial exposure. Record stop."

With a few discrete gestures, Eve's details were brought to the forefront on the right, and a scan option in the stream was opened and executed with her as the subject. The response from SENTRy was immediately negative. A drag and a tap or two later and the search was enhanced to use the timeline from the extraction, Eve, and the entire library of the Collective streams as criteria. A couple of breathless moments passed and again, the response was negative. He had hoped she would show herself, after all, she had taken an enormous risk to hide Joshua, it was hard to believe that her investment ended there or that she would leave him out in the open, unprotected. Unless... he was protected.

He restarted the streams from the beginning and watched the events unfold at full speed several times. Someone was missing. The moment his team arrived in view of the diner, Joshua was clearly looking at a table nearby, but not at the table really, rather, someone sitting at the table who wasn't there. Not an invisible or cloaked, or otherwise masked-from-view person, but someone who had been there moments, maybe even seconds before the streams would have found him or her. In that first frame, the waiter was walking away from the table with a water pitcher, about two glasses-worth, just shy of full, and the water glass on the table was full. The Leader had dismissed it initially—not enough information to draw conclusions— but Joshua wasn't looking *for* someone he was looking *at* someone, as though he hadn't yet registered that the person had left. This fourth patron had avoided the streams entirely, although his team had approached from all angles with exits and windows well in view.

"Record...," this time with an inquisitive slant to his words, "The manifestation was of a duration and strength that would certainly have drained the subject." His voice became more direct, as though he'd answered an internal question, "Based on previous subjects, I expect at least a twenty-four hour period of dormancy, then death."

"Speculatively, evidence suggests that he has accomplices, known to him or otherwise, but more than just Eve. It is not clear whether this unknown actor or group of actors is colluding with Eve or working independently. It is clear, however, that Eve, at a minimum, is aware of the existence of this actor or actors. She was not present at the time of the failed extraction attempt."

He heaved a sigh and settled himself deeper into his chair, completing the report with the requisite perfunctory language, "Effort in order of priority: Retrieve Collective Officer; Eve alive, preferably; Interrogate detained diner occupants; Debrief extraction operatives personally; and place an alert for Joshua Falken's body." *He'll come to me soon enough.* Continuing, "Send Notifications:

"Laterali Liaison: Full Report."

"inSpire Media Control: Composed Report, suppressed Laterali activity at local diner."

"Gene Enhancement and Replacement Systems: Full Report and request interpretation of manifestation."

127 stopped and sent his report with a few swift keystrokes then slid the entire key display away. The stream and report controls and keys were replaced by a standard QWERTY layout. His fingers were deft on the keys and he typed out several paragraphs in a matter of seconds. Leaning back and reading it over to himself a few times, he decided on a few changes then sent his memo out. Something was wrong in the Upper Spire. The Leader filed his reports as regularly as ever before, but the responses had come slower lately. In fact, his communication with his superiors had completely ground to a halt. His letter was a curt but professional reminder that the Apple Project was becoming a liability. It was the fifth one of a similar nature that he'd sent in the last few weeks.

What the hell was going on up there anyway?

The Leader put the thought aside and chalked the silence up to the typical nature of management. He washed the displays away and the smooth surface of the Desk became dark, a semi-translucent black. He stood, walked to the front of his Desk, and faced the

Wall. It dimmed slightly to compensate for the lack of internal light. Minutes passed and the Wall dimmed even more as the sun glimmered on the horizon and gradually set the ocean on fire with chaotic, ephemeral sparks on each cresting wave.

He closed his eyes, "Filter off." The full brightness of the rising sun filled the office, and the Leader was bathed in golden light. He imagined warmth on his face and the pleasant scent of the salty ocean air.

He opened his eyes, irises turning silvery and reflective almost instantaneously, "Where are you, Eve?"

In Sickness

Thirteen

She was there, walking on the walls, crawling along the ceiling. Lines of silken thread followed her, spoke to her, protected her. She saw me. She knew I was watching her watch me. Her long legs were relaxed, her body weightless, her movements effortless.

I wanted to touch her.

One shaking pair of small wings emerged from my chest, unexpected but welcome. Despite the weakness of their movement, the tissue-thin and malformed wings fluttered to life. Flapping limply, they finally managed lift-off.

My little friend flew up toward her, but it wasn't easy. The butterfly was weak and seemed to stumble, alternately rising and falling, trying and faltering. The bobbing motion matched my breathing, weak and shaky, but enough... enough. One flutter, then another, closer and closer to the waiting, watching creature. A last push...

... and then she struck with a preternatural deftness. Agile arms and legs knifed out from where they were tucked neatly into her body. They grabbed the fragile fly. They snatched and snared and twisted, and spun and wrapped, and packaged up the little spy, suffocating it. Then slowly, delicately, the appendages dangled my friend down to die.

I didn't want to look anymore and my eyes were thankfully too tired to even try. The darkness behind my lids was an endless field of lurid red heat. There were bodies floating into my vision. Faces appeared that I did not recognize and stared back at me blankly. Mutated memories of places I'd been got mixed up with each other and created an impossible landscape. It was fragile though, and the landscape washed away like a sandcastle with each wave of heat and pain that crashed against my body.

Someone was touching me.

There was a sudden coolness on my forehead and a silky voice in my ear. Her words were sweet and thick, and I didn't understand any of them. The shape of the sounds though, the roundness and softness of the whisper, were enough to dull the sharp pains.

...

"Shhhh, don't try to speak. It's okay," Sara spoke in her softest whisper, "It's okay. You're alright, Joshua. Just sleep," She tried to find stronger, confidence-inspiring words to say, but she had none.

She was holding a damp, makeshift washcloth to Joshua's head. The rag was nothing more than an old t-shirt and it didn't hold water well. She had to dunk it frequently into the large bowl of hot water she held in her lap. Dabbing his forehead and cheeks, she washed away some of the sweat from his face, trying to offer him some solace from whatever pain or sickness had come over him.

He hadn't spoken an intelligible phrase in hours, just the occasional moan or desperate inhale. At least three times she witnessed his eyes open and stay open for several minutes, without blinking. His body appeared calm in those moments, relaxed. The marble-blue eyes, crystal clear and wet, stared at something she couldn't see. He appeared almost curious in those moments, as though he wasn't entirely sure what he saw either.

The last time she caught him staring, Sara had positioned her face directly above his, close enough to feel his fevered breath on her cheeks. He seemed not to notice at all. He had continued to stare straight through her to whatever had caught his attention. She had looked closely at his eyes. There was no white at all, just opaque marbled-blue. At the center of each was a jagged vertical black slit, as though the marble had cracked open and there was a vast expanse of nothing inside. She desperately wanted him to look at her, to make contact, but just as before, he eventually closed his eyes and went back to his feverish sleeping.

Sara wanted Joshua to wake up, so that she could talk to him. So much of the morning was a mystery to her, not the least of which was how they'd ended up here. Joshua had carried her home the three miles from the "All-Niter," though really, he'd seemed to almost fly them here. The location of her apartment was nothing they'd discussed at any point, but he'd managed to bring them straight here without hesitation. She had never even mentioned that she lived in the city.

Sara was paranoid about her identity and living arrangements. Even before she'd believed herself a target of the Laterali, it was her nature to be secretive, to never reveal important details about herself to anyone. She drifted to a new place whenever people got to know her well enough to want to know her more. Average people were so well-connected to each other that being connected to any of them meant she could be found.

It was simple enough for her to start over in a new place. Sara knew how to find the types of people who wanted to live anonymously. She would quickly change the subject if someone tried to get anything specific out of her. She was full of disguises and ruses, conversational blockers, and ready excuses. There was no way Sara had mentioned anything to Joshua about her cubicle of an apartment. Still, here they were.

The room was small. The roles of living room, bedroom, and office were shared by the same fourteen-by-fourteen foot square. Shared is too civil a description of their cohabitation, judging by the competitiveness of the clutter. Hair products and styling implements obscured the Desk input area, there were wires of various colors and terminations on the disheveled bed, and there were clothes crumpled up into every visible space, including her overalls from earlier that night. A thong, the kind that seduced and teased the eyes by virtually not existing, hung languidly off the back of a chair that doubled as a bedside table. The only door in the place, other than the exit, was the one to the bathroom. It didn't have much in the way of modern amenities, but it had the necessities. And though the bathroom was cramped, there was enough space on the counter beside a half-used roll of toilet paper for an induction plate and a small frying pan.

The morning was still young, and although she'd been up all night Sara didn't feel like sleeping. She was too lost in the replay of the events at the diner to even consider dozing. Not to mention, Joshua had pretty much gone catatonic and feverish within moments of their arrival at her place. She'd given him the bed, which meant her only options were the chair or the floor, neither of which looked comforting. She only guess at what really happened with Joshua, but whatever he had done, whatever he had become, was taking a toll on his body.

Sara dunked the washcloth into the bowl of hot water again. She was nervous, helping a man that she barely knew. Last night had gone from strange to stranger at light speed and she was pretty sure that Joshua was responsible for most of it.

A little water spilled over the edge of the bowl and down her inner thigh. It was cooler than she expected. She had been absent-mindedly stroking Joshua's face, washing away the sweat, and not even noticed that the water had become room temperature. How much time had passed? Sara wasn't sure. Adrenaline had quickly turned into exhaustion, and suddenly she was nodding in and out of consciousness.

She was beating herself up for sticking around the city. Once, in a different life–she'd called herself Pillo then–she'd been panicked into relocating by a grocery clerk who swore he knew her from somewhere. He'd looked familiar to Sara, too, and that was it. Too risky. She'd had to move on.

Last night she'd seen enough Collective at close range to run and never look back. And yet, here she stayed. With a stranger in her bed who knew her real name and where she lived, the situation was bad and getting worse. She should have been halfway to nowhere by now, but instead, she wrung out the water from the old shirt, set it aside, and took the bowl to the bathroom to refill it with warm water.

She splashed some water on her face. She would normally have been asleep by now, even after a really late night. She had that exhausted-acceptance calm, the kind that settles in after the adrenaline fades, and she abandoned any hope of rest.

Staring into the Wall over the sink, she looked closely at herself. She saw the first signs of her youth transitioning to maturity, especially around her eyes. She didn't recognize any beauty in the new subtle texturing of her face, especially with the tired scowl staring back at her, though, anyone else looking on would have been charmed.

Sara couldn't explain it, but she felt safe with Joshua. Feeling safe wasn't exactly a regular aspect of Sara's life. Whatever happened last night, whatever she thought might have happened, there was no doubt about the presence of a kind of protective voice, urgent and strong, willing her to stay at Joshua's side.

There were no actual words, nothing recognizable, but the voice was there. It was calm, but forceful, and it had been the only thing that kept her from screaming back at the diner. The voice sounded like her father. So despite her instincts, her well-worn pattern, she was compelled to stay with the sick man. At least until he was better.

She splashed her face one more time, dried herself off with her shirt, and did a last practical examination of her appearance before returning to the bed. Joshua was staring wide-creepy-eyed at the ceiling again. It was as though he was listening to someone that she couldn't see.

Sara looked down, deep into the fissures of his glassy blue eyes. He continued to look through her, beyond her. After a moment, she looked up and began scrutinizing the ceiling.

What the hell is he looking at?

Peering as hard as she could into the vacant, white ceiling, there was nothing.

He's dreaming. She shrugged and stopped staring at the ceiling.

The heat of his fever rose up through the air and warmed Sara's still slightly damp skin. That kind of sick-warm was usually enough to make Sara nauseous but this illness was different, clean. Instinctively, she was confident whatever he had wasn't contagious, so it didn't bother her to stay close.

Joshua's lids quivered a little, then covered his gaze again. Fresh beads of sweat broke out all over his forehead. Sara sat and repeated her ritual. She wiped his face, dunked the shirt, wrung out the excess water, and wiped his face again. She didn't entirely believe the chant herself, but repeated it anyway, "It's okay," a soft whisper, "It's okay. You're alright, Joshua. Just sleep. It's okay."

Eve 'n Flow

Fourteen

"Ezechial, I need you to go there today," the voice was female, Eve's but not Eve's. She spoke into the air, but the air did not speak back.

Eve had entered Joshua's apartment many times, but this time she had no need for subterfuge. The Collective had already come and gone. And she had already circumnavigated the surveillance equipment they'd left behind.

She had employed one of her more elegant devices. The Relay looked like nothing more than a square-inch piece of foil. She had wrapped the foils around each of the cameras in the apartment. Each Relay calculated the aperture of the lens, compensated for any wrinkles, took an instant data shot of the room, a broad spectrum image that could stand up to analysis, and continually projected that image into the surveillance camera.

The circumvention process produced a lot of heat and the Relay's surface was not sufficient to dissipate it, so the thin foils had a short lifetime before they became unreliable. Although she'd never solved the heat problem directly, she implemented a reasonable work-around solution. When the temperature in the vacuum between the foil and the lens was high enough, the foil simply melted. It was possible the surveillance system would flag the momentary distortion, but not likely.

Eve hadn't exactly been surprised by how quickly the Leader put together the details of her deceptions, but she had hoped for better. She thought her methods were clever enough, disguised well enough to give her more lead time… to give Joshua more time.

She'd seen test subjects like Joshua go from normal to nova in less than three hours. Not all of them exploded either, some melted. All in all, Eve had personally witnessed 1,977 "evolution events." There were three survivors past that initial three hours, counting Joshua, and his odds were slim and getting slimmer.

"Yeah… he doesn't look good…" Eve spoke to the air in her filtered, not-quite-Eve voice. "Without your help this morning, I'm not sure he would have made it."

She was wearing tight-fitting pants and a stylish, silver thermal tank top. Coupled with a backpack and tennis shoes, Eve could pass as "the girlfriend." But the pedestrian look was not a disguise. She was winding down. She'd been pushing her internal Spikes to the limits and her filters were complaining. Her endocrine system was flush with toxins and her nerve impulses were slowing and misfiring.

Eve was equipped with every known form of mounted hormone injection and stimulation system, several nerve accelerators, and even the latest electro-chemical regulators to prevent jitters and noise in her body that could lead to errors in judging distances, missteps, and mistakes. Eve had all of those GEaRS and she'd been pumping them to the limits for the last several days. All of her monitors had red-lined over an hour ago, which meant that the scrubs and filters were also on overtime. There was no way around it, she was vulnerable. She needed rest.

Her clothing helped her body cool down, and effused dermal emollients when heated. The emollients were medicinal and provided moderate pain relief, hydration, as well as a small level of toxin extraction through the skin. All of her GEaRS were on standby, powered down. They were available if she needed them, but the results could be fatal if she pushed them further at this point. Staying awake much longer would only result in heightened pain and slower recovery.

"I'm at his apartment right now…"

Eve ran her fingers along the surface of the Desk. It wasn't locked. The Wall came to life and several streams were displayed, each vying for her attention by playing various portions of the latest news, reviews, and music to which Joshua subscribed. Eve selected one of the videos and smiled as a lurid pornographic scene filled the display. She raised an eyebrow and tilted her head slightly as the woman in the stream became particularly energetic. After a few seconds, Eve slid her fingers along the Desk and shut down the porn.

She began searching for images, videos or frames that might be personally linked to Joshua. He didn't have much. Looking around the tiny apartment there were no decorations, no displays of personality. She knew he was cagey based on the file she'd picked up on him, but he seemed to maintain privacy even with himself.

Becoming anxious and frustrated, sure signs that she was in a bad way internally, Eve put her hands flat on the desk and smeared them around.

"I can't find anything and if don't leave soon, I'm going to be stuck here," Eve's true voice came through this time which was sure to trigger a match and draw some attention from the Collective. The Leader would have put a watch out on all of her identifying characteristics by now. Officers would be dispatched to her location as soon as her voice was recognized… probably less than two minutes. Every second she stayed increased her risk but she still didn't have what she came to get.

"I'm made, I have to go. Please, Ezechial, tell me you're already on your way?" Common nervousness edged her voice making it seem alien even to her own ears. For the first time since she'd entered the Collective, she felt real fear. But she was trained for all contingencies. Physically and mentally strong regardless of her Genetic Enhancement and Replacement Systems, Eve hoped that she had enough willpower to overcome the extreme strain she'd put on her body.

She took a deep breath and rested her chin on her chest. With her eyes closed, she took a moment to feel her way through the joints and muscles of her body. Eve asked each fiber if it had more to give.

Mapping out the city in her mind, she picked the closest location that would still be outside of the Collective Net when they came here to capture her. She asked her body how fast and how far it could go. Breaking down between here and there would be guaranteed capture. Stowing away in one of the other apartments, in a ceiling vent, or in a closet, hidden in the Sniper's Hold in her back pack, was a huge risk, but if she couldn't make it out of the Net, then here was as good as anywhere else.

Still considering her options, Eve opened her eyes and noticed for the first time that Joshua's Desk had an open drawer. She reached out and pressed the drawer. The closer didn't activate and the drawer slid back out to its previous position, not quite flush with the rest of the Desk. Feeling around the perimeter of the exposed front, she placed the pads of her fingers on the smooth edges and tugged the drawer open.

Among the other random contents, a tooth stick, some chocolate candy bars, and a pack of gum, there was a tin box. Eve removed the box and pulled off the lid. Inside there were a variety of pills, a pipe, a lighter, and sheets of tiny colored squares. There was also a silver marble, which made a satisfying rolling sound on the bottom of the container, a miniature plastic figurine holding a cane that would have been human except for the pointy ears and the green skin, and a single photograph on non-digital paper.

The photograph was of a young man, handsome, sitting on a set of cement stairs, holding an ice-cream cone. He was smiling at whoever took the picture and the sun was shining on his face. Eve didn't have to scan the photograph to know that the man depicted was related genetically to Joshua. The easy way he sat and the casual confidence in his eyes, though not the same color as Joshua's, described a cousin, or more likely, a brother.

"I found something... I'm sending it to you right now..."

She scanned the photograph and put it back in the tin box, then placed the tin box in her bag. Standing and looping the straps of the bag over her shoulders in one motion, she prepared herself for her escape.

Eve surveyed the apartment one last time and took a deep breath. The Collective had treated the surveillance set-up as routine, believing there was nothing of value here. She would have done the same. Strictly speaking, there was nothing here… except fragments of Joshua's life, items that were meaningful to him and to no one else. Now that she'd returned, and unwillingly revealed her position, the Leader would not be so casual with his orders. It would be impossible to return here again. If the photograph didn't work the tin memorabilia box would have to be enough.

Thirty seconds, no more, and her voice would be recognized and the closest C.O. would be on the way. The closest officer couldn't be more than five minutes away or at least she couldn't count on more than that.

Eve took out her Glass and checked the stream to Joshua's apartment. Her camera had not been disturbed by the surveillance team. It hadn't been detected. Either her basic counter-measures were enough to defeat the standard sweep, or they'd left it there to make her feel comfortable in case she did return. If the latter was true, she was already caught. She accepted that they'd simply missed the ceiling-mounted SPYder, and that she could trust the stream.

Enough, I've got to go.

Out in the hallway, all was quiet. Even in these older buildings, the apartments were effectively sound-dead. Doors and adjoining walls reacted to vibrations with energetic impulses, stamping out sound instead of passing it on.

No one was in the hallway, but who would be? The low-quality EFL dissuaded most people from considering living here, and those that had no choice but to live in the low-rent complex avoided the hallway light whenever possible.

Joshua's complex had never upgraded from the first attempt at eternally fluorescing light systems. A conduit that ran the length of the hallway was filled with two perfectly symbiotic organisms. The creatures were engineered to live off of each other's excretions, and together they produced a bright florescent glow, which was amplified by mirrors at intervals along the conduit and projected into the hallway. It was enough ambient light to navigate the corridor safely.

A small portion of human waste had to be introduced to the system regularly, but other than that, it was a no-cost solution for lighting. Unfortunately the light produced by the early version of the system was an eerie and disquieting green, which generally made people feel extremely uncomfortable, even after short-term exposure. It even made some people physically ill. Eve entered the hallway already nauseous, so she moved fast down the hall, even though her body complained.

Rounding the corner, Eve made her way quickly to the elevator. Not ten feet from the doors, the arrival light turned on. Her nerves tight and paranoid, she jumped to the stairway exit and slammed open the manual door. It didn't make sense. She couldn't outrun the Net if the Collective was already on the scene, but she pushed on regardless.

One step at a time, the stairs reminded her rubbery legs that they needed rest. The first C.O. to arrive at Joshua's would have a single objective; set up the Net. There was no reason to check for the target in the area. If the target was still in the room and got the drop on the first operative, there would be two more operatives close behind and even more distance to cover before the Net was inevitably cast. It would take the officer five minutes, minimum, to set up and activate it. If she was lucky, the first on the scene would be a rookie.

Eve hit the ground floor and began making her way toward the entrance. Joshua's apartment was an inner-room, meaning that it had no true windows, and that she still had a few hundred feet of nauseating lighting to go before exiting the building. She was sweating profusely now, waves of heat rolling off her skin.

Her legs complained as she broke out into a dead run. The layout was mapped in her mind, along with her entire escape route. She needed to make three miles in the next nine minutes. There were three motorcycles parked out front when she arrived. If just one remained, she had a chance.

She hit the double doors, threw them open, and ran out onto the sidewalk. The flow of pedestrians slowed briefly to assess Eve, the sweaty and frenzied, albeit seductive, woman breaking up the cadence of those going to and from work. Mostly though, they walked on without interest.

Eve did not anticipate the afternoon sun, bright and sharp through the cool autumn air. The filters on her eyes were off, needed to be off, and her pupil contractions were unaided, tired, and sluggish. The over-exposure pierced through her eyes and out the back of her head, resulting in throbbing dizziness and momentary blindness.

She stumbled forward and reached out for a lamppost, which caught some new attention. A few pedestrians looked at her with disgust and gave her a wide berth.

Eve folded over and heaved her lunch, a black-colored nutrient-rich gel, onto the sidewalk. That was enough for most of the commuters to clear ten or more feet around her, and for some of the suits passing by to turn on their germicide fields. The fields weren't that effective, in truth, but it made those who were wealthy enough to own them feel better. Besides, the occasional static discharges were an impressive spectacle, a declaration of status.

Blinking her eyes slowly, Eve spit the acid from her mouth. Calming herself down, she reached around to her backpack and grabbed out a small capsule. She split to tube open with her fingertips and held the two pieces beneath her nose, breathing slowly. The smelling salts relieved her nausea a bit and sharpened her senses.

Dropping the halves of the capsule to the ground, she reached into her pack again, this time retrieving a thin, flexible, clear packet. She ripped the top open, tilted her head back, and squeezed the contents of the packet into her mouth. The blue, translucent gel coated her tongue with a cool and pleasant sensation. Her mouth filled with liquid as the gel reacted with her saliva. She swallowed, her mouth filled once more, and she swallowed again.

A little over seven minutes and still three miles to go. She surveyed the motorcycle parking and found better than she had expected. Not only were the bikes she'd seen earlier still there, but a better one had arrived. The hot metallic red of the farings was an unmistakable trademark of the best cycle the Italians had to offer. The bike was outfitted with everglow trim, which screamed to her, "Steal me, I'm owned by a poser." The custom detail probably indicated expensive theft protection, but there was nothing available in the common market that Eve couldn't bypass.

She pulled out her Glass and noted that Joshua's apartment was still undisturbed. Placing the middle three fingers of her right hand on the surface of the Glass, she executed a series of slides, each finger working independently as though she was flipping a set of dip-switches in a specific sequence. A new interface appeared and she began navigating it with familiar ease and quickness. And like that, she disabled the cycle's proximity alarm.

In a single motion, Eve threw her leg over the bike and placed her Glass into the Glass channel interface in the dash. She pulled the straps of her backpack tight and secured an additional strap around her waist. Her Glass flashed a signal at her and she held her pinky finger against the surface for a couple of seconds. The soft whir of the engine came on, and a throbbing, pulsating strength revved up against her inner thigh.

She sat down and pushed the handlebars forward, sliding them in an arc over the front wheel. The bike stood itself up and Eve tucked both of her legs into the sides of the chassis, feet on the pegs. The power of the motorcycle was remarkable. She doubted that even a 300-pound linebacker could overcome the gyro and tackle the bike to the ground. Pushing her butt back into the seat, she felt it give and slide in a slight arc over the rear wheel, similar to the way the handle bars worked over the front. She pulled her stomach muscles in, found the spaces for her elbows along the chassis, and pulled her shoulder blades down her back so that she was in a strong, controlled and tucked position. She locked the position with a flip of her right thumb on the handlebar. The side mirrors adjusted to accommodate her position, and for the first time in days, Eve smiled a genuine smile.

She rolled the throttle forward slowly and the bike reversed out of the parking spot smoothly. The agility of her turn-out was surprising, the sensitivity of the gyro-stabilizers was masterful. She tapped the brake down with her right toe and stopped immediately, parallel to the street.

Eve took a moment to assess traffic, and decided she couldn't wait any longer. She rolled back on the throttle hard and her rear wheel slid around behind her like she was trying to ride a slimy wet worm. Surprised, she released the throttle quickly. The waft of smoke and the smell of burning rubber were brief, but potent.

Apparently, the cycle's owner wasn't a poser. The torque control had been removed… a custom job, entirely illegal. Again, a blissful happiness, a kind of joy filled Eve.

Maintaining her posture on the bike, now a little askew from the street, she looked around to make sure she hadn't drawn too much attention.

Trying a more delicate hand, she eased open the throttle and accelerated into the flow of traffic. She merged elegantly, the bike responding to her every movement. In her side view, she saw the approaching Collective as they were about to arrive at the front of Joshua's building.

Less than six minutes and less than three miles to go. Easy, if not for the merciless traffic and traffic cameras. Though they weren't constantly streaming like the Collective Agents' ocular cameras, crossing through reds would tag her instantly. Although the connection between Eve and a random traffic violation might not be made immediately, or at all, if Watcher spotted her, her chances of escape fell to null.

She leaned hard to the left and swept the bike into the space between opposing flows of traffic and opened up the throttle even more. Riding the double-yellow, she made it several blocks before hitting her first red. When she nailed the brakes, her Glass reported that the inertial dampeners kicked on. Her nausea came back up into her head as the dampening field pushed through her molecules. She fought the feeling down before the light flipped to green and she blazed off the line.

Using the thumb of her clutch hand, she manipulated the Glass controls. It was a little cumbersome navigating the interface through the thumb controls, having not been designed to access anything more than rudimentary instrumentation like speed, RPM, and time readouts. Nevertheless, she managed to get back to the stream from Joshua's apartment. She glanced down and saw a C.O. setting up a tripod for the Net. He had already plugged into to at least three separate circuits. Casting the Net would blackout the entire block, drawing maximum power from the grid.

The Net requires an extraordinary amount of power. It operates on a quantum level, a vibrational fingerprint. Each person is made up of multiple unique frequencies on a sub-atomic level. This property of existence, this phenomenon was observed and studied extensively after the End War. The results, so far, were primarily academic, except for the Net. Knowing the quantum fingerprint of an individual meant that a field could be generated that precisely targeted that individual. Not only could such a field precisely pinpoint a target within a sea of people, but with enough power that same field could deliver a sub-atomic knockout punch.

It would take a city block full of power, and some time to rig up and calibrate, but when the Net was cast, if Eve was within three-miles of the origin, she would feel like she was hit by a truck, pass out, and the Collective would simply pick her up.

The intersection ahead was jammed up. Eve weaved through the slow-moving cars over to the sidewalk, jumped the curb, and simultaneously flexed the front brake and rolled on the throttle. She was counting on the owner to have disabled the linked front and rear brakes. Her hunch played out as she was able to swing the rear tire out to the right, and use the crosswalk to cut through to the other side. Using the crosswalk from the sidewalk allowed her to avoid any camera-triggering barriers.

She hugged the sidewalk, going against traffic on the other side until she was able to split back into her makeshift center lane. Looking down into the Glass again she was startled to see that the C.O. on the scene was already running the calibration program. Well, she couldn't tell for certain but since that was the only fully automated aspect of the task, the fact that he was standing around idly looking through Joshua's mail was a pretty good indication that he was waiting for something. Eve adjusted her estimates and opened up the throttle even more.

The light ahead was green and even though it was a ninety degree turn, Eve didn't slow up a bit. She leaned hard into the turn and hugged the chassis of the bike bodily, taking it down to the asphalt and back up in a flash. Coming out of the turn she hit the split between the lanes and kept the throttle open throughout. The rush of adrenaline she felt, cars flickering past her periphery, inches from her shoulders, was a surge of hope, helping her to focus. Time was collapsing in on her and she needed to stay sharp.

There it was.

Up on the left.

A vertical sign.

"Backbone."

The facility housed most of the city's servers, both residential and commercial. Inside would be a layer-cake, wall after wall of servers, stacked to the ceiling, and floor after floor of hardware decorated with sprinkles of LEDs, and hundreds of thousands of lines of multicolored cables. The frosting of course, was between the floors, the huge spaces used for cooling the facility and all of those cores running virtually non-stop.

Eve went for the frosting.

Before she could make a move through the opposing traffic though, the motorcycle locked up. The gyro came full on, along with the brakes. The seating and handlebar positions returned to 'park,' lifting Eve up at first, until she realized what was going on and erected herself. The owner had activated an anti-theft protocol. A set of physical keys would be necessary to unlock the bike, one held by the owner and the other by the manufacturer.

She hopped off the bike and reached for her Glass, but the Italians didn't take theft lightly… the physical docking site for the Glass had locked it in.

"Shit."

Taking a last look at the stream, she noted that the officer was still sifting through the apartment, entertaining himself while he waited for the 'ready' signal from the Net-caster. She put her fingers to the surface of the Glass and executed the musical dip-switch motions again, locking out all of her identifying data, all of her Collective secrets.

Her legs were shaking as she looked across the street. She saw her opportunity and ran for it. A couple of honking horns complained loudly about her blocking the way but she made it across to the sidewalk. Bolting between pedestrians, pushing through the stream of people, she dashed down the block toward Backbone. When she made it to the alleyway, the one just in front of the building, she ran down it.

The old fire escape along the outside of the Backbone building had probably never been used, and probably never would be used, save for Eve. Looking up, the first floor ladder was well out of reach, and her body echoed painfully at the thought of climbing, jumping, or stacking objects to get up the wall.

Unclasping her pack from around her midriff, she swept the bag around to her front and reached inside. She pulled out her massdriver and pointed it at the old cement weight hanging down from the cable-and-pulley system that suspended the ladder. She decided it was too risky. Even though most of the commuters were too busy to care at all, the noise would inevitably draw the attention of one or two of them.

She looked out to the street and aimed into traffic. It was the only way.

But before she could create a disturbance, one happened. Horns blared and tires screeched as cars crunched into each other in the street. Eve, didn't waste a second thinking about it. She turned and shot the weight, and it exploded in a cloud of fine, grey dust and huge fragments of cement. A large chunk of the original cylinder fell intact to the ground. It shattered on the pavement and shards of cement flew from the impact. The ladder swung down in a huge arc, ejecting the telescoping portion down to the ground with a loud metallic *slam-clank*.

Eve looked back out to the street. Drivers were still honking and some people were arguing loudly. Then she noticed that the shop across the street, which was clearly open for business, was lights out. She put her massdriver into the waist line of her pants against the small of her back, and walked to the mouth of the alleyway.

There was definitely a blackout. Every shop and building as far as she could see was without electricity. The traffic lights were all blinking, operating on back-up power. There was an accident in an intersection down the road from where she had come, and some people were standing around gawking, while others pushed past, going on with their business.

The Net had been cast and she was out of range.

The threat of immediate capture gone, Eve turned her attention to her imminent bodily crisis.

The excitement in the streets kept anyone from noticing her return to the shadow of the alleyway. She climbed the extended fire escape ladder carefully, the fatigue in her muscles turning slowly to soreness. Soon it would be pain. On the fourth floor, she spotted an exhaust vent for the air-conditioning system. Backbone was off the city power grid, so their power was on, and the fans were still running.

Eve tested the grating, pulling at it with both hands. It held fast to the side of the building, half-inch bolts anchoring it into the cement. The grating was hot enough that, although it probably wouldn't burn her, it would be painful for her to wrestle with it for very long. However, the temperature inside the vent, especially farther in, would be more than enough to hard-boil Eve's head if she entered unprotected.

She reached around into her pack again and pulled out a slender, metal capsule about the length of her middle finger. Squeezing the capsule in the middle, she twisted it and it unlocked, end sliding from end, increasing its length an inch or so. Then she pulled the ends apart, separating them from each other. She attached the ends like magnets to the outer metal surface of the ventilation grating, one at the bottom left and the other at the upper right.

Eve had to climb up the railing of the fire escape a bit, and reach across the vent to place that last one. The exhaust was dry-hot against her face. She had to fight back the urge to close her eyes as they welled up with tears against the abrasive air. Before letting herself back down from her semi-perched position, she pushed the far half-capsule hard against the grate. There was a satisfying *thwak*, and she released the half-capsule then retreated hastily from the front of the exhaust. Eve repeated the activating action with the closer half-capsule, pushing it strongly in toward the grate. The affirmative *thwak* sounded once again.

Eve wiped her face and rubbed her eyes, took a couple of breaths of the surrounding cooler air, and looked back out to the street. The yelling had mostly died off, but there was still some amount of jostling and honking in the street as people tried to get around the accident. Drivers were having difficulty negotiating turns at the blinking lights of the intersections, which had delayed the arrival of Civ-level C.O. units to the scene, but Eve couldn't see any of that from her vantage.

She looked back at the vent, having her first doubts about her hiding place. Reaching into her pack, she removed the last object within. It was a large, tightly rolled cylinder of silver fabric. The material was cool to the touch and the roll was heavy. Holding the roll to her stomach, she squeezed the two retaining clips, releasing them.

Her hands were shaking and a chill went through her body. Staring at her fingers, she concentrated and tried to steady them, but found she couldn't. She tasted the sour quality of her mouth, and thought of the flu. She'd had it once, one of the rare and deadly cases. Her body had ached then as it was starting to now. The memory of that illness was accompanied by another chill. Her short, chocolate hair, damp with sweat, blown back by the ride and heated by the exhaust had become a thick matted mess on her head. The whites of her eyes were irritated and red. Although she didn't have a mirror, she imagined she looked just like she did when she had the flu.

The roll had expanded somewhat the moment the clips were released. Eve fumbled it around a bit and found the edge. She unrolled the fabric unceremoniously onto the narrow space of the fire-escape. It was a Sniper's Hold. Only slightly smaller than a sleeping bag, the military had employed the bags as both an environmental suit, capable of protecting the occupant from heat, cold, biological and chemical weapons, and also a means to increase stealth as the material absorbed all forms of active detection.

Eve pressed her thumb against a flat red disc embedded in the material and the mouth of the Sniper's Hold opened. Grabbing her massdriver out of her waistband, she dropped it into her backpack, closed it up, and dumped it into the bag.

Click–clack, click–clack.

The two halves of the capsule detached from the ventilation grate and fell to the ground, one after the other. Eve looked over the grate and hoped that her little capsule had done the job.

She reached out and tested the grate again. This time she tugged hard at a single rib of the grating and it snapped clean off. It sounded more like a dry twig than a piece of steel.

Snapping off vane after vane, she created a hole large enough for her slender body to slip through. Her hands were still shaking as she slung the weighted, closed end of the Sniper's Hold into the shaft through the jagged opening she'd created. She climbed over the railing of the fire escape and holding the rail in one hand, the open mouth of the Sniper's Hold in the other, she put her right leg into the bag.

In a graceful maneuver, she propped her foot against the inside of the ventilation shaft, pushed against her hands on the railing, and deftly knifed her left leg into the Hold, into the duct. For a couple of seconds she was suspended horizontally with nothing but her upper body strength and coordination preventing a forty-foot fall to her death. She wormed the rest of the way into the Hold, wriggling into the protective material, as she went deeper into the ventilation shaft.

When she was fully inside, the total darkness blinded her. Even if she'd had reserve enough to activate her Cat's Eye lenses, she would have been blind in that pitch black bag. She felt around with her hands for the controls on the interior of the Hold. A dim glow responded to her touch and as her eyes became accustomed to the dark, the glow was just enough light for her to read the interface.

She sealed the shell of the Sniper's Hold, set the temperature, and changed the alert status to green, which deactivated all of the external sensors. Deactivating the active sensor array increased the battery life, increasing the time before the shell would shut down. The prediction on the display said that the shell now had a little over twenty hours before running out of power. She hoped it would be enough.

Eve thought about very little in the next few minutes before she passed out. Luckily, it seemed her scrubs were going to stay ahead of all of toxins and wastes building up in her system, but that wouldn't be enough to stave off the pain.

She had been on overdrive for too long… way too damn long. Her knees, shoulders, and hips, moved like coarse metal tools rasping against each together, shaking, vibrating and grinding. The throbbing ache in her head came in regular pulses. With her eyes closed in the darkness, the pulses seemed like a white hot flash of light. Electric pinpricks randomly erupted from her spine, shooting sparks through her body and out her fingertips and toes. She calmed herself, focused on her breathing as much as she could, and tried to slow down in order to diminish and control the pain.

If she was really lucky, there would be no permanent damage. When she purchased her first exotic implant, it was an adrenal spike, she'd been warned not to use it more than three times in a twenty-four hour period and only for short bursts, no longer than a minute at a time. Using more than advised could result in all kinds of damage. Her kidneys might burn out, her muscles might tear themselves apart, her blood could become toxic, or her heart could tear itself apart. She wasn't 'planted with a full DiagStat augmentation until years later. Before that, she'd just had to keep track. Old-fashioned though it was, she never lost the skill of keeping track of usages and times with her memory alone, but at best, it only offered a guesstimate. With the DiagStat, she could do a lot better than ballpark her risk, so she felt reasonably safe. Still, her monitoring systems didn't check everything.

Suddenly remembering one of the nasty side effects, reaching down between her legs and around to her butt, she checked herself. She was clean. The fact that she had to check at all though, that she hadn't known for sure until that moment that she hadn't shit herself, was a little scary. In her delirium, she wondered how and why the Pinheads did it.

The crazy fuckers paid equally crazed 'planters into doubling or tripling up their Spikes. The results were fairly impressive. Pinheads could execute super-human feats of strength, speed, and coordination in short bursts, but the ability came at a huge cost. They invariably walked around all day in a rank cloud of piss and shit. How else could their bodies react to the flood of chemical and electrical information suddenly and forcibly poured into them? But the Pinheads didn't care, of course. If they cared, they wouldn't double- or triple-up in the first place.

The thought of pissing herself randomly in public disgusted her. It was such a gross display of weakness. The more she pictured it though, the more she wanted to laugh. Pissing and shitting all over the Leader's office, smearing her name all over the Wall… it was some kind of joy. Light-headed and delirious, she finally passed out.

SPIRE

The Doctor's Inn

Fifteen

Gabe came to consciousness slowly. His body was stiff and sluggish, dull from the meds he'd been taking. The Wall at the foot of the bed displayed the time, temperature, a forecast of the weather for the coming week, and a ticker which rolled through the day's headlines. It was just after five a.m. and it was chilly outside, not expected to break sixty all day. He would need to wrap his leg before venturing out, for support and for warmth.

No nightmares had followed him back to his body as he woke this time. He was grateful for the dreamless sleep. It gave him a break from his frightening reality. Shooting Vanya, hobbling on his severely injured leg for miles, and stealing pain medication, were so far from the context of his life, the events might as well have been dreamed. For a moment, he found himself hoping that he had lost his mind, but there was little solace in it. Insane or not, it all felt real, out of context and strange, but undeniably real.

His leg was going to require more than PainFree to get better. That was real. He had to deal with it.

The room was softly lit by the combination of the Wall display and a few night lights. The night lights were LEDs mounted in each corner of the room, ceiling and floor, that offered just enough ambient glow to help someone to the bathroom and avoid tripping

135

over luggage. The effect of the diffuse, ever-so-slightly blue glow was reassuring – no dark corners, no lurking dangers.

He pulled the covers back and began scooting himself to the edge of the bed. To his surprise he found an almost empty container of PainFree clutched in his left hand. He reached over to the bedside table, set the container down, and found his glasses. The lenses were smudged and dirty so he worked them between his fingers with his shirt. It didn't really help, so he gave up and put the spectacles on anyway.

Helping his leg with both hands he continued the task of simply getting out of bed and began to doubt if he could walk at all. The pain was manageable, but it was only a symptom, indicative of a serious problem with his knee. He couldn't trust the leg to support his body weight. A true cane would help, something sturdy with traction, but inevitably he needed some hospital time. It wouldn't take long to repair the ligaments or whatever had snapped in his knee, but it would be tricky getting admitted and remaining anonymous.

Moving slowly and carefully, Gabe navigated himself into an upright position. He sat on the edge of the bed, hurt leg straight out and resting on the floor, good leg resisting the floor a bit in order to relieve the pressure from the hurt leg.

Touching the top of the bedside table, he activated the tiny console and slid the room lighting to three-quarters maximum. He looked at his room for the first time, or at least consciously looked around for the first time.

The carpet was dark and tightly woven low-pile designed to prevent and mask stains. Nevertheless, it looked old and dirty. He wasn't sure from his vantage, but he thought he saw an area where the carpet had been melted. The walls were marked by years of chipping, repairs, and repainting, all of which were done with great speed and without great care.

The place was a dive. It was exactly the right place for him. It made sense.

The only currency Gabe had with which to negotiate was a small container of 'O' that he'd manufactured weeks before, forgotten, left in his coat pocket, and found while limping around in the cold. The disreputable, toothless clerk had accepted the drugs as payment without so much as blinking a twitchy eye. It was obvious she knew her drugs, and 'O' in particular, because she licked her lips and eyed the container lustily when Gabe offered it to her as payment for the room.

'O' was a masturbatory sex drug, which, at the peak of the experience, elicited multiple orgasms and most notably, drooling. Most people salivated uncontrollably throughout the high. Some even drooled and licked their lips for hours after the high was completely over. Whether they had a little self-control or a lot, most users carried a fairly reliable 'tell' with them forever after just a single session: they always licked their lips at the suggestion of taking more.

When Gabe created 'O' and began running experiments with it, he solicited testimonials through his Runners. They reported that people were "tasting sex," which Gabe later concluded was a temporary type of synesthesia. There were side effects of course: diminished physical sex drive, addiction, and rarely short-term catatonia. Gabe had expected some number to become permanently synesthetic, but oddly, he'd never heard it reported. The end result was that 'O' became one of Gabe's most lucrative products.

The total value of the 'O' in the container that he'd given the woman at the front desk was enough to pay for a room at a five-star hotel for several nights, so he expected to be left alone for at least a few days. The over-payment would, he hoped, tighten her lips a bit, despite the drool. At any rate, it would be better for Gabe to be gone before she came looking for more, or sobered up long enough to be curious about his misfortune and what angle might be in it for her. And with that thought, he began the arduous and lengthy task of preparing himself to leave.

It was surprising to find a fully stocked bathroom in such a rundown motel, but he was happy to discover a full personal hygiene kit on the sink. He unwrapped the clay-like, U-clean product and placed it in his mouth, positioning it so that it rested on top of all of his lower teeth. Then he bit down until all of his teeth were encased in the clay and ran his fingers around the outside, smoothing the U-clean up to his gums. It was already working, frothing a bit, and filling his mouth with banana flavoring. Gabe hated banana. He chewed it a bit, working his jaw up and down and left to right, as it scrubbed and dissolved. Then he swished and spit out the remains into the sink.

The shower looked clean enough, so he stripped off his shirt and undershirt. He unbuttoned his pants and noticed himself in the mirror. Not much to look at, really. Middle-aged, pasty white, jiggly around the waist, and on this particular morning, extra puffy in the face. His eyes were light blue and kind, or at least he'd always thought so. The hair on his head had begun to thin out a bit, and the dark brown had faded to light. It wasn't the most pleasant view the Wall had displayed, he was sure of it. Gabe smiled at himself anyway, and started to work his pants off carefully to avoid stressing his knee.

The bruising was worse than he expected. Extending from the middle of his quadriceps, down his knee, it ended in a sharp, splotchy red-purple mess partway down his shin. It scared him. He wasn't a doctor. What he knew of medicine and biochemistry had almost nothing to do with the treatment of illness or injury. Unable to trust any evaluation he could make from his armchair of knowledge, he decided he would have to seek medical attention regardless of the consequences, the risk of being found.

Gabe pulled the curtain of the shower stall back as far as it could go, making room for him to enter. A support bar, which looked more or less like an exposed pipe, was mounted vertically, closer to the curtain than to the far wall of the stall. The atomizer was there just on the other side of the support. It was mounted similarly to the support, matching it in color and texture, though it was thinner and looked much more fragile. There was also a horizontal support, but it was out of Gabe's reach so he grasped the vertical bar with both hands and helped himself into the stall.

His leg hung limply at first, but then he lost his balance for a moment and stiffened it up out of habit. He felt an immediate and painful rebuke from the bad knee. With both hands still clutching the support bar, he held his forehead to the metal and wished the leg would just get better, just be better.

He wished the situation was different, that he'd made other choices. The regret was so strong that he began fantasizing about the specific moments that he thought would have changed everything.

The most vivid moment was a woman. Her name was Kara, and the night they met she was wearing an off-the-shoulder dress with an extreme low back. He'd had minutes to try to figure out how the dress stayed on while standing behind her in line at the campus convenience store. The time was long enough to burn the silhouette of her body into his memory forever.

It was late, or early depending how you looked at it, and Gabe was dizzy-tired, so he'd come to the convenience to purchase some caffeine pills. Kara was there buying prophylactics, more like she was buying a pack of gum than planning for anything, anyone specifically. If he had just stayed in his room, or been a little slower walking to the store… if…

But he hadn't stayed in his room or walked slowly, instead, he was there in the store, queued up behind the sensuous and kinetic Kara. The line moved forward. He stumbled. He fell forward and clumsily knocked over a stack of boxes displayed on the counter. The clerk, a student, laughed until Kara leaned down and helped Gabe pick up the boxes from the floor. Both boys were treated to a show of her cleavage and the lovely curve of her back, but only Gabe got the smile.

She walked him home that night. He showed her his projects; his room was a chaos of monitors, chemistry glassware, and stolen lab equipment. She was delighted, amused, and excited. He was nervous, so he blathered on for hours about neuroscience, chemistry, and genetics. She might have understood all of it, or none of it, he was never sure. He didn't realize it at the time, but that night was pivotal in determining the path his life would take. It was that encounter… it was her who gave his chemical pursuits personality and direction.

Hardcore Recreation.

Kara stayed that night. She stayed many nights, for almost two years. Whenever she came, she brought numerous illicit options with her. Gabe would carve a sample from her stash and run it through a series of tests. Sometimes it would take hours. For Kara, it was all foreplay.

She sat, watching and listening as his hands went to work with his equipment. He explained, in great detail, what effects it would have on her body and her brain, revealing every hidden secret of the drug. He compared and contrasted and ran more tests. He disappeared into a world of molecules, atomic structures, chemical attractions and kinetic energies.

Watching him fade into his research, sending messages from his arcane world to her and her alone, Kara would rev up mentally and physically. The anticipation would build until Gabe felt the analysis of whatever fantastic substance she'd brought him was complete.

In those closing moments, she often began taking off her clothes, recognizing that he was returning to her world by the gradual tapering off of his excitement, the slowing of his speech. Gabe would turn from his monitors or look up from his microscope and see her on his bed, a pill or capsule or paper in her hand, waiting for the greenlight, and be stunned by what he saw each and every time. He had only ever nodded his head in those moments and then it was his turn to watch her journey into another world.

They'd only ever made love one time in the two years that he knew her. Kara brought him a caffeine pill that night, remembering how they'd met, and pretended it was something else. He dove right in, as usual. He didn't even look at the pill; otherwise, it would have been obvious that she was teasing him. But he hadn't noticed. The ritual was so compelling that his hands had gone to work without thought.

Looking back on it, he could see the more-mischievous-than-usual facial expression, the 'I'm-hiding-something-from-you' eyes, but in that moment, he'd failed to understand and had just gone to work. When he finally figured it out, he turned to her, a little hurt, maybe even angry, but she laughed and smiled, grabbed his face with both hands and kissed him fully on the lips. The ritual was so compelling that her hands went to work without another thought.

They returned to the routine for the remainder of that semester, not because there was anything wrong with that one night, but because it was their nature. It was the way of their relationship. When Kara left school there was an attempt to stay in touch but it failed quietly, trailing off into nothing after less than a year.

They lost touch, but Gabe never lost his lust for plucking the chemical strings of the human body. That was his addiction and he'd never been able to shake it. If he hadn't stumbled that night… if he had gone to a charging station off campus instead… if…

Gabe pulled himself more upright and shook the thoughts from his head. It was a ridiculous line of reasoning. *My life, this mess, isn't the result of a single moment or one fateful choice. I'd still be here regardless of Kara. This mess is entirely my own.*

It wasn't a fatalistic perspective necessarily, but it was his analysis of the variables involved. So many choices were made every day that each one became less and less significant. The night he met Kara was definitely special, but it hadn't dictated his path. His path was created by the choices he made every day, the results of which had clumped together and built a probability for where, when, and who he would be. How could he place so much import on one moment when so many moments were responsible? Kara was just one of the million choices he had made to bring him to this. It wasn't her fault.

He pressed his finger against the shower activation button and circled clockwise until the display reached his desired temperature. The atomizer came to life in a rush and the tiny stall was filled from top to bottom with a fine heated fog of sterilizing mist. With one hand holding the support firmly, he began rubbing his chest and then the jet stopped abruptly.

"What the…?" The background of the display where the temperature had appeared previously had turned bright red, and the foreground stated that the allowed time had elapsed.

The motel had never reset the allotment for Gabe after the previous guest. Standing there, naked, wet, and partially clean, he couldn't decide whether to laugh or weep, and then laughter won out. The laughter was tainted with a touch of hysteria, but it felt good regardless.

He leaned onto the horizontal bar, which was just below waist height, took some of the weight from his good leg, and allowed himself the moment. A couple of tears formed, and he wiped at his whole face with one hand to get at them, and to rub some of the moisture from his cheeks.

"Well, this really is a moment, isn't it?" Asking himself, hearing his voice in the emptiness of the stall, woke him up a little.

He could bring up the front desk from the Wall to get more time, but he wouldn't. It didn't matter anyway. Gabe was going to risk a walk-in clinic today, and they would clean him up there. Whoever was looking for him, if they had the means, would know exactly where to pick him up and he didn't care anymore.

It was a relief, actually, to make up his mind to come out of hiding. He was valuable and didn't need to be afraid. Apple – whether he completely understood it or not – was generating a reaction, a condition, never before seen, and he created it. Maybe the Collective had a use for him? Marius was his connection. Tracking him down might explain how the Collective had gained possession of the Apple compound in the first place.

The remaining process of getting himself ready was tedious and uneventful. Gabe swallowed more PainFree with a glass of water while waiting for the closet to finish cleaning his clothes. He located the nearest clinic on the Wall. It wasn't far for a healthy person, but he imagined it would take him a couple of hours. A cane would help, but finding one along the way was unlikely. Although some of the more fashion-forward in the community of young business types considered the antiquated accessory stylish, he didn't imagine much in this area of the city catering to that crowd. Still, he would keep an eye open for one.

As he exited the room, he made sure he had everything. He shrugged to himself, sheepishly remembering there was nothing he could have accidentally left. Smiling sardonically, he wedged himself completely out of the doorway before removing his broomstick from where he was propping the door open with it.

After about ten minutes of struggling toward the entrance, he approached the front desk nervously. He wasn't sure what the reaction of the clerk from last night would be and he didn't really want to have any conversation if he could help it. Pleasantly surprised, he noticed that it wasn't the same woman behind the desk. She looked Gabe up and down with almost no sympathy, and then suddenly recognition.

"Oh hey, mister!" She was younger than the woman last night by probably ten years, and definitely much younger than Gabe. "You're the one that paid in 'O,' right?" loudly.

Gabe was stunned. The girl's nonchalance was sending up every paranoid flag he had in his skull. He looked around a bit and thankfully saw no one, but who knew what kind of recording devices were present? He had worked so hard to distance himself from his occupation, being identified directly as a dealer by a stranger was unsettling and completely out of his comfort zone.

"Hahahaha! Relax, limpy. There's no one around to tell your little secret." She reached down behind the counter for something and Gabe had visions of a gun, this crazy young woman gunning him down and laughing, shot after shot.

She brought up a cane and set it down on the desk. "It's a little thank you from my mom. From me, too… I stole a few caplets from her."

She winked at Gabe, and he thought he saw her swallow hard, not quite licking her lips.

"I ain't gonna bite you, little man, you can come closer…" she trailed off at the end.

The woman came around the desk. She was dressed in a frumpy outfit of baggy clothing attempting to hide her weight. It didn't really work, though, as her movement demonstrated her heft with slow, over-encumbered footfalls. She was also wearing glasses, not completely unlike Gabe's.

"Here," she offered Gabe her hand. He still hadn't moved or spoken a word.

She took his weight as she exchanged the broomstick for the cane. "There you go," she smiled.

"Good as can be… ooooh, I like your glasses," then, hesitatingly, "Think I could try them on?"

He blinked a few times, dumbfounded. A few tumblers finally fell into a place, "Oh, uh, um… I'm sorry miss, these glasses are, well, they are corrective, not for looks. The lenses are for a severe astigmatism, I don't think you'd like them."

The woman seemed annoyed and looked at him suspiciously. She roughly pulled her glasses off and held them out to Gabe, "I KNOW what real glasses are. Let me see."

Again, he was stunned stupid, but he managed a shrug of his shoulders. Apparently that was enough of a go-for-it for her to pull the glasses off his face and put them on hers.

"Ugh. How can you see with these things?!" She spoke too loudly for how close they were.

Stammering, "Th-thank you, miss… uh, for the cane. I really have to leave now. I'm late and I just need… "

"Eh. Here," as she shoved his glasses into his cane-free hand. She shambled back to her position behind the desk.

Gabe, unable to sort out the interaction, gave up and tested out the cane. It felt firm and steady. It still took him longer than it should have to pass the front desk, but he was gaining speed, figuring out the motion as he looked at the clerk.

She was peering into a display, watching a show or something. He set his keycard on the counter. She didn't look up.

"Thank you." She still didn't look up. "Uh, for the room and the cane. Thank you."

"Sure. Whatever." She didn't look up.

As Gabe limped out of the motel, he heard the woman laugh, forced and loud. He thought about her, what a weirdo she seemed to him, and at that same moment, he could've sworn that he heard her say, "Weirdo," back at him. Then the door closed behind him.

Outside the air was bitter cold, biting at the skin of his face. He looked left and right to orient himself, to get his bearings so he could make his way to the clinic. At first, he didn't notice the tall handsome man in the long charcoal gray coat, but the man noticed Gabe and began striding toward him. Gabe did a double-take, as the man was so completely out of context.

A coincidence…? No, it couldn't be him.

But it was him. It couldn't be a coincidence.

The man was groomed, obviously wealthy, and he exuded extraordinary confidence. His face was thin but healthy, clean shaven. The hair on his head was full and silver. Tucked into his buttoned trench, he wore a dark purple scarf around his neck. His collar was turned up and he wore black leather gloves that matched his shoes. The manner of the man was strong and in control as he approached Gabe.

He stopped a foot or so before Gabe, his stature imposing, "Gabe." The seriousness of his face softened, as he looked down at the wounded Chemist.

"Marius?"

"I think it is time we get you to the hospital, old friend."

Marius came around to Gabe's side and offered him his arm. Noticing Gabe's hesitation, "I know, I know Gabe. I haven't always been upfront with you about the terms of our business together. It's nothing all that conspiratorial or strange, I assure you. Sometimes it's just the nature of this line of work… better to keep some things hidden, even from yourself," he smiled.

He offered his arm with greater emphasis, "Come now. We'll talk after the hospital."

Then he pointed up the street a bit, "My car is just there."

Gabe gave in, relaxed for the first time in days, and took the extended elbow of his tall friend. They might have been a couple, the gentle way Marius helped Gabe to the car. He held Gabe close, hugged him into the passenger seat, and helped him into a comfortable position for the ride.

It felt good. Too good to be true, too good to refuse. Gabe relaxed into the seat of the luxury sedan and closed his eyes. Marius came around to the driver's side, opened the door and smoothly entered, then closed the door.

"That's right, Gabe," he placed a gloved hand on Gabe's shoulder, "Rest."

"Everything is going to be fine," he started the vehicle with a thumb press, followed by a few other strokes.

"Yeah, boss?" from the car speakers.

"I've just picked him up."

"Oh, good. I was beginning to think we lost him."

"Me too. Anyway, the search is over. Thank you."

"Sure thing."

Marius took a moment, looked to Gabe to make sure he was secure and comfortable, then watched traffic for an opening. He pulled out into the street, and set his destination.

No words were spoken. No music was played. Gabe waited and wondered. What exactly would they want from him? It didn't matter. He didn't care. He would just be glad to be out of pain. That was first. Beyond that, who knew?

Wait, maybe Vanya was family, and close to Marius? Gabe felt hysteria bubbling up in his chest again but managed to suppress his laughter at the thought. If that were true, he doubted he was on the way to the clinic. He tried to push the thought out of his mind. He would just have to wait and see. Patience was actually pretty easy at this point, because he had no choices. Taking solace in that thought, he drifted to sleep.

The Picture of Health

Sixteen

Sara was startled awake by the bowl of water tipping into her lap. She quickly stood up and righted the bowl, but it was too late as most of the water, now cold, had spilled out onto her pants.

"Great," a defeated whisper. She stared down at soaked sweats, her facial expression a mixture of disbelief and frustration. Then, for a sleepy moment, she was actually amused with herself and she smiled. She couldn't think of a reason why she would have a bowl of water in her lap in the first place.

Seeing Joshua brought her back to reality, and the easy smile faded from her lips. Joshua twitched a bit, and she could see that he had continued to sweat while she'd slept. The sheets and blankets needed to be changed.

Sad and worried thoughts began running through her imagination. She wondered if she could just put him in a taxi for the hospital or if he took a turn for the worse, if she could hide his body. She thought about leaving the apartment and all of her belongings, this version of her life, behind. But if she acted on that impulse she would be left with no conclusion, no explanation of Joshua. She was too curious to let it go.

Sara had connections with the underbelly of the world, enough to get fake Creds and decent drugs. She even dealt with some crazy GEaR-heads now and again, but she'd never seen anyone move through his own clothes before. *Must be high-ranking Collective. Had to be.* It was the perfect reason for her to turn tail and run, but her gut kept telling her to stay. Anyway, it seemed pretty clear that he could find her if he wanted to, so running away probably wasn't a realistic option. What could she do, but stay and hope something good would happen if Joshua woke up with her taking care of him?

The entire situation was too dramatic, and now that she'd had a little sleep, her pragmatism stepped up. Resolute that she would stay until Joshua was conscious or dead, she knelt down and picked up the damp rag from the floor. She dropped the rag into the empty bowl and set it aside on the chair.

She examined Joshua more closely. He was sick and getting sicker, his breathing shallow and labored, his chest moving slowly and weakly.

Peeling back the blankets, Sara thought about how uncomfortable Joshua must feel because he was so wet and sticky with steaming sweat. Then she smirked at her own uncomfortably cold, wet pants. She pulled her pants off and threw them toward the closet. They hit the wall beside the opening with a thud. Her naked legs exposed, she gathered up the soaked blankets from the bed. Bunching them into a damp pile, she was disgusted as she lifted up the heavy mess. She carried them quickly to the Closet and dumped them on the floor.

It took her a few minutes of separating and hanging, making room, but eventually, all of the blankets, and her sweatpants too, were layered into the Closet. The Closet was small, the smallest she'd seen in the city, the kind of appliance only housed in the cheapest of apartments. Sara had never had one that worked better though. For whatever reason, everything always came out smelling amazingly fresh. On the other hand, she was lazy when it came to laundry, so she didn't use it all that often. Still, she was proud of her little Closet. She would be sad to say goodbye, which seemed inevitable at that point; probably sooner rather than later.

Sliding and locking the closet door, she set it to full clean. A soft, barely audible hum told her it was working. Turning around, she walked to the bed and knelt down beside it. Peering into the darkness beneath the bed for a few moments, she found what she was looking for and reached for it.

She pulled out a stack of heavy plastic containers, each about three feet on a side, maybe three inches deep. She slipped the top one off, and the next, leaving the bottom container exposed. Sliding her finger across a red bar on the top changed the color of the bar to green and initiated a slight sucking sound. Air was pulled into the container and the lid popped, allowing Sara to remove it effortlessly.

She pulled out a set of fresh, lavender-colored sheets, and a forest green blanket. Holding the sheets to her face, she inhaled deeply and decided they were fresh. Certainly, the bedding was fresh enough for the comatose Joshua. It was difficult getting the bottom sheet out from under Joshua earlier, but she'd managed it. It was amazing that he hadn't woken up as she rolled him from one side of the bed to the other, then back again. She had left him on his side facing the door, mumbling to himself, but definitely not conscious.

"Okay, Joshua," softly, "Let's try this again."

She considered trying to clothe him. She had some sweat pants that would have fit him easily. With greater difficulty, she might have even found a shirt, but she liked him better naked anyway. It made him seem less threatening, at least when his veins weren't black and popping out of his skin.

Sara put her hands on his shoulder and chest and began to push. He resisted.

She looked down at him, "Joshua?"

No response. He seemed pretty damned unconscious. Even if he was willfully resisting her a moment before, he'd gone back to languid ambivalence now. His skin was warm beneath her fingers and covered with a slick of sweat.

She stood up and went to the bathroom, grabbed her shower towel, and returned to the bed. Rubbing him down, from top to bottom, she soaked up as much of his sweat as she could. She lifted his arm up from his side to dry it all the way around, and even tried the same with his leg, but less successfully because of the weight and awkward nature of her position. Trying to roll him over again, towel draped over his waist, she pushed from the top of his shoulder and his hip.

He resisted.

She pushed harder.

He matched her strength.

"What the…?" she looked down, then jumped back, startled by his wide open eyes.

He wasn't mumbling anymore. He was speaking, but his words were weak, "… the door… Winter's at… your door…"

He licked his dry lips and closed his eyes again. Sara looked over to her door, back to Joshua, and then to the door again.

"Joshua?" she pleaded, "Joshua!" a harsh whisper.

Shit, she thought to herself. She walked over to her bag, which was lying on the floor near the bathroom, and rummaged through it. Finding her canister of mace, she flipped the lid and removed the safety.

She tiptoed over to her door. She couldn't turn on the viewer without alerting whoever might be out there that she was watching. Still, there wasn't much choice. Standing there waiting for whomever was out there to come barging in didn't seem like a great idea.

Standing to the side of the door, she reached across and activated the viewer. The screen lit up with a view of the hallway. No one stood in the corridor. She waited and watched. Her neighbor, a couple of doors down on the right, opened her door and set out some garbage, then shut her door again. Nothing, the hallway was empty. It was possible someone was hiding just out of view, but there wasn't much room, not enough to conceal a whole, adult body, at least not in Sara's mind.

She relaxed, "Joshua, bud, I think you're hallucinating."

His eyes were closed again, and although she couldn't really trust her Engagement system with Joshua, the read agreed with her feeling and stated that he was unconscious, sleeping. "… and I'm a little nuts acting on your sleep-talking."

Securing the mace, she walked back to the bed. She neglected to turn off the viewer. It stayed on for several seconds before automatically turning off. Before it shut off, a man appeared down the hallway, seeming to emerge from a fog, as though he'd always been there but had been obscured.

The man strode toward the viewer, looming larger with one step, dissolving into foggy, energetic wisps on the next. The alternating continued and he approached faster than the motion of his walk could explain. It was the man from the diner, the man who was there, but wasn't… the wintering man. He knelt down outside the door as the viewer flickered off.

Joshua's eyes shuttered open, "… the door…," a harsh and urgent whisper.

"Sick boy," Sara sympathetically, "There's no one at the door."

She gave up on the bottom sheet, not wanting to struggle with Joshua again. Instead, she moved on to the top sheet and unfurled it with a flourish. It was a well-practiced motion, and the bed and Joshua were covered completely on the first wave.

Sara gently tucked the sheet around his body. His eyes were still staring eerily wide toward the door. She looked down at the blanket, but before she could reach down to grab it, Joshua's hand reached out, covered by the sheet, and latched firmly onto her arm. It would have scared her, but it happened too fast for her to react.

He was looking at her with clear, blue, completely normal eyes. Not through her anymore, but at her directly, into her eyes, "… the man… at the door.…"

"Wha?" but his eyes had already closed and his grip loosened, and then released. He rolled limply onto his back all on his own.

Frustration ate at Sara. *What is he talking about? Is he having a flashback?* She couldn't understand and it was beginning to bother her.

She looked over at the door and noticed that something had been slid beneath it. Standing and running at once, she hit the door and opened it with a fast wave of her hand.

No one.

She looked back to Joshua. He was resting on his back and had resumed his shallow breathing. New beads of sweat were clearly visible, dewing up all over his face. He was dead to the world again. Down the hallway, there was only silence and the soft glow of the hallway light strips. Kneeling down, she picked up what looked like photopaper.

She stood and closed the door without looking up from the photo. The man pictured looked similar to Joshua, but it definitely wasn't Joshua. He was taller, obvious even from his position sitting on some concrete steps, and more traditionally handsome.

She flapped the photopaper in the air and looked thoughtfully over to Joshua. Looking back to the picture, her face bunched up on one side. Curious, she held the photo in her palm and ran her finger along the surface. She wasn't sure what she expected, maybe another picture, maybe a whole album, but instead it was just two words.

Joshua's brother

She ran her finger back and forth on the photopaper, but nothing else appeared. Walking over to the Desk, she set the photopaper onto it and slid her finger along the surface. The Wall lit up instantly, displaying the contents of the photopaper album as side-by-side images. A toolset appeared with options to manipulate the pictures and the photopaper. The picture of Joshua's brother was highlighted and the properties were displayed in a side panel. The image, or this copy of it anyway, was created earlier today.

She noted the time, "Damn." She'd slept for several hours beside Joshua. It was already late in the afternoon.

Sara selected the picture of Joshua's brother, stretched it by splitting her fingers apart, and dragged a question mark icon over to the man's face and dropped it there. The Oxford WhoIs Library window appeared, and listed 2500 suggestions for the person selected. The first ten were displayed, each accompanied by brief, public-zone Credentials.

The scan identified the building based on a plaque embedded in the brick, visible over the right shoulder of Joshua's brother, so the suggestions were ordered by residence proximity, then by percentage of phenotypical similarity. There was a request dialogue open, asking for another picture of the subject for cross-referencing. If they really were brothers, a picture of Joshua might help narrow the search but Sara decided to browse through the first several hits instead.

If she could find someone to take Joshua to the hospital, or someone who could tell her more about what was happening, she would feel much better. Maybe the brother was her ticket to an explanation and freedom from responsibility.

As it was, Sara just felt helpless and vulnerable. Whoever slid the photopaper beneath her door certainly knew more than she did, probably knew she had Joshua, and obviously knew where she lived. Apparently, that wasn't much of a secret anymore. Conspiracy theories aside, she always believed she'd done well flying beneath the radar, lived a quiet enough life, that no one would ever notice her. What happened to her anonymity?

"What's wrong with me?" More annoyed than anything else, she brought up the keyboard input display on the surface of the Desk and typed quickly, filtering by "Falken."

Five results. Joshua was fourth among them. Second from the top, she was sure she had found the man from the picture. His name was Bradley. But she was immediately disappointed by the deceased notice that appeared when she selected him for more information.

Sara took a moment to pull up the obituary page and found that the young man had been in a fatal car accident about ten years previous. There wasn't anything particularly astonishing in the article except that it was sad to lose someone so talented, and apparently well-loved. He had his doctorate in physics and was working with the World Science Foundation on quantum-level communication systems.

Sara thought about it for a moment and vaguely remembered that that research had been dropped. It had made all of the news streams at the time. The WSF had made a breakthrough in nerve generation that would supplant the older, less reliable method, yielding results in hours instead of days or weeks. The communications research was put on hold in light of the breakthrough. Nerve generation tech was a far more profitable and predictable line of research and development than the speculative quantum communication Bradley was apparently working on. She hadn't followed the story all that closely then and certainly hadn't looked it up since, so she wasn't sure if Bradley's research was ever continued.

Bradley. It was an old-world name, like Joshua or Sara. She felt a connection with the boys, superficial as it was, just because of those names. The names weren't that uncommon, really, but she was comforted by the thought of some sort of bond among them. She wanted some karma, some destiny right now.

Sara was never connected to anything, never had any roots. She didn't have a god or gods to rely upon, few did. A sentient being or a spiritual, disembodied benevolence just didn't fit into her world view. Instead, she had a strong sense of destiny, a kind of faith in herself and the world, which gave her a sense of stability.

It was simple really. She believed in a continuity that existed outside of her, beyond people's choices, unqualified by human value judgments. A consistent and continuous force of life… she rarely ever spoke of it. It wasn't a well-thought-out philosophy or religion. It was more like an excuse to not worry.

It was an excuse for many things… her parents, her life. Right now, she didn't want to worry, so she thought about the relationships of the old-world names and thought the connection made sense. She convinced herself she was in the right place, doing the right thing.

So, if everything was in its right place, who the fuck slipped her this picture, and why? Joshua's brother was dead. Communicating with him seemed pretty unlikely. The parents were unlisted, or at least, they would have appeared as matches if their profiles existed, or were publicly available. Maybe Joshua took this picture? Or maybe he was there?

Turning away from the Wall, Sara walked over to Joshua and picked up the fresh blanket. Once more, she deftly threw the blanket out over him and over the bed. She gently nestled the covers against his body and noted the heat. His temp was rising again and his lips were parched. She probably needed to try forcing some fluids into him, but she wasn't exactly sure how to do that while he was unconscious.

She would have to leave the apartment to buy some gel packs and probably some basic meds. Sara hesitated to leave Joshua alone, but she knew there wasn't much she could do to protect him if the Collective or the recent visitor decided to come get him. She had to hit the pharmacy if she was going to help him. The one around the block would have something, she hoped, to reduce his fever. It wouldn't take long. She could pick up some packets of hydrating gels there, too.

"Joshua," she began softly, somewhere between a question and a statement, "I think I might have to leave you alone for a bit. I would have taken you to the hospital, but... well anyway, I didn't, and I'm not going to."

Sara sat down on the bed, her naked legs folded neatly to her side as she leaned over his waist, facing him, "I filtered my news streams for anything about the 'All-Niter,' but nothing's come up... I'm pretty sure you hurt or killed two Collective Officers... soooo, that's a whole lot of surprising. You'll have to explain all of this when you wake up."

Sara leaned a little closer. Her natural pose was flirtatious, as always, the front of her sweatshirt hanging down loosely, exposing two significant testaments to her gender. She'd once been told that she could "raise the dead" with those two, but Joshua didn't make a move.

Lost my touch.

"Anyway, I don't know who, but someone's keeping the Diner story offline. Oh, and uh," she smiled, "there's something else. A photopaper was slid beneath my door. One of the pages says that the picture is of your brother, Bradley?"

She stopped for a moment, looked around and found the towel she'd used earlier to wipe away some of the sweat from Joshua's face. Grabbing it, she folded it a couple of times and wiped at his forehead and cheeks.

"It was strange the way the pic just appeared there. Nothing as spectacular as whatever you did this morning, but still, whoever delivered the photopaper was pretty tricky."

Sara realized how thirsty she was as the words caught in her mouth a bit, "So, right, I have to go out and get us some supplies. I don't know if you're in pain… I'll get you a few different kinds of meds."

She cupped his cheek in her hand, "I'm sorry I stunned you and tied you up. You didn't deserve that. Anyway, I feel guilty now, so you've got that going for you."

Standing up, Sara went to a pile of clothes and pulled out a pair of jeans. She sat on the bed again, hard—hoping it would disturb Joshua—and pulled her pants on, both legs at once. Standing up into the pants, she buttoned them up and found a jacket. She put her hands through the sleeves of the jacket and grabbed the photopaper from the Desk.

"Here," she placed the picture on Joshua's chest.

"Do me a favor and wake up before I get back. Mysterious is only cute for ten-year olds and one-night stands…" she considered it honestly for a moment, "Actually, if this was your idea of a one night stand, then do me one better and be gone before I get back. You scored big points with your open, but I have to say, your finish? Disappointing."

Still, no reaction.

Not one for the jokes, eh?

"Anyway, Joshua, I'll be back in about fifteen minutes. I'll lock up on my way out."

She moved toward the door, looked back at Joshua and decided she could use some meds of her own.

Stepping out into the hallway, Sara looked for any sign of activity. There simply wasn't anything extraordinary about the corridor. She rarely ran into her neighbors and she'd only chosen to live here because the landlord had billed the place as a quiet, keep-to-yourself residence. She closed the door behind her and flashed her Creds, mounted in her wrist, toward the door panel in a downward motion. The locking mechanism engaged with a thick, metallic *thwack*.

Her trip to the drugstore was entirely uneventful. She picked up some PainFree, some anti-inflammatory pills, two kinds of sedatives—she wasn't sure why—and FeverBreakers, which were recommended by the pharmacist. Also, she grabbed a handful of nutrient-rich hydrating gels. The nutrient-rich version of the gels was more expensive, but it was the only way she thought she would be able to feed Joshua if he decided to stay unconscious.

The walk cleared her head. The cool air sharpened her attitude, her reasoning. If Joshua wasn't conscious, wasn't speaking coherently by tomorrow morning, she would dump him into a taxi and send him to the hospital. At that point, she could leave town. A new continent was probably the safest bet. She had no interest in the Midwest and she'd lived up and down both coasts. There were a few cities in the European states that had always intrigued her.

She could hop in one of the intercoastal Javelins and be in Florence in a couple of hours. On the other hand, the inoculation to prevent IDS was expensive, and hers had certainly expired. They wouldn't let her fly without it. Even if she could slip past the inspection, she would rather swim in shit than suffer Inertial Dampening Sickness again. She needed to procure some high-quality forged Creds and expedite an appointment for the inoc, something she should put in motion sooner rather than later.

Sara was so distracted by her thoughts that she nearly knocked over an older woman who stopped inexplicably while staring into her

Glass. As it was, Sara only bumped the woman a little which got her legs started up again and she walked away, oblivious.

The minor collision brought the world into focus for Sara and she noticed that she was in a rush of pedestrian traffic. So many people, face after face, flashing by, a blur of personalities plugged into their networks, far away. It was business as usual, a business almost completely foreign to her. Being up at this hour of the day was strange. Luckily, her feet knew the way home. She crossed the street with a flood of people at the light and entered her building.

On her walk to the elevator, she considered that she would be okay if Joshua didn't wake up. Sure, she would feel bad for him, but that Javelin out of town was beginning to sincerely appeal to her. Pulling out her Glass, she summoned up a picture of one of the bar's better customers. She'd found him without too much trouble within the first couple of weeks as Lily. It was important to connect with an Exit right away. Peace of mind only came when she knew that she had a quick way out.

Mark was one of the best she'd ever seen. He was even somewhat mythological, people saying that he could be anywhere at any time. If it were true, though, then how was he so often the guy ordering White Russians in the corner of the bar?

The guy made his entire living sorting out various grades of Creds for those in the underbelly of the city. He had high-class, clean tools for the extraction and replacement of the sub-dermal interface. Sara had paid him for the Engagement system and the install. Even though she didn't know him well, she trusted him.

Mark had chosen his line of work for the love of the GEaRS, seeing how it all worked. He was always the first to offer the latest Enhancements, simply to be the first to install it and know everything about it. In his trade, his expertise had served him well, and Mark had been able to procure early, more volatile and more innovative versions of systems. That was the true key to his happiness and his success… he was the bleeding edge.

She left Mark a video-message as she boarded the lift. Simple and sweet, "Hey, Mark, it's time for my Exit."

A seductive wink and a slight movement of her lips, and she closed the connection. It would be enough. Whether he'd ever bothered to dig her and identify her, she never knew. Regardless, he was a class act and would understand that her statement was a request for a job, for his help. He would hook her up, no questions, no gouging.

The lift door opened up on her floor. Sara hesitated. If she was going to leave, she should just leave, lingering wasn't going to help. Mark would be ready for her tomorrow at the latest, or so she hoped, and then she could be on her way out. She could leave this madness behind her. Right now. Turn around. So easy. *So easy.*

But she faced forward and after a moment, her feet carried her forward. She wasn't scared of whoever left the photopaper. She wasn't scared of Joshua. She wasn't even scared of the Laterali anymore. Or even if she was scared of those things, she was more scared of completely losing her sense of self by running all the time. It had nothing to do with Joshua or last night, but it was the thought of starting over again. How many Credentials had she skinned and shed? She liked herself as Lily—truer to her character than she'd ever been before. She wished she could stay Lily, a little while longer at least.

Tension built within her, each step tauter than the last. When she arrived at the end of the corridor, in front of her door, she was filled with fatalism. She'd made the right choice. Joshua would be awake on the other side and he could give her some kind of explanation. And maybe she would be herself, for a little while. He'd seen right through to her after all. Maybe…?

But her door opened on a quiet apartment. Staring at the ceiling again, or through it, Joshua laid perfectly still on the bed. The photopaper was undisturbed on his chest, the room exactly as she left it.

Sara let out a sigh, disappointed and defeated by her own imaginings. She was tired, thoroughly exhausted. Dropping the small bag of medicine to the floor, she pulled off her jacket and levered off her shoes. She reached into the bag and found a gel pack. Ripping the top off, she held the small plastic pouch to her lips and sucked a bit of the gel out. Her mouth filled with cool comfort as she worked her tongue through the gel. Swallowing once, twice, three times, she continued to play with the gel and let it fill her up. For whatever reason, she'd always liked the feeling of squishing the gel up against her gums, around her teeth.

Her whole body relaxed and she felt comfortable, wanting to sleep even more. She pulled a bit more gel for herself then leaned over Joshua and tugged his chin down gently. She squeezed a small amount of the thick blue gel onto his tongue. Holding his mouth closed, she waited and watched as she continued to work the cool liquid in her own mouth, around her cheeks and gums.

It seemed like several minutes passed. She got nervous that she was drowning him, but before any real panic hit, Joshua swallowed. And soon after, again. A sense of relief rolled over Sara, like the gel over her tongue. She gathered up the remaining jelly in her mouth and swallowed it herself. Time for sleep.

She unbuttoned and unzipped her pants and stepped to her Desk. Setting the lighting to nighttime, the room took on the magical feel of full moonlight. She slipped out of her pants and then into bed beside the comatose stranger and closed her eyes.

"Don't try anything," she spoke to the wall, away from the fever-hot Joshua, "I'm not sleeping with you… I just don't think I should have to sleep on the floor."

Business as Usual
Seventeen

"We found him," Marius addressed the Viewer, which displayed only a few lines of text. The messages detailed the security of the connection, but also reflected an uncharacteristic lack of information in the form of repeated "insufficient data" lines.

"You recovered the sample?" the voice was odd.

The voice lacked inflection, but more notably, it had a mechanical slant to it, a sort of flatness. The sound was unnaturally even. Marius was accustomed to the flatness because it was the same voice he'd always heard when dealing with this particular man.

Marius had never been able to identify the man. Unmasking him should have been easy, especially with that voice, but when Marius sent a sample of the voice to his insider among the Watchers of the Spire, the voice came back as unknown. Not unknown as in, classified or restricted, but the voice was completely unrecognized. It was curious and unsettling. Even Marius, careful as he always was, has his voice recorded *somewhere*.

The blank screen—indicating total lack of identifying material— was representative of a man who had never once owned a Glass, never been admitted to a hospital, had never gone to school or been incarcerated for any reason, or he was in the Collective at a rank far out of Marius' reach. Since most of those possibilities were improbable at best, or at least impractical to entertain, Marius had decided on the last. To his advantage, the last possibility could potentially provide valuable benefits, could result in a very powerful ally.

Marius had worked with the Stranger for some time. He was a stranger to Marius but not to the business. He understood the advantages of working out from under the watchful eye of the Spire. The black market could afford the risk-expensive experiments that the Collective could not, experiments that sometimes led to great advancement. It was progress that benefitted everyone, even if the method could not be condoned by the general population.

The Stranger had come directly to Marius, unsolicited and unknown, which had never happened before in Marius' recollection. He had built a life on his ability to know everyone and be known by no one. He had, in fact, considered himself unidentifiable until he was contacted by the Stranger, a true ghost. It was unsettling to be at such a disadvantage with an associate, but if Marius had shied away from every risky encounter, he would never have built his underworld, would never have remained so strong for so long.

Besides, there was implied leverage. Clearly, despite his considerable resources, the Stranger was not able to work completely outside the bounds of the law. He needed Marius. And so, they did business.

The courting period of their relationship had been short. A few odd pieces of information, nothing more than seeds really, passed from the Stranger to Marius. The documents were frequently white-papers, but sometimes less formalized, describing fabrication techniques for controlled and volatile substances, requiring a high degree of expertise to produce, handle, and store. In return, Marius needed only to put the experimental substances to use, and report the results. The arrangement felt like any legitimate business.

The first few objectives were straightforward with clear results. The prototypical inertial dampeners worked well. They went into production mere weeks after Marius concluded the tests.

The new shield-defeating measures were highly effective; of course they were completely fatal against unshielded biological targets, disintegrating flesh and bone at an alarming rate, but that was hardly a drawback. It didn't make the cut for the Collective but Marius thought that it worked perfectly. Tidiest work he'd ever done, no loose ends.

The anti-depression drug... well, it worked anyway. In addition to relieving depression though, it also caused a near total loss of cognitive ability for several hours, a condition that was often permanent. The test subjects didn't really seem to mind in Marius' estimation. Unfortunately, he had felt a few seconds of sadness initiating "the cleanup," considering that the subjects were blissfully happy, finally.

Over the last few years, there had even been some dramatic advancements of which Marius was proud. The High-Density Mass Accelerator, for instance, worked exactly as desired. Marius didn't necessarily understand how it worked, but the results spoke for themselves. Lightweight, discrete, ridiculously powerful, the HDMA could put a hole of the desired size through almost any material.

Theoretically, you could run out of ammunition, but he'd never seen it done. The HDMA was still listed as a prototype for the Collective, but that was their problem. Marius had been supplying his people with the weapon for several months.

And there they were again, not quite face to face, discussing the latest endeavor. Marius had come to rather enjoy these encounters with the Stranger. Each conversation was a challenge to try to gain some understanding of the man, or woman, behind the Wall.

"My old friend swallowed it," a proud smile imparted a mild softness to his gaunt face, as he told the Stranger the location of the Sample. "I think I will talk to him before removing it forcibly. At this point, we can still use his help explaining and defining the effects of the Apple Compound. I assume that is still our primary objective?"

"We do not share objectives, Marius. You, on the other hand, have been paid well and have yet to deliver. Convince him to help you, force him to help you, or take the sample and figure it out for yourself… I don't care."

The silence that followed the statement was a gaping maw, swallowing up the words Marius thought he might say. The options were limited, and it wasn't at all clear yet if Gabriel would cooperate, or what level of coercion it would take to make him cooperate if he chose not to.

"I'll be in touch," the connection closed.

Was there a threat in there? Marius couldn't decide. He supposed it didn't matter. No threats were necessary to keep him focused and on task. He wanted to know for himself what Gabe had created. He'd thought it was a failure, causing more than one death, and often causing nothing at all to happen.

When Gabriel had called a halt to the distribution, results of testing almost entirely negative, Marius had obliged without question. Soon after that though, the Stranger had made it clear that the distribution must continue. Apparently, Gabriel had been keeping secrets about the effectiveness of the drug. Marius had never confronted him about it—a regrettable decision, one Marius expected to rectify, even if it meant sacrificing the Chemist.

But why even consider that possibility? Marius and Gabriel were old friends.

…

"Double espresso," Marius ordered for himself, and then turned to Gabriel who was hurriedly examining the list of teas.

"Sir?" the barista prompted Gabriel, reminding him impatiently that she was waiting for his order, even though there was obviously no one else in line.

"Green tea, please?" he leaned a little to one side, his leg-assist strapped neatly around the repaired knee. Gabriel looked uncomfortable in his body and insecure in his choice of beverage.

"Um…" she pointed a patronizing finger at a flickering menu, "… which one?" The look on her face exuded annoyance, and she raised her eyebrows sardonically.

"The Dragon Leaf will do," Marius cut in gracefully and completed the transaction with a wave of his wrist on the counter.

"It's one of my favorites, although I don't honestly drink tea all that often," pleasantly smiling at Gabriel.

The coffee house was set up in the old-time style. Earth tones, browns of various shades, dark greens, and a smattering of burnt orange and red decorated the establishment. Lots of modern coffee houses didn't have employees at all, but this one was proud to provide lattes with a heavy helping of sarcasm and wisecracks.

It was similar to a place where Marius and Gabriel had frequented when they first met many years ago. Gabriel was still enrolled at the university at that time. He was there for the easy access to lab equipment more than anything else. Kara had been gone for a year or more, and Marius had strolled right into the on-campus coffee house, sat down across from Gabriel, and begun their friendship.

Marius seemed to have already known Gabriel, to already have respect for him and understand him. Employing his natural charm and confidence, Marius won over the socially awkward Gabriel with a joke and a smile, and grew the relationship with genuine interest in Gabriel's experiments.

It was as easy then as it was for him now, free-flowing conversation. Marius was always the exceptional listener.

"I'm sorry that I didn't tell you." Looking deeply into the bottom of the glass, Gabriel searched for forgiveness.

"Well, I'd be lying if I didn't say I was disappointed," Marius looked across with concern, his salt-and-pepper brows raised slightly and softened. "I've always considered myself your confident and your aid. On the other hand, I'm not certain that I could have offered much… not sure that I understand."

Gabriel looked up from his tea and met Marius' eyes, "I'm not sure that I do either…"

He looked around a bit, fumbling the words around in his mind before venturing them aloud, "Most of the test subjects experienced nothing, but those that did react," he found the words and implored belief, squaring himself to Marius, "They burn… inside out."

"Burn?" hard-pressed to respond without skepticism or judgment, Marius prompted for more of an explanation. *Burning is hardly an explanation, unless these subjects actually caught on fire… that could be useful.*

"I don't know. Burn. It's like all of their senses turn inward, external stimulation ignored for the sake of some dramatic internal event… when these few special subjects look outward again, they know things they cannot know…" his voice became quiet and lost some of his momentum.

After faltering a bit, Gabriel recovered and surged on with new urgency, "Marius. Marius, one of them opened his eyes and looked straight through me. He talked about my feelings and my thoughts as though they were his own! Then, all around him, all around me, the air became thick… it was difficult to breathe and to move. And when I did move? It was like swimming."

Gabriel licked his lips and realized he was talking louder than he desired. He observed the few other patrons, busy at their keys, music in their ears. No one was listening to him. No one cared.

"So, you shared some kind of hallucination?" Marius put forth a guess at an explanation.

"No! No. Not at all," Gabriel showed his exhaustion, shoulders slumped, lips and brows lax. He tried again though, "He pushed objects around the room, Marius. The place was wrecked by the time he died."

"Mmmm…" he sipped his espresso thoughtfully then returned, "But you said these people *burned* up? I do not take your meaning."

"Well, the man that I've been describing? He moved through the room, in some inexplicable form—delicately at first, then faster and more furiously. Eventually, the room became chaotic and dangerous. Imagine… imagine a man possessed by rage was having a meltdown in your office. Then imagine him uninhibited and unfettered by his corporeal form."

He looked around, avoiding eye contact, "I was scared. It was like this guy had tapped into some new understanding of the world, an understanding that gave him power but was out of his control... no, that's not quite it... I don't know what was happening. Maybe he didn't burn? I don't know." He sipped his tea.

"Relax, my old friend," with the disarming smile came so easily to Marius. He sat up strongly in his chair, a posture that commanded confidence and strength. "We will find the answers together, eventually. It does not have to be today." *Today would be better, of course, but I'll give you until tomorrow. No rush.*

Gabriel took a deep breath and another sip. After Vanya—after the last two days—it was good to be back in good company, to feel less alone. He wondered why he had ever excluded Marius from his findings. With the sample and Marius' help and resources, Gabriel felt a resurgence of hope that he could unlock the secret of the Apple.

The sample!

The PainFree had slowed his digestion considerably, but the sample would soon be available, and Gabriel could just show Marius. Everything would be much easier then.

"Marius," eye to eye, "Thank you. Truly, thank you for everything."

He flexed his leg and the assist-servos kicked on without hesitation. There was no pain. In a day or two, the assist would be removed and his knee would be good as new. "I never explained why I disappeared, why I stole your equipment... and you haven't even asked for an explanation. You came for me and rescued me..."

"Come now, Gabriel, I know you far better than that," the casual, if not a little arrogant, smile, "You were scared and suspicious. Understandable considering that you'd found me out, that I had continued the distribution and experimentation on my own."

"We deceived one another and a divide grew between us. I let desire for results get the better of me," he played into Gabriel's past, *that was your mistake with Kara, right old friend?* "I'm sure you know what I mean. I am truly sorry for that." The apology sounded genuine, even to the ears of the deceiver. "We can forgive each other and move on." Marius sipped his espresso.

"I have to admit," a guilty but mischievous smile showed off Gabriel's growing crow's feet, "I continued, too."

"The equipment you *borrowed* was put to good use then?" a friendly jab.

Smirking, "Yeah, yeah," then, excitedly, "I have something, a sample… tissue from one of the reactive brains. It's in suspension, caught at the moment of the reaction!"

"Really!?" again, genuine surprise. His feigned ignorance was not even slightly detectable. Marius was an artist.

"Yes! I can't wait to show you!" excitement coursed through his veins, rejuvenating him. "It isn't even a reaction. It is unlike anything else. It… I've been trying to articulate it to myself, trying to describe what I've seen. It's amazing."

Gabriel closed his eyes and took a deep breath then continued, "A rabbit recognizes the shadow of the hawk from birth. The rabbit doesn't react with the shadow directly… sure there are chemical reactions taking place, photons pummeling receptors in various patterns and shapes, exciting electrons, eliciting chemical and neuro-electrical signals… but the rabbit recognizes the shadow of the hawk as opposed to other shadows, even though the measurable chemical reaction is the same!" He pulled his glasses off his face and began rubbing the lenses absentmindedly, smiling a knowing smile at Marius, "Perception, right?"

"Mmm…" *How whimsical.*

"Recognition written into the DNA! Well, what if we, humans you know, have a latent ability to recognize a shadow?" Gabe shook his head at himself disgustedly, "I mean, what if, in the evolution of mankind, some of us have retained or developed a recognition for a chemical, a shape of a particular molecule? Some kind of internal perception?"

170

Marius studied Gabriel for a moment, trying to decide just how serious he was, "But for your premise to work, your analogy requires an eye. What organ *sees* inside?"

Shrugging, and waving his hand dismissively, "For the sake of this discussion can we say the mind's eye, the third eye... something like that? I mean, you're right, I don't know how some of the subjects identify the *shadow* of the Compound, but they do. The point is that there is no chemical or electrical interaction, no explanation for what the brain does in the presence of the Apple's molecular structure because it isn't reacting to a traditional vector, not in any way that we understand. I'm suggesting an innate preternatural recognition occurs. The brains that have developed this internal vision recognize the structure, like the rabbit recognizes the shadow..." he trailed off a bit, seeming to lose some of his conviction. "I don't know, something like that..."

"So, some internal sensory organ—something undiscovered?—*sees* the molecule floating around in the body... and...?"

"Well, maybe it isn't a new organ precisely," he tilted his head to the side, "More like an aggregate of the known senses? I can't define it or explain it... I'm just suggesting that maybe inner sight exists literally... that human beings are sensitive, able to sense and interact with their own bodies through some mechanism we have not yet measured."

Marius displayed his skepticism clearly on his face, "Interesting," *insane.*

After an uncomfortable silence, "Isn't it more likely that you simply have not figured out the reaction yet? That you have not been able to observe it because of lack of appropriate tools or timing?"

"I know, I know, it sounds crazy," smiling proudly, he downed his remaining tea, "but it is real. You'll see... the sample, it made me a believer."

Sitting rigid, and leaning in slightly, "Believer of what, exactly?" his cadence was mechanical as he pronounced each word discretely, biting off each syllable.

"Spirit, soul, chi, something unlike anything I've seen before exists in us... well, some of us anyway. The Apple Compound just unlocks it, a powerful and raw connection with the world."

Gabriel's eyes glazed over. He stared at nothing for a few moments, blinked and looked to Marius, full of hope for acceptance or approval... for understanding.

"Well, certainly this is more than a little to digest," he shrugged and then raised his brows, "Will you continue your examination of the sample, or are you satisfied with 'other-worldly' phenomena as an explanation?"

Somewhat disappointed, "I was hoping for a more open-minded discussion, Marius, but to answer your question, yes. I will poke and prod at that sample probably until I die... or I reach a more tenable understanding."

"Do not be cross with me, Gabriel," he leaned back in his chair and folded his leather-gloved hands together on the table, "I'm only looking out for your sanity and your safety. From the condition in which I found you, I can only assume that the people who are after you are interested in something more concrete than a prayer and a sprinkle of holy water."

"That, I cannot explain either. I have to admit, I thought maybe it was you that sent Vanya after me," Gabe was unsure if he was telling a joke or testing Marius as he spoke.

Looking for some reaction, some telltale sign of innocence or guilt, Gabriel paused and examined his companion's face, but there was nothing. "Fact is, I have no idea who would even know about our research... and if you don't know?" he was caught off guard by his own suggestion, finally voiced, that Marius had to know, "...that would be surprising." He realized that his tone was accusatory, but it was too late to take it back, and maybe, just maybe he had the strength to handle the answers.

"Killing a man has improved your self-confidence I see," Marius took his gloves off his hands methodically. He placed one on top of the other in the palm of one hand and then pointed the sagging leather at Gabe, "No sense in debating the reasons… Vanya was mine, or rather he was yours until I made him mine. His methods, however, were his own."

Gabriel's posture changed dramatically, his face was dragged down by disbelief and fear. "He said that I had no idea what I was up against…"

"That is decidedly the case. You do not."

The gravitas of his response dragged down the air between them. The moment opened like a noose and it was Marius holding the rope around his neck. It was loose for now, but it was clear that it didn't have to stay that way.

How had the conversation turned? His thoughts screamed out at him. *Why didn't I just keep my mouth shut?! He's helping me now. I can't do this alone! So tired of running… I'm so damned tired.*

Marius decided to expedite the conversation, seeing his companion's strength flagging. *No sense in drawing this out,* "I suspect that you have always known that the money funding our research has not come from the most forthright of characters."

His tone was matter-of-fact, but the edges of the words were sharp, "You are no fool, Gabriel. You must understand that these investors expect a great deal in return for all of their considerable allocations."

"But, we've had more failures than successes," he pleaded with reality to undo itself. He wanted to believe that somehow this was all a misunderstanding. His leg complained for the first time since that morning's surgery. "Why is it a problem this time?"

"You curtailed the research, omitted some of your findings from your report and fled." Marius raised his eyebrows and softened his face sarcastically, challenging him. "See it from their perspective, Gabriel. Sounds more than a little suspicious, don't you think? Intentions pure or not, you are a thief. A cutpurse stealing from a ghost…" He shook his head, "If not for me, you would already be dead."

Gabe stared at him for several seconds, unmoving. Marius tilted his head and watched his words burrowing and chewing into the brain of the Chemist like insects. He sat back after a bit, confident that his point was made clear.

"What... what can I do?"

"Well, that's the attitude for which I was hoping," again with the winning smile, although most of the charm had gone from it, "Those pain pills slowed down the efforts of your intestine, but I imagine you will begin in the bathroom."

Realizing that there were no secrets that he could keep, even in his bowels, "I'll do what I can but, as I already said, it doesn't make sense. I cannot predict who will react, and no one has ever survived anyway... will I survive?" he shook his head roughly, "I mean, will I be okay, Marius?"

"I hope so," he dragged the gloves back on and motioned that it was time to leave. He stood up, "You would be difficult to replace."

Found

Eighteen

The sand was hot. It was so hot that it burned the soles of my feet. I was too weak to lift them out of the sand fast enough to escape the heat, so I dug them in, painfully pushing my toes deeper. The abrasive grains were like tiny white-hot coals scarring my skin. I felt them carving into the prints of my feet, rubbing them raw as I went deeper, searching for the slightest relief from the sun-scorched surface. Then the skin around my ankles began to scream as a ring of pain formed a sharp cuff where the thin skin touched the surface of the sand.

I couldn't take anymore, so I lifted that foot back up... I took another step.

Burn. Burrow. Lift. Burn. Step. Burn.

I was breathing in the acrid air, chest constricted and shallow, staring at my feet. Each breath caught in my lungs, shuttering, quaking from the caustic air. I expelled the miasma, but it was a cloud of acidic barbs; the harder I pushed them free the more they pulled and cut and ripped my insides out.

I waited, not wanting to need the air, not wanting to endure it again, but the need won. It always won.

Burn. Exhale. Breathe. Burn.

The entire world was bleached by the sun. My colorless skin limned against colorless sand and sky. My eyes felt wounded, like they were bleeding, but they didn't bleed. *What could possibly bleed here?* Emaciated and dehydrated, my blood was syrup and my eyes were cauterized by the insane star cooking the world.

A pleasant dizziness began to slowly fill my head. It felt like spinning laughter, it felt like hysteria, it felt good. The spin swirled down to my chest and out to my limbs. I lurched a step forward then back, and then raised my hanging head until my eyes were level with the horizon. The even line of dune meeting the sky was interminable in all directions. Nothing but sand, and sun, and forever.

Was I staring straight ahead, or was I perpetually spinning?

The vertigo felt like a crocodile with rows of razor sharp teeth in a vice around my ankles. I could not pull my feet from its jaws, and it rolled and rolled, around and around, and twisted my flesh around my spine. Taut and stretched, my bones felt like they would break and tear through my skin.

Urgency, alarms pounding and ringing in my head, told me I had to breathe again… but I'd been dragged down, dragged under, by the croc's death roll. I was drowning.

Get to the surface! But as much as I struggled against it, the vertigo grew stronger.

Where is the surface! I have to breathe.

Breathe.

The thought echoed deep inside of me, bouncing around while I spun, and began a slow fall to the ground. Time stretched out and slowed and before I hit the sand, I felt okay… I felt okay. I was glad to die trying…

I drew in, hard and fast, filling my lungs, opening my chest. The burning air rushed into me like a live flame exposed to propane.

And I fell.

And I kept falling.

The fiery heat flowed through my blood and coursed through my body. I was in the furnace, cremated… incinerated… consumed.

I was far away from my body, numb and falling, or floating, I couldn't tell. I exhaled and breathed again. Deeper, drawing strongly into my lungs, opening my chest as wide as I could, I hoped to expand my ribs until they broke. I embraced the flame. I drank it down. I consumed it.

I overcame it.

Taking huge breaths, filling and expelling my lungs to the limit, I felt relief from the heat. The dizzy spin slowed down and I became steady, floating in cool water. Rising and falling with the waves of each breath, I closed my eyes and heard my heart thudding in my ears. One powerful and loud *thud-thud* followed another as I rode up and down on the swells and troughs of the ocean. Calm and open, softly up and gently down, I was extinguished.

My eye opened and there was nothing but cool blackness all around me. I looked around and floated through the infinite space. I was satisfied with the blackness and I explored it. There was something out here, someone to find or to find me. I looked on effortlessly. There was no sense of time. There was no understanding of distance. More blackness, more darkness, expansive and full.

And there it was.

Was I tasting it? Smelling it? I heard it touching me… a confusing joy of overwhelming sensations.

There it was.

A body. My body. The details were more clear, my posture more defined. My lids were closed, but my eyes jerked around beneath them like two mad moles dancing. The veins on my body were raised up and black, pulsing with the strong beating of my heart. As I stared at the black branches, I massaged them and cooled them, and watched as they calmed and faded beneath the skin. Black to purple to green, softer and softer until they were blues, olives, and teals. The lid-blanketed, dancing moles slowed and synchronized.

I smiled, he smiled, we smiled…

Like pulling on a pair of thin leather gloves, I felt my fingers then my hands. I was plugging into the nerves. I felt the saliva on my tongue, the hairs along the back of my spine, and the working of my intestines.

My chest expanded and contracted, my heart beat, and I felt a weight—like heavy blankets—as my muscles turned on. I curled, flexed, and extended my fingers and toes, squeezed my thighs, my ass... pulled back my ears, raised my brows. I smelled something sweet.

A flower? No. A woman.

...

My eyes fluttered open. I was soaked with sweat. Testing my body, I moved around a bit beneath the sheets. I was weak, and the sheets and blankets felt heavy and wet, so each movement was a little harder than it should have been. Even so, it felt good to move around. I rolled to my right, and there she was.

Sara.

Sara. She was on her side, curled up, facing me, and glowing softly. A lavender fog spilled off of her onto the bed. I could feel her. As her chest moved up and down, she tugged gently at the covers stuck to my body. She looked beautiful and fragile, hardly the woman that electro-shocked me and tied me up. There were lines of stress in her face, more exposed while sleeping, drawing a picture of each cold moment in her life. The lines of being alone and afraid, I felt myself drifting into those lines and had to stir myself from them.

Where am I?

This was her place, cozy close and endearingly unkempt. I examined Sara closely for signs of consciousness, but she seemed deep asleep. Although I didn't want to disturb her, I propped myself up on my elbows to see more of my surroundings.

The clutter felt like a home not unlike my own. The biggest difference was that everything here was connected to her, a diorama of where she'd been. The mess was the story of her most recent life as Lily. Each item reflected her misty, milky lavender glow, some objects stronger than others.

I knew so much more about her than I remember her telling me… what it was like being the daughter of one of the most powerful women in the Syndicate; how she came to be free of that life, so young, so abandoned; and how that old life followed her even now, preventing her from ever really moving on.

She was strong. Perhaps she was a little lost, but she was impressively alive despite never quite being herself, despite the ever-present edge beneath her feet.

The ceiling was unfamiliar. There was something fixed to it, over the bed, in the center of my vision, staring down at me. I floated up to the device. It had eight silvery legs that ended in sharp points. The points dug into the plaster, gripping and holding it in position. At its widest, it was three inches across and there was a slight telescoped neck at its center. At the end of the neck was an open aperture, pointed down, pointed at me.

The Collective.

I was slowly waking up to the situation, vivid memories—of the diner, of last night, of the last several days—suddenly flooded me. The Collective was there for me, hunting me. Eve. What about Eve? She warned me, said they would be coming for me. But she seemed to have her own agenda, not necessarily my best interests in mind.

Did I ever come down? I felt unreasonably good. A little warm and sticky perhaps, but good overall. I felt as though every part of my body was connected, that each nerve was speaking softly to me and that my mind was hyper-focused.

I folded the covers down halfway, diagonally, careful to leave the portion covering Sara undisturbed. The skin on my chest, still damp with sweat, prickled a little as it was exposed to the cool air of the apartment.

Sara stirred a bit, wrinkled her nose, and turned over away from me, but did not wake. In that moment, I realized how much I wished she had woken up. It would have been nice to hear her voice and maybe clear the dreaminess from my mind.

I found a dry portion of the sheets and wiped the sweat from my right hand. I couldn't resist—I reached out to her, touching her shoulder gingerly. Her skin was silk. The lavender dust—the fine purple pollen that surrounded and drifted around her entire body—floated up from her shoulder and swirled around my fingers. I shook her shoulder briefly, gently. It was just a nudge, a reminder that I was there beside her. Again, she stirred. The dust solidified somewhat, and became floral petals rubbing against my hand.

I imagined the sound of her name spoken in my voice. Staring at the back of her shoulder and her chocolate hair, I saw the purple petals settle on my hand. They shaped themselves to the shape of my fingers, melted through my hand and moved back into her body. There was a rush as the resting, drifting petals were sucked into her.

"Huh?!" she woke with a start.

She rolled off the bed, somewhat clumsily, but caught herself well at the last moment. Standing, facing me down defensively, Sara looked down at me with her glowing, soft purple eyes. She was at once astonished, confused, and angry, and then happiness lit up her face. A smile lifted up her cheeks and brightened her eyes.

"Joshua!" her voice was an excited exaltation.

Even though I knew she speaking loudly and clearly, her voice sounded distant and almost muffled to me. Similar to being under water, the syllables were dampened and thick. It wasn't just Sara though, the entire room felt unusually quiet. There was no buzzing sound, the usual hum of the electronic world, the kind that flows beneath your hearing most of the time. It was absent as though the world had flooded.

Her lips began moving quickly, hard to follow. There were sounds too, and echoes, but the specifics were lost on me. Still, I think I heard her. She was astonished and happy for me, for herself, to see me awake. I'd been out for a long time. She was worried about me, and also about herself. She'd brought me meds and tried to hydrate me. I just gazed at her, staring deeply into the lavender, glowing clouds of her irises.

I touched her lips in my imagination, and in reality she pulled back a bit and touched her own fingers to her lips with a curious expression on her face. I thought of kissing her and holding her, and felt myself enveloping her, but she moved away.

She stared down at me fearfully. Then with frustration and not a little anger, she interrogated me about the diner. How did I know where she lived? Am I in trouble with the Collective? What the hell had I done?

My thoughts and conscious energy came back to more concrete concepts. I felt myself more in my body... more uncomfortable with the sweat and the sheets. I pulled the covers back the rest of the way and exposed myself.

Sara looked at me, a little differently; not totally unwelcome, but I decided to pull the covers back up a bit anyway. I wasn't exactly sure what was happening. Then an odd look came over her face. It was fear mixed with fascination. She said she could hear me, but that I wasn't talking.

I'm not talking?

"I'm not..." I heard my own voice as though through a filter. The volume and timbre were as strange as any stranger's voice. "I'm not talking?" I finished chewing the words, jaw and lips carving into each sound as though my mouth was full of halvah.

"You weren't a second ago, anyway," Sara seemed disappointed, but at least her fear had somewhat subsided.

Her legs were sexy-long, completely exposed. Actually, her entire body was exposed, the lily tattoo laser-engraving itself into my mind. She wore only a delicate pair of underwear, slender and pink.

She knelt down and picked up a sweatshirt that was crumpled up beside the bed, discarded at some point while she slept. Propped up on the bed, covered in a thick film of sweat, I watched her liquid movements as she slid easily into the sweatshirt.

"You are… stunning," my gaze taking her in completely, enjoying the strong curves of her legs and her ever-present, hazy-purple glow. My words echoed around the room, bouncing off the walls and settling nowhere. Realizing that now was not the time, I stifled the compulsion to continue gazing at her.

"Um…" she gave me a look as though I was a child, and an unwanted one at that, as though she was babysitting her neighbor's kid and not getting paid enough for her trouble. It was more than that, though, like she was disappointed that I didn't have something more astonishing to discuss than her sweet ass.

She was right, consciously or not, to change the subject, so I pointed to the silver, eight-legged creature staring down at us from the ceiling, "Does that belong to you?"

Sara followed my gaze and looked up, "What…?"

"I guess it doesn't belong to you," the words came quicker and more comfortably than the moment before, "the spidery-looking thing. Right there?" But she just squinted toward the ceiling for a moment then looked back down at me as though I was testing her patience.

I stood up, allowing the sheets to fall away from me, and reached up to the spider. Electric blue discharged from the device when I touched it, startling Sara. *She sees it now.* I pulled at it a bit and without much effort, pried it from the plaster. The sharp feet pulled away some paint, leaving marks in the ceiling.

I turned the object around in my fingers, examining it. After a few moments, I noticed a lavender radiance, slight but certainly there, around my fingers. It went all the way up my arm, and then curiously, up and down my entire body. Looking up to Sara, I realized she was staring at me. Finally, she saw me see her, and she immediately looked away. She preoccupied herself with the electronic intruder in my hand and the purple radiance on my body faded away.

"What the hell is that?"

"I think it's a camera," I looked at it, eyebrows raised in frustration, not really knowing what it was. "Well, anyway, whatever it is, I think it is safe to assume someone else knows where you live."

Sara walked over and took the little device out of my hand, then looked up and saw where I'd ripped it out of the ceiling.

"You kept staring up… the whole time you were out," she was talking to herself, to the room.

I smiled at myself, imagining how I must look, standing on Syndicate Sara's bed with a fascinating piece of metal in my hand, naked, and a little hard. I felt good. Really damn good. Powerful and tall, I seemed to dominate the room. I decided that I didn't like someone watching me, watching Sara and me. A strong sense—a feeling of betrayal and invasion—stirred me up. I focused on the creepy spy, felt the cool, lightweight metal against my skin. I understood the nature of the camera, its legs and lenses. I could see into it, see how it fit together, see all of its separate pieces and their connections to each other. Fascinating really, how fragile it seemed…

I dismembered it, one leg at a time. Each slender silver knife-like limb was pulled savagely from the abdomen, then left to hang in the air, ignoring gravity. I held only the base, still attached to the neck, between my finger and thumb. Small thin wires poked out from the leg sockets, reaching out toward the legs floating beside it.

Swiveling the eye around and around, I unscrewed it from the base along with the neck and ripped it from the few hairy wires that clung to it. I crushed the lens, imploding it like a tiny, juicy seed. Driving them one at a time, I impaled the body with the legs, metal sliding through metal with no resistance. Satisfied, I crushed all of the parts together into a small silver ball, and it dropped into my palm. I held it out to Sara like a gift.

But it was not as well-received as I had hoped.

She stared at me, unblinking, "How did you do that?" Stepping closer, she reached out and plucked the metal berry from my palm.

Testing it with her fingers, squeezing and pulling at it, she tried to crush it or pull it apart, unsuccessfully in both cases.

"I didn't think you liked being watched."

Sara looked back up at me, impressed, "No. I mean how, like… look at your hand."

The veins in my fingers and most of my hand had blackened, but were now softening back to a more natural green. "I…"

"You just stared and stared at it, and your eyes went all weird… and your veins…," she hesitated for several moments, closed her fingers around the ball, "Then I swear, I saw, I don't know, talons or claws or something, forming out of the air," she shook her head to herself. "What the hell was that?"

"I… I felt like I could do it, that I could take it apart," I shrugged, "so I did. I felt so strong." Looking around the apartment I took a deep breath, "I feel so damn alive."

She gave me another uncomfortable look, "You look high, but this," she holds the ball up like a gem, "is no fucking hallucination." Sara twists her face in a kind of self-mocking pose, "*I'm* not hallucinating anyway, sorta wish I was."

The soft lavender glow of her body was still pouring out, mainly through her eyes. The rich color stood out against the gray apartment, like a splash of feminine wild. The filtration system of the apartment was moving the air around, stirring up the dust into a charcoal fog, and pulling the last of the sweat off my skin. I was getting cold, actually shivering slightly.

"Hmm, finally cooling off, huh?" Sara read my mind. "I have some clothes that I think will fit you well enough."

She moved to the closet wall, pressed her hand against the panel and it slid open. There were a few options; some club-diving shirts and a random assortment of pants. They might fit me. I supposed it wouldn't be okay for me to just walk around naked, at least not in the middle of the day. She pulled them down, one after another, gathering them up into her arms. She took the two steps back to the bed and dropped the load at the foot of it. "Here. Try them all. Something should work."

"Great," I stepped down from the bed, unsure if I really wanted to wear anything in the pile. "Thank you," I held the dark yellow mustard T to my chest apprehensively.

She went to her desk and turned the environment lights to daytime, reflected by an icon change and some text displayed on the Wall. The brightness hurt my eyes at first, and I flinched away a bit, blinking rapidly. She dimmed the lights, seeing my discomfort and I felt an overwhelming sense of gratitude.

I had never really thought much about my emotions, what was appropriate with strangers or among friends. I sometimes cried at the movies, or when listening to certain music or reading certain books. It didn't really matter to me one way or the other. I felt what I felt, and if someone saw, I guess they saw. This moment though, this outpouring of thanks wrapped itself around my head like a wet, hot towel. It was almost too much to stand at first, but then the heat washed over my whole body in a release of acceptance. I thought I might cry as I imagined myself holding Sara, hugging her.

Looking at me, again a little unnerved, "What are you doing?" Sara stepped into me, deep into my personal space, looked into my eyes, and touched my left cheek with one finger.

She traced the outline of my jaw and chin, "Your eyes… it is like they turn inside out, and on this side, they're unlike any…," her voice trailed off as she followed my chin down my neck, across my collar bone, and over my shoulder with her fingernail. "…your veins swell and pulsate, and turn dark," she looked inquisitively at her finger on my skin, dragging it down my arm.

Looking down, I looked at her finger. Strong and lithe, it ended in a sharp polished nail. For a moment, I thought the nail was pleasurably cutting me open as a small pool of lavender, like a thin liquid line, had formed beneath it. But that was when I noticed that she was right about my veins, swelled in an arcane pattern of black branches, pulsing with my heart.

I focused on the pulse, examining the back of my hands and then my palms one hand at a time. The veins were black, gauzed by a thin covering of skin. But it wasn't just the veins; there were patterns, almost like writing…

The yellow shirt was on the ground at my feet. I didn't notice when I dropped it. What was happening to me? My eyes searched for Sara's, but what I found was a lens of fear and uncertainty. Her softly radiant dust swirled tightly within her eyes, and not a single particle floated out to me. She had withdrawn completely into herself, and even recoiled a bit, taking a half step away from me, no longer touching me.

I wanted to go to her and assuage her fears, but reaching out to her only made her step quickly back even farther. She bumped into the Desk, knocking a bowl that had been resting there with her hand, sliding it off the edge. The moment of the bowl falling through space and flipping over itself yawned open. I reached into the mouth of it and snatched the bowl out.

There I was. Up against her as she leaned back over the narrow Desk surface, I held the bowl between us with both hands. My posture was an offer, and simultaneously a kind of challenge. I felt my awareness stretching out, filling the room with black smoky tendrils. I felt the bowl, I felt the walls, I felt every surface in the apartment. I smelled her. I touched her skin. I was potent, in control, and impossibly powerful… and it felt un-fucking-believable.

I grinned.

"What the fuck was that?" her fear replaced with curiosity and desire.

"I don't know," my grin broadened and deepened, "but I like it."

Hallow Eve

Nineteen

Eve woke with an abrupt burning inhale. Alarms blared in her head from ear to ear. She was dizzy and blind and soaked with sweat. *I'm trapped.* The container was fabric, rubbing against her skin, hot-hot. A red light blinked slowly off and on in the distance.

She was buried alive. Someone was after her, some evil thing, and she had tripped and fallen into this cave. She was being digested in the belly of the devil that chased her. In space, underwater, buried, caught, trapped.

Her mind was folded onto itself several times over. Layers of imagination and memory stuck together forming a strange and otherworldly explanation for her predicament. But her eyes eventually found the light, slowly found focus on the blinking red beacon. It was right in front of her, two inches from her face. She felt the muscles of her eyes holding the close focus, and the layers peeled back and became discrete again.

The Sniper's Hold was out of power. The bag was like a greenhouse and the heat that got in stayed in. Eve quickly took stock of her body and her GEaR, wriggling around in the cocoon—slowly at first, then more vigorously as she found she had strength and flexibility. Some soreness and stiffness were revealed, but nothing she couldn't handle, especially since her medicinal spikes were all back online. The spike's related toxicities had been reduced sufficiently, so that she could use them again. She dumped a potassium-based muscle-emollient and fired up all of her auxiliary and peripheral augments.

Her scrubs were dead, her kidneys were dry—*and damn sore too*—and she still had high levels of vaso-constrictors in her blood. Serotonin was overloading her system, the reuptake receptors were probably pretty nuked, and the only solution for that was genuine rest. Openness, creativity, and clever solutions were off the table, or at least she could not enhance her innate capability. She had to lean on her innate abilities more than she would like, but it would have to be enough.

Her training kicked in, reminded her to be wary of fatalistic responses to situations. That didn't stop the thought, though, that lying there and roasting to death, sounded pretty good.

Shaking the image from her mind, she was immediately irritated by the heat and the stickiness of the Sniper's Hold. *Fuck this.* She wanted to scream. Clawing at the bag, she finally found the opening and slid her fingers along the seam. She reached out, felt even hotter air, and tried to pull herself forward.

"Fuck," she growled through clenched teeth as she pulled her hand back from the hot surface of the duct. Blinking hard and quick, she tried to access light-enhancing lenses, but her eyes were sore and dry and it hurt to make the switch.

Pain seared straight through to the back of her head when she peered out of the bag, trying to find some light. A blinding glare burned trails and images in her vision. She returned to her natural sight reflexively, like she'd put her face into an open flame.

She hissed and spit.

"Damn it," her tear ducts should have automatically responded, but they were bone dry, even with the synthetics and spikes. Gritting her teeth and squeezing her lids tightly, she tried to stifle the throbbing echo of the light.

Eyes still closed, but with less pressure, Eve began folding and unfolding her body away from the bottom of the duct like a caterpillar. She inch-wormed her way forward at an agonizing pace—hotter from the exertion, boiling from the exhaust pushing around the bag. She found a groove, levered herself against it, and thrust hard.

Some sharp piece of metal bit into the top of her head and snagged the Sniper's Hold, and Eve found herself falling. The rush of falling caused her to panic and open her eyes, but it only lasted a split second. She landed hard on her breasts and felt one of the remaining grate vanes grind into her armpit before it snapped off and fell, flipping end over end, to the ground below. Partially out of the vent, her head and shoulders hanging out, she felt renewed and a desperate to get out of the superheated duct.

It was early to mid-morning judging by the light. She looked around and found the fire escape out of reach to her right. As she strained to see better, she wriggled farther out of the opening. Gradually, farther and farther out of the opening, her center of gravity moved dangerously close to the edge. She was slow to react and made herself dizzy as she desperately tried to keep herself from going over.

It was too late though, and she began to slip. Slowly at first, she slid, terror growing exponentially in her heart. She reached out and tried to embed her fingernails in the concrete, but the result was her left hand going numb from the returned force. A moment away from total free fall, she reached with her right hand into the duct. Her fingernails, used like claws, went straight through the Sniper's Hold and easily into the soft metal beneath it. Although the heat-resistant material was pinned beneath her fingers, her fingernails conducted the heat straight to her skin. She had to bite back a scream.

She reached up with her aching left hand and dug in, same as the right. She began to swing herself right and left, gaining momentum. The heat ache crept up her hand and up her forearms. Just when she thought she would have to let go, she managed to catch her feet between the bars of the fire escape. One more good push from her arms, and she released her claws. She was swinging by her ankles from the fire escape, feet hooked in the bars. Her joints from her ankles to her hips were twisted and strained, but she held on.

The cool air gave her strength. She breathed it in deeply and curled her upper body up to the escape in a slow, controlled, serpentine motion. Pulling herself over the rail, she gathered herself up for a moment before collapsing against the wall of the building, arms and legs limp but vibrating internally from the use. She heaved volumes of open air in and out of her lungs. Her chest stuttered and shook intermittently with overwhelming relief.

Looking through the back of her lids at her HUD, she examined herself more closely. She highlighted links on the Inter-Ocular Display by focusing on them, and read the resulting reports. She was going to be fine. A starter colony of new scrubs were necessary, her population had eaten itself to death entirely, leaving nothing to repopulate. But that was it really.

Suddenly, a wave of nausea hit Eve. She was barely able to get to her hands and knees before retching. It was a strong convulsion of her stomach—a full-body flex—and the contents of her belly spilled out over and through the bars of the fire escape. Two more heaving motions and she sat back in a couched, fetal-like position.

Unfortunately, that wasn't the end of her expulsions. She felt the next wave of nausea coming and automatically rocked back onto her heels, more upright, using one hand to hang herself from the rail of the escape and the other to pull her pants down around her knees. She prepared herself for the next convulsion.

Sitting lower than if she was on a chair, back against the railing, both hands over her head gripping the top of the rail holding her up, she felt the irresistible push and opened up. Pissing and shitting simultaneously, she felt the pressure turn gradually to relief.

Covered in sweat and nearly in tears out of both relief and disgust, Eve stayed in that position for several minutes. A couple after-surges went through her, but they were nothing compared to the first shock.

She shook herself dry and dreamed of a warm bath, but she didn't indulge the fantasy for long. She had work to do before she could rest.

Bridging herself up and propping her mid-back on the top of the rail, she reached down with both hands and pulled her pants up. She gingerly moved her feet to the side, then stood up and moved away from the stink. She had to admit she felt a lot better and sort of wished she could do it again.

The mingling smells caught in her nostrils and the sour-sweet of it was the only signal she needed to get out of there. She spit a few times off the side of the escape and wiped her mouth on her shirt. Coolness comforted her exposed midriff and relaxed her well-worked stomach muscles.

It wasn't her most graceful descent but she made it to the ground in one piece. In fact, as she touched her fingertips together, it seemed to her the only real damage she had sustained were some minor burns and some general muscle soreness and fatigue. She wouldn't be fully operational again for another day or so, but considering everything, she felt good. Maybe she stank, but that was a small price to pay. *The Collective probably wants me dead, but other than that... fuck, I'm great.*

Eve looked over her clothes for anything that would draw too much attention and discovered that she simply looked like she'd been out for a vigorous run or workout. She would pass right into the population without turning a head.

Walking to the mouth of the alley, she welcomed the sounds of the heavy traffic, both foot and vehicle. It was the sound of anonymity. Her reports, the never-ending streams of data she used to send almost continually, were cancelled. She was alone. Well, not entirely...

Eve executed all of her usual protocols, masking her voice and modulating the frequency of her transmission. Only one other person had the multifactor decoder. She opened the connection to him. It was time to find out if this was all worth it.

"Old man, are you listening?"

"Eve," his voice was clear and deep.

"How's our boy?"

"Awake."

She smiled and grinned, staring out at the world moving and flowing before her, totally self-important, completely ignorant. "Holy shit, the pinkie lived."

"He's not a baby mouse anymore…"

"How do you mean?" concern pulled at the curve of her smiling lips. "What happened?"

"I have to go. I'll shadow him the best that I can."

"Thank you," her gratitude was genuine. Joshua could go nuclear at any point and erase Ezechial from existence, or… who knows really? They were still in the shallow end, but not far from the first drop off. If Joshua survived the day, he'd be the first to have made it that long. "Good luck, Ezechial," she closed the connection.

At least she had been right about Joshua. The Collective had been picking up test subjects based purely on genetic similarity. The genetics obviously weren't the only factor, though the scientists working for the Leader had nothing better to go on. Experience mattered. Subjects who had responded to the Compound had common histories. They had similar social problems and general difficulty fitting into the system. They couldn't hold down jobs or keep themselves in school. They were all bright, but the standard measures of intelligence showed great variance among them. Most of them used drugs regularly, but none showed any signs of addiction.

Inexplicably, most had lost siblings or parents at a young age. Eve thought it might have more to do with role, the loss of an influential mentor, than blood, but biographical reporting wasn't always detailed enough to support or refute her idea. Many of the stories she read about those subjects that survived, albeit briefly, contained no globally definable characteristic that would have made it into a cross-referencing program. No way was the Collective going to see the similarities in the abstract.

Reading over the genetic potentials, she spotted all of the markers in Joshua's past. You would almost think he was desperately trying to find an addiction the way he lived his life, but he never found it. There were other factors too, but the point was that Eve had read and read, and whether fact or intuition, she'd spotted Joshua and given him the highest chances for survival on the list of scheduled test subjects. That was enough for her to set the wheels in motion, to find his supplier and ensure that Apple would be his next purchase.

The world kept moving before her eyes, crowded but efficient. The engines were a quiet and collective whir, cycling up at green lights and down at red. The sound of the wheels on the road could only be heard occasionally over the din of the pedestrian chatter. She couldn't guess at the number within the crowd who had the potential to be like Joshua, but there had to be at least a few angels among them.

SPIRE

The Devil's Tail

Twenty

There wasn't much in the selection of random men's clothing Sara had accumulated, but there were a few options that at least fit pretty well. Joshua chose a slate grey pullover, which was heavy and cool against his skin. The pants he picked were charcoal black jeans with swirled textures throughout and copper pinwheels on the back pockets.

Along with the outer-wear, Sara had an abundance of boy-shorts and boxers because they were her preferred sleepwear, but none of them fit Joshua. Despite her proportionately voluptuous hips, they were too slim for him, so he went without.

Finishing the look was the only pair of shoes that fit, a dusky orange casual wear shoe. They were tight so he wore them sans socks.

All in all, he looked pretty good for pulling clothes from someone else's wardrobe. Sure, maybe the look was confused, but it wasn't really that far off the mark from his usual attire.

After taking a fast shower, exhilarating in ways Joshua had never before felt, he'd become obsessed with his image on the Wall. While he was busy with his look, admiring himself, Sara was quickly closing all of her connections with the world. She'd been busy at the Desk for several minutes, disabling, discontinuing, and cancelling various accounts. There were transfers going on as well, but Joshua hadn't seen the specifics. When he did look at Sara, he ogled her witlessly. She seemed flattered whenever she noticed him looking, but that was only once or twice, briefly.

There was a consistent lavender mist flowing down her skin to the ground where it pooled around her feet. Joshua thought it was beautiful and almost irresistible. The flow was dense enough to give the impression that Sara wore a fine, delicate, living dress. At times it moved like a jelly fish, flowing and rippling as though it was a single entity with a single motivating direction, but at other times it was merely a mist of independent particles.

He was staring at her as she began the tenancy termination protocol on the Desk, eliminating all of her local personal data and resetting the preferences for the next resident.

She kept almost everything on her Glass, which was sitting on the Desk absorbing data. Looking up, she caught him staring again and smiled. The way he looked at her, it was different from anything she had ever experienced, as though he was actually touching her with his eyes. Was it possible to kiss and couple visually? Sara welcomed the thought, but her survival instinct, her motivation to leave was greater than any emotional thrill. She finished up at the Desk and moved to the closet.

Grabbing a duffle bag, Sara began packing her clothes. It looked more like she was looting than packing, carelessly shoving random articles into the large bag.

Joshua had clearly recovered from his illness. Although his eyes remained somewhat spacey and glassy, they weren't cracked marbles and his veins weren't popping out of his skin. There was no sign of fever either, so Sara figured it was a good time to get on the move.

Finding a pair of brown, seamless linen pants, she pulled them on quickly. Joshua was disappointed that her legs were suddenly covered, but he still thought she looked beautiful. The loose fit of her pants made them seem more like a long dress than anything else. She appeared comfortable, casual, and feminine. The sweatshirt only teased his eyes—breasts obvious, but somewhat obscured, the details left to his memory, enhanced by his imagination.

He felt drunk or high. It was impossible for him to honestly distinguish. Certainly, he felt powerful, powerfully connected and aware. He was desperately trying to articulate the sensation to himself, he wanted to share it.

Sara handed him the picture of his brother, Bradley, then went back to work getting ready to leave.

He held the photopaper and for the first time in his life, he recognized how similar they were to each other. In his fevered, burning dream he'd been trying to find his brother. They looked different in many ways, but they shared the same spirit. He had missed him so much for so long, but suddenly, he felt a sense of peace, as though he now held his brother within himself.

Joshua had snapped the picture on the day Bradley launched his own business. He'd broken through on his quantum communications research, but the funding stopped in favor of something more militaristic. Bradley wouldn't allow that to end his research though, because he was too close to finalizing the process. It was a method of instantaneous and perfect transmission of data across any distance. He'd done it.

Well, on a small scale anyway. It would have proved itself out.

But there was an accident.

Joshua stared at the picture. The dream, the fiery walk across the desert, the searching through a timeless, immeasurable space... it might have been a test, it might have been torture. But maybe the fever had brought out the hardest moment from his life and exposed it. He just wanted to see his brother again. That's how he wanted to think of it, looking back on the dream from the waking world.

Then the chill came. At the base of his tail bone, creeping crawling pricks like icy snow flakes, landed. Up his spine they climbed, encasing his body in a slick of sober cold.

Looking around the room, feeling through the room, he sensed their hunger. They came for him. They wanted him. And there was something else, someone familiar, close and strong, waiting and watching.

"We have to leave," his voice was unrecognizable, far away and strange, "Now. We have to leave now."

Sara slid her fingers along the opening of the now full duffle and it sealed up neatly. She looked up, "I know, I'm…," she saw Joshua, veins black, solid eyes staring at nothing, seeing everything, "…what?"

They've found us. He tried to be clear, to speak in her internal voice as she would speak to herself. *We need to leave.*

Her face fell. The exhilaration of packing and closing up, of getting ready to start over, the prospect of an even better 'Lily,' flew from her. A sense of dread replaced the excitement as Sara was reminded that they were on the run from the Collective and they were close. At least that was the emotional impression from Joshua… and there was someone else.

Knock, knock.

They gazed toward the door.

Knock, knock. Harder, knowing they were home. Impatient, calling them out, *open the door.*

The door lock opened, and the door slid away. A man stood there in the doorway, his grizzled face stern and strong. It was the wintering man from the diner, scruffy as ever. To Joshua, he looked smoky and liquid, oily almost, a thick shadow of a man.

"Sorry, about the lock," he spoke with confidence, not a low voice, but calm and quiet, "You have to leave."

Joshua put his arm around Sara. *We don't have to trust him. We were already on our way out. Let's go. Stay close.*

"They don't know you are here," Winter moved into the room, "They're just part of the team sent to find you. Shouldn't be too many of them yet, because they're expecting a corpse and not combat," he floated quickly over to the Desk and dropped his Glass down. The apartment building blueprints flashed up onto the Wall. "Take this lift," he highlighted the location of an elevator, "and leave out the south entrance."

Sara looked from Joshua to Winter and back again, uncertain and tense.

"I'm Ezechial," he stared intensely into Sara's eyes, "They're coming for you, too," reading her posture, her expression, "Get Joshua out of here. I'll meet up with you later."

Ezechial's head jerked up and he stared down the hallway, "I have to stay and slow them down." He took stock of Sara one more time and slid into her personal space, a deft movement from a dangerous man. "You have to leave now, Sara."

She threw the duffle around her shoulders like she was going hiking, pulled her shoes on, and grabbed Joshua by the hand. Stepping through the door, she turned around, "Thank you."

She trusted the gruff man. Ezechial reminded her of her father, the few memories she had of him. Abrupt and confident, he was an authority not to be trifled with. Above all though, he had gray eyes, her father's eyes. And behind those eyes was that same deep regret her father's had, from having worked outside the bounds of common morality for too long.

He mouthed the word, *Run.*

She turned and fled, dragging Joshua with her by the hand.

Ezechial faded, shifted to the entrance, became solid, closed and locked the door. He assessed the room, as he had many times previously, and found nothing of significance had changed. He would hide and wait. The bones were cast, the dice rolled. He would watch and hope that he'd placed the right bet. Two on one to start, back up to follow.

He pulled up Sara's Desk chair and sat facing the door. Calmly, he breathed in the space of the tiny apartment, lids closed. Filling his nose and lungs deeply, he found Sara's smell, he found her comforts. He felt Joshua, his powerful presence left an unfamiliar residue on everything in the room. Ezechial still couldn't grab it or understand it, but it was there.

Without opening his eyes, he reached out and plucked up his Glass. Lifting his right hip, he slid the slim device into his pocket. He repositioned himself, more upright, but still fully supported by the chair, head tilted up slightly, resting against the back. He placed his arms across his chest, weaving his hands beneath his forest green jacket.

The soft, well-used leather handles were perfectly fitted to his palms. With a quick flick of his thumbs, both weapons were released from their hangers. He could feel the ever-so-slight drop and expansion of the coils, the extra weight against his hands. Holding the handles, the same as each time he'd held them before, he felt the urgency for action. The long cords, still coiled at his sides, tightened and relaxed reflexively.

Ezechial worked his focus to hide himself from the perception of the Officers outside the door. They activated the exterior Viewer, a little trick reserved for firemen and the Collective, and took a look inside the apartment before entering. Unable to see anything in the room, they unlocked the door and stepped in cautiously.

They scanned carefully and readied their weapons. They stayed close to each other, and the bulk of their well-armored bodies overwhelmed the small room. Moving away from the door, following the wall, they pointed their weapons wherever they looked. Clearly, they were making their way toward the bathroom, the only conceivable hiding place in the small apartment.

Ezechial stood up and kicked the chair back toward the far wall away from the entrance and quick-stepped to the door in a single motion.

A thin line burned and ripped through the air as a bullet embedded itself in the back of the chair. A discharge of blue branches spread out from the point of impact, around and through the chair.

Both C.O.s stood staring at the chair, one forward and down on one knee. The kneeling Officer remained facing the chair while his standing partner began scanning the room more aggressively, his back to the wall.

Pulling and unwinding the Devil's Tails from his sides, Ezechial readied himself. The two heavy cords of synthorganic material slid down to the floor, each ending in a tuft made of hundreds of three-inch-long bone quills. They were whips, ostensibly, but they were alive in Ezechial's masterful hands. The handles were complex chemical and electrical receptors. The slightest squeeze, the pull or drag of any finger, would cause the Tail to come to life, to move and writhe like the tentacle of an octopus.

The first year he trained with his chosen weapon, just trying to hold a Devil's Tail felt like losing a wrestling match with a python. He'd seen terrible accidents. Amateurs, full of arrogance, ripped their own arms off and lay open long flaps of their own skin with a Devil's Tail. That's how the almost-living, sensitive, and deadly weapon had received its name. The only way to use one was to have no fear of what it might do to you if you let it loose. To master such a weapon, you had to put the fear back in the Devil… what you would do to him if he tried to get away.

Ezechial had mastered two.

His arms down at his sides, Tails laid out on the floor in a 'V' extending out from his feet, he decided it was time to announce himself to the Officers. "Over here," he spoke through the apartment's audio.

Two shots were fired.

Each C.O. picked an audio source and shot it dead, and then Ezechial unleashed his whips. Dancing the chords along the floor, his arms began to swing languorously, and then one Tail leapt forward and ripped at the air while the other went back and snapped behind him. He lunged forward, two steps, Tails exchanging places with each step, snapping behind him then flying out ahead of him. He hit his marks with lethal precision, the bone quills shredding the Officer's throats. Blood began pouring out of the open wounds with no sound but gurgling attempts at screams.

The C.O.s dropped their weapons and fell to their knees, grasping at their throats, trying to keep their life inside. Ezechial maneuvered the Devil's Tails like two snakes along the floor. They slid around the officer's bodies as Ezechial stepped forward. He deftly, and almost simultaneously, severed their uplink connections. The whipcords seemed to look at each other before sliding down from the corpses and recoiling themselves into Ezechial's waiting hands. They were well-fed anyway, absorbing the blood of the officers. He reached beneath his jacket and returned them to their hangers.

He took a quick look around the room, decided there was nothing important, and walked out. Shutting the door and locking it behind him, he made his way casually to the north lift. The Collective backup was on its way and he needed to know if he ghosted the two in the room, or gave himself away. The quickest way to find out was to walk right out into the light, into the open, and see what happened.

Just as he arrived at the lift, the doors slid open. Inside, two C.O.s stood and stared back out at him through protective visors. He knew they were scanning him, trying to identify him. Either they would come up with nothing, or they would open fire. Ezechial gave nothing away though, "Good day," smiling, "How's it going?"

"Stand aside," a woman's voice, a commanding tone. Her weapon was pointed at the ground and remained pointed down as she stepped forward. Her partner was more anxious, rifle held in both hands, but pointed away from Ezechial.

"Uh, sure thing," he put on his best annoyed, slightly hurt face and stepped aside.

As the lift doors closed, the two C.O.s he'd just met were intersecting pairs of other C.O.s from their respective entry points. None had even attempted to open the door to Sara's apartment yet.

Pretty clean.

...

"Joshua's DNA is all over the place, sir."

"Clearly." The Leader was hot-connected to his retrieval team. "What's that…," he placed his finger in the display.

The C.O. walked forward, knelt down, and picked up something from the ground. "Photopaper, sir. Sending you the image now."

The Leader set the picture to full scene. He sat back and stared at it intensely.

Several minutes passed, "We're about done here, sir. Unless there's anything else?"

"Notify me personally when you get back to the Spire with the bodies. I will examine them myself. Do not allow any of their gear to be removed." He took a moment to digest the scene. Definitively not Eve's handiwork. "That's all Ra'bella."

"Sir."

SPIRE

Unknown

Twenty-One

"No closer now than last we spoke?" the unusual evenness of the Stranger's voice.

"No closer," Marius was clearly disappointed. It was the middle of the night, but some calls could not be put off until the morning. "I think he wants to believe that it cannot be understood. It satisfies his cowardly world view, that if he can't figure it out, it must be indecipherable." He leaned forward at his Desk smiling at his thought, "The man's been witlessly killing people for years... of course, now he has discovered his conscience."

Several seconds pass.

"Hello?"

Silence.

"You know, video would be nice for moments like this," Marius tapped his finger with dramatized impatience on his Desk.

"You consider yourself a Ghost, Marius, do you not?"

"Uh...?" intrigued, nonplussed.

"I know you, who you are. I've seen you."

"A point that has concerned me for some time," under his breath, edged with strong, quiet anger, as though he wanted to strangle the answers from the Stranger.

"I see the residue of your influence like a glowing beacon on everything that you touch. You have not abused me or extorted me because you can't. Yet, you consider yourself a Ghost? Untouchable, off the grid – what then, does that make me, Marius?"

"You're finally going to tell me? This is so much easier... I should have just asked you," a virulent sarcasm poisoned each word. He was surprised to find himself genuinely wondering if he might get an answer, some hint or clue about the nature of this powerful and elusive contact.

Marius had always believed he would catch the Stranger, that he would have the upper hand in the end. He had kowtowed and placated. He had been subservient and willing in every correspondence while waiting patiently for the scales to shift in his favor.

He allowed himself one last indulgence, the thought that maybe he had haphazardly pulled the right string to get the answers he needed to have the leverage he deserved. Then the laughter began.

The Stanger laughed the strangest laugh. It stuttered and stopped and spiked irregularly. The sound was broken and irritating but it smoothed out again quickly. Eventually, the remaining sigh of laughter subsided, "If Gabriel needs something to believe in, something omniscient and omnipresent that he cannot see or understand, tell him to believe in me."

"I will pass that along," begrudgingly.

"Have faith in me, Marius," the voice smiled, "Continue the distribution and do whatever is necessary to expedite the results. I want another survivor, sooner rather than later."

Connection Terminated.

Marius sat back in his chair. His chiseled face was gaunt and drawn down, lit dimly by the few displays open on his Desk. He could think of no escape. After all this time, he was no closer to uncovering the identity of the Stranger, and even if he had that, it took time to put hooks into a person to find exploitable weaknesses. No, he was too far behind with this one to try anything like that now. There might have been an element of bluff in the Stanger's cavalier attitude, but how could Marius call him on it?

Thinking about the situation more, Marius realized that he had always considered the Stranger his equal. If he was right and they were equals, then there truly was no escape. The Stranger had the higher ground. If the tables were reversed, Marius would have already prepared an all-out assault. He had to assume that the Stranger had done the same.

Moreso, if they were equals, he and the Stranger, if they worked in similar ways, then the Stranger did not require the sample, Gabriel, or Marius at all. *We are merely more convenient than his alternatives.* There was no doubt in his mind that the moment his utility was outweighed by liability… he would be dead. It was just good business.

An uncomfortable realization drew Marius' farther down. If the Stranger *was* like Marius, he already had at least one person on the inside. First point of business was to know your client, his or her past and present pressure points. The second was live coverage. You had to have someone on the inside.

How long have I been under surveillance? Who works for the Stranger now? Questions asked too late to be meaningful, but he knew the answers: *forever* and *everyone.*

His reign was over. It had probably ended the moment he first began working with the unknown contact. No sense in dwelling on it. The mistake was made and he wasn't dead—not yet anyway.

Marius was pragmatic, icy. It was one of his defining characteristics, one of the attributes that enabled his success, at least until now. He was unattached, able to free himself from vulnerabilities at a moment's notice. No love, no kin, no assets he could not live without. His goal, his interest, had always been to be invulnerable and powerful.

Marius chastised himself for entertaining the notion. *'Almost?'* Only fools measured their success in terms of proximity. "So, close!" then poof... gone. There was no "close." You either had it or you didn't, win or lose, succeed or fail. Gradients only existed to help losers feel better about themselves. The concept of "close" messed with your perspective, corrupted your judgment, and made allowances for risks you would never otherwise consider. How *"close"* was Marius to being invisible and untouchable in this world? *Almost!?*

"Fool," the word burned his lips. He embraced the heat of his frustration for a moment before the ice kicked back in. His reign had been a good one. He was no Ghost. As far as mortals went, he wasn't bad. How many in his line of work lived to see grey? The Stranger had the better of him, no question. Time for an Exit.

He leaned forward and executed several complex and agile strokes along the surface of the Desk. There was no need to delete or destroy anything, he was simply looking for the man that he would become, a purchase he made long ago.

Marius was confident that no one would have found the Credentials. The bits were spread out across various systems and networks all over the world. And the trick was that he hadn't written any information at those locations. A thousand addresses for identical portions of data were catalogued. His Credentials existed out there in a picture, in someone's game, in a movie, and in a random feed. The assembly of the data was all that mattered. And the system for reassembly was organic. A measurable, regular, predictable chemical reaction was the key to the distribution and the retrieval. Mark was commissioned to design the system exclusively for Marius, but even he had no idea what key Marius had chosen.

Marius had chosen the neurotoxic venom of the black widow spider as his key. A million sources existed for that reaction, but no one knew it would be the key to unlocking a set of unused, crystal clean Credentials. Marius would be no more.

The pieces of data were already being retrieved and written directly to a sub-dermal implant. As clean as it could be done.

Marius stood up resolutely. He walked to the door, opened it, and stepped out into the hallway. Heading to the implant lab, he felt urgency, but knew that he should not show it. Walking confidently, as always, he nodded at the lab tech standing at the entrance to the lab.

It was uncommon for him to exchange many words with his employees. Most of them had no idea who they worked for or even what they were working on. He couldn't erase all of their memories, but within a few hours, he expected it would not matter. The beaches of Zihuatanejo were made of miraculous sand that ground identity into anonymity.

Passing smoothly into the room, he walked up to a Desk and pulled a small rectangular dish down from a shelf. He extracted a slender translucent capsule from the dish and placed it on the Desk, then returned the dish to the shelf. Looking around, it had been awhile since he'd been in this particular part of the lab, he tried to find the Credential Cuff. Spying it on the other side of the room, he pinched the capsule from the Desk and walked over to it.

There were three others present in the lab that day, representing the softer side of the business. They were scientists. Sure, they were engaged in illegal activities, but they were hardly capable of violence or even self-defense. Still, he had to consider them a threat. They watched him surreptitiously, but what did that mean? He was their boss. It was only natural to be on guard with Marius in the room.

The scientists were paid well. Most of them never even inquired about the end results of their work, if they even cared. *It's like they work for the government.* And like government employees, paid well or not, their loyalties were for sale. He strode passed them and pulled the Cuff down from a shelf.

He set the Cuff on the Desk and removed his long trench. He folded the jacket over the back of the chair and sat down in it. Sliding his finger down the front of his shirt, it parted neatly down the middle and he sat. He slipped the sleeve of the shirt off his left arm revealing a lean-muscled bicep and forearm, marked with thick, olive veins. Pulling the Cuff up over his wrist, he positioned it carefully in the middle of his forearm and turned it on. It pressurized and secured itself, hugging tightly around his skin.

Marius set his arm with the Cuff onto the Desk in front of him. A menu appeared on the Wall and he made some choices. The Cuff came to life, rotated around his wrist and a small band moved up and down the length of it. When it finally found his currently embedded Credentials, the Desk prompted him for confirmation. He confirmed and there was a sharp prick in his wrist. A few moments of pressure and discomfort, then a small capsule popped into a clear-covered dimple in the Cuff. If not for the bloody smearing, the capsule would be identical to the other one he brought with him to the Desk.

A few more strokes, the Cuff cleaned the Credentials and ejected the capsule. Marius placed his new Credentials into the Cuff and waited. The memory-material could only be written to once and could not be modified. It took a couple of seconds and a couple of confirmation prompts, and then the Cuff went to work again.

The Wall usually displayed the progress with a bar and a video, but Marius quickly disabled the video so that his activities would be less obvious to the others in the lab. Besides, he knew the process well enough.

The Cuff was precise. It would mount the Credentials in exactly the same position as the previous capsule. The mounting barbs of the capsule would only be released when the rotation and position of the capsule were within half a micron of the old one. The procedure would easily pass any casual inspection and trick all but the highest resolution tissue scans. It was a paranoid level of precision.

Marius didn't intend to put himself in the way of any kind of scan in his retirement.

The mounting barbs fired. It felt like nothing more than a mosquito bite. The Cuff made a couple of passes and the Wall displayed that the deployment was secure and complete. Marius slid his finger down the side of the Cuff and it released from his forearm. He slid it off and returned it to the shelf. He inspected his arm briefly and rubbed at the marks left by the grip. Touching the deployment site, he noticed that it looked just like it felt; a mosquito bite and nothing more.

That was it. He put his hand back through the sleeve of his shirt, pinched and slid the front closed with his finger and thumb. He grabbed the ejected capsule, found the bio-waste container and dropped it in. There was a satisfying crunch and pressurization sound as the capsule—Marius' life—was crushed and treated.

Marius grabbed his trench from the back of the chair and slipped it on as he made a round of the Lab. He looked over the shoulders of the employees, no longer his. He had to be honest with himself, if one of these were a spy, he was fooled. Appearing satisfied, he left the lab.

The hallway was empty. The lights were low for the night, creating a somber aesthetic. He walked toward one of many exits. He would be walking until he purchased a new Glass and new vehicle, two stops Marius would have to make before embarking.

Rounding a corner, he almost collided with Gabriel, who was walking stiffly and quickly, staring at his feet, in the opposite direction.

"Marius?"

"Gabriel?"

"Marius! I've done it!" his eyes were sparking wildly. He held Marius by the shoulders.

"What, what have you done?" Marius was exasperated but curious. Even if Gabriel had solved the riddle of the Apple, or had learned how to predict who would react, it effectively meant nothing to him as a new man.

"It is the soul! They are so thin now…" trailing off and looking beyond Marius, "… so thin. The soulless masses, the vacant eyes…"

Stepping away, Marius shrugged Gabriel's hands from his shoulders, "So, you have finally gone mad then?" He was overwhelmed with a righteous feeling about his decision to leave this life, *my former life*, behind.

Gabriel, eyes glassy with tears and still sparking as though thousands of maniacal thoughts were crossing his mind all at once, "No! No, my old friend. Not mad... enlightened." The last word was fevered and desperate.

"Enlightenment, last I checked, could not be achieved through poisoning and exploiting the weak in order to satisfy your curiosity," it had always nauseated Marius that Gabriel had never accepted the truth of what his experiments did to others. Marius, *in my former life of course*, acknowledged that he was a murderer and a fiend. He had to live with it. He couldn't deceive himself, like Gabriel had, or remain blissfully oblivious. It grated at him.

No reason to hide it anymore. He'll never see the mad little man again, so why not let him have it. "Enlightened? You've studied history haven't you?" He took a long, overly dramatic pause, "You're a damn Nazi! The only thing I can't decide is if it makes you better or worse than them, that you don't discriminate... you're just equally cruel to all humanity!"

Gabriel's eyes welled up until, unblinking, a single tear was born from each. Marius' posture was imposing, tall and strong, challenging. Gabriel had never seen his old friend unmasked. He had never, in his recollection, seen Marius angry. Marius was a rock, a steel-willed man with a present and lucid mind. Gabriel hardly recognized him in this new form, especially considering the aim of the anger and frustration.

He reached out with one hand, and touched the sandpaper-rough cheek of his oldest companion.

Then he allowed his hand to drop to his side, but he did not look away, "You were my friend." Gabriel's pupils grew, and his flashing eyes calmed. "We were friends. You've left this life...," the words became slurred and his head sagged. "You are already gone... this conversation... phantom..."

Marius did not shy away from the touch. He stared coldly back into the insane, wet eyes of the Chemist. His anger would not be assuaged. His bitterness would not be quelled by the weak gesture. He would not leave this moment, allowing Gabriel to believe that they had ever truly been friends. His partisan arrow, tip dripping with betrayal, was aimed for the insane man's heart. But before he could let the shot loose, Gabriel spoke again.

"I ingested the Compound. I took it…," it was a moment of clarity and it pulled Gabriel's face sober and serious, "not long ago."

Then he softened again and looked around, like he'd lost something, "What time is it?"

Marius could do nothing but stare back. He opened his mouth to say something, but his thoughts disintegrated before they could become words.

"It's judgment and I deserve to be judged. The worst thing that can happen is nothing, that I am completely forsaken. That's what I think…" his shoulders sagging down, his voice a whisper, "… it's what I believe."

He would be dead very soon. The mortality rate was astronomical.

"Do you see? Do you see, Marius?"

Marius stepped slowly around the wavering man, "I see, I see." He completed a half-circle with Gabe at the center and took his first backward step away from the Chemist.

Gabriel reached into his pocket and pulled out a blood red gelatin lozenge. He stared at it in his palm for a few seconds. He held it out toward Marius, offering it to him. "You need this."

Narrowing his eyes, Marius saw the Chemist as threatening for the first time. "I rather think not." He took another backward step.

Gabe stepped forward, "You need this!" hissing the words between his teeth.

"You've lost it completely. I'm not interested in suicide. You and that fucking Stranger can pursue your salvation together."

"Take it," aggressively.

They step back together again.

"Please, just take it with you. In case… you change your mind?" Gabriel's voice was desperate and pleading.

"I won't." Marius turned his back and began walking crisply down the hall toward the elevator. He listened closely for pursuing footsteps, but heard not one.

From within the elevator, looking down the hall, Marius saw a frightened, lonely man standing and staring back at him. Gabe held his open hand out a moment longer, but as the doors closed, so did his hand.

Outside the building, Marius breathed in the cool night air of his new life. He was on his way. A new Glass first, and he knew just the place.

Walking confidently, already feeling lightness in his step, the weight of his former life lifting, he headed for downtown. It was quiet on the streets but the city never slept. The world never slept. Jasper Raines though, he didn't belong here, wouldn't see much of it. He had to leave town immediately. Business.

Bone Tie

Twenty-Two

"Containment, Leader 127, I believe that directive was made abundantly clear."

The Leader had rarely ever been contacted directly by the upper Spire, and never in person. On this particular early morning though, Secretary Deliah, was kind enough to stop by. The Secretary walked around the office as though he was a wealthy investor considering a purchase—interested of course, but ostensibly disappointed in the deal. The Leader only sat calmly behind his Desk, making no effort to improve Deliah's disposition.

"You have, of course, seen all of my reports? The details there are as clear as your directive, are they not, Secretary?" The Leader was matter of fact, but allowed slip at least a touch of sarcasm, a wisp of superiority. *I know my role, Deliah, do you know yours?*

The Leader had been afforded a luxurious amount of freedom, more than any of his peers. In fact, his record of unqualified successes had elevated him to a position *above* most of his superiors. The title and responsibilities of a "Leader" had only remained at 127's request, not wanting to become an administrator, not wanting to move even farther from the field. The Leader's believed that those in management positions invariably became the tools of the subordinates: the nature of control to be controlled. Although his title did not accurately reflect his influence within the Spire, few ever questioned his authority. He was a busy man and the level of inspection implied by the presence of the Secretary only slowed him down.

"Eve was one of your highest ranking Officers. She was, by the details of your regular evaluations, the most trusted and most capable of all of your personally trained agents."

The Secretary was casually walking around the Leader's office, hands clasped behind his back. As a Secretary for the Upper Spire, he took notes and ran errands. It was the content of the notes and the nature of the errands that made his visit a threatening one. According to the Secretary, the Leader's progress with the Apple distribution was his top priority for the day.

"Yes," his voice was deep, resonating powerfully in his chest, "Eve was my best." The inflection hinted for the Secretary to continue. *Just what is he suggesting?*

Secretary Deliah was tall and slender, the typical Spire garb of loose linen pants and shirt were hanging from his body. As he moved purposefully around the office, he twice snapped a quick hand out. In the first flash he altered the settings of the Wall, and then a moment later he deftly turned off the Leader's Desk projections. It was an arrogant display of his agility, a not-so-subtle reminder of the training and responsibilities given to Secretaries of the Upper Spire. In an even greater show of arrogance, he put his ass on the Leader's Desk and leaned across it casually.

"You know where this is going of course," Deliah leveled his clear, amber irises at the Leader. 127 stared back unflinchingly. "How is it she is corrupt and you are not? How else could she have so masterfully and successfully eluded you?"

"Ever my best student," the Leader smiled, "She's showing off."

"Is she better than you, Adam?" he leaned, bending deeply over the Desk, surprisingly close to the Leader's face despite the width.

"Maybe," he raised his brows inquisitively, "But she hasn't the resources." He sat forward and his hands went to work quickly bringing up displays that showed his team's positions and directives. The displays were positioned vertically so that the Secretary's face was suddenly framed in colorful distorted lights.

"As you can see," the Leader gently motioned with one hand for the Secretary to move back to a more comfortable viewing distance, farther away from the Leader's face, "if you will step back a moment, my teams are collecting information right now. The gap is closing."

Playfully annoyed, Secretary Deliah erected himself slowly, maintaining his unblinking stare throughout the motion. Finally, standing solidly, fully facing the Leader, "See to it that it closes entirely, Leader." He turned and walked to the door. It slid open for his departure, but he hesitated in the doorway. For a long moment, the Leader simply stared at the back of his head.

The Secretary eventually slumped in exaggerated disappointment, and then he looked over his right shoulder, "Leader?" Deliah's dark chocolate skin was silky smooth and his high cheek bones shined a bit in the light of the room. He focused his gaze somewhere between the Leader and the exit, not quite turning his head or his eyes far enough to see the Leader's face.

"Is there something more, Secretary?" The Leader turned in his chair toward the tall man standing in his doorway.

"It is customary to stand and greet a member of the Upper Spire when one enters your office," then flatly, "I'm disappointed."

"Is it?" borderline sarcastic, the kind of inflection that can easily be denied, "Then I must extend my sincerest apologies," but Adam made no effort to stand even now.

"Mmm...," Deliah nodded his head deliberately, slowly, "I'll try not to take it personally, Leader. Merely a..., a misunderstanding then?"

"Certainly."

"I suppose each of us is culpable of indiscretions to some extent. It would be unfair of me to leave without claiming some for myself."

Posture tall and strong once again, the Secretary turned his head to face the open door. "You'll have to forgive me for disabling your personal security system. It was, of course, only customary."

The Leader's face was grave.

"Your chair and Desk will require some maintenance," a casual advisory. "I've never seen a system like that, so I removed the activation and response sensors for our mutual comfort. I fear I may have damaged unrelated components in my zeal to ensure a safe and trusting environment."

The Leader offered only a stony stare.

"Good day, Leader," the Secretary left. The door hushed closed soon after his departure, but it was several minutes before the Leader relaxed. There was no rational explanation for the Upper Spire to send a Secretary to his office. After all, the UpperS were rarely concerned with the details of whatever happened beneath them. Even if they were concerned about Eve—and he sincerely doubted they were—the usual course of action would have been to file a request for explanation. Easy. Impersonal.

On the other hand, maybe he'd stirred up some trouble for himself demanding some sort of reason for continuing the Apple project. In that regard, it had almost been a month since 127 filed his first request for an explanation and he'd filed several more since then. No response had been forthcoming.

I suppose this little visit was the response.

Still, it seemed like overkill. The UpperS could have silenced the Leader's concerns with the usual, 'need-to-know-basis,' line. There was more at play here than the Leader knew and he didn't like that at all. He'd have to find some pressure points—perhaps Deliah, even?—and begin squeezing some information out of management. Apple was apparently worth a lot to someone and knowing who and why would be valuable.

He took a few moments to inspect the damage done to his personal security system, the one that he had implemented personally. The device was hooked into the standard tracking unit built into his Desk, and the projectile was a needle only twice as thick as a capillary tube, and it should have been entirely undetectable.

Either Deliah had been tipped off—although by whom the Leader couldn't guess—or there was some flaw, something tell-tale that the Leader had not seen in his implementation. Regardless of how the Secretary had known, the butcher had found and scrubbed the drivers and burnt out the circuitry in both the arm rests of his chair and the clandestine back panel of the Desk.

Surprises... the last week had been full of them. Luckily, the Leader had more than a few of his own left up his sleeve.

He brought up a new display, "Jacobs?"

Jacobs attention, initially divided among various displays which were reflected in his eyes, turned entirely to the Leader. All of his other display windows faded away when the Leader's channel took focus, "Sir?"

"My chair and Desk are in need of repair."

"Sir," Jacobs' eyes dashed quickly over to his right and back, "I'm not showing anything..."

"You wouldn't. I don't hold this station because I trust people," he offered a disarming expression, an exonerating smile, "The systems were off the record, or so I thought." He paused for a moment, running his fingers over the top of his Desk, "Anyway, some of the diagnostics had to be shorted in order for me to prevent detection. Please ensure that everything is brought back up to snuff. Restore the systems to what you would have expected to find."

"Of course, sir."

"Also... wake the dog, Jacobs," the Leader was uncharacteristically happy, contemplating a plan that would put him into the action, "It's time I went for a walk."

"No problem, sir. You'll be in the field personally then? Would you like your full personal deployment?"

"No, thank you. I'll handle it."

"Yes, of course, sir."

"That is all."

"Sir."

The window and connection closed simultaneously. The Leader opened the door to his room. He imagined that the level of privacy within his personal chamber was no greater than anywhere else in the Spire, but nevertheless, he desired the illusion of privacy, so in he went.

Metallic, modern, and Spartan, his room contained no items of personal significance, save one. A two-tiered display sat atop a black marble table in the center of the room. The Wakazashi, an ancient weapon and side-arm of the samurai, was held horizontally on the table by a wooden fork. Its sheath was held by another wooden fork, lower and in front of the bared blade. It had taken the Leader more than a decade to find the genuine article. It was the embodiment of what he expected of himself, and what he desired to be in life.

He lifted the sword up from the display and studied it for a moment. Then he deactivated all of his personal augments, all of his GEaRS. Adam began a practice that he had begun many times before in his life. He needed solace and focus, and he needed his mind to be clear.

Executing one Kata after another, he formed his body into deadly shapes and performed a lethal dance. He stomped and thrust, he spun around, cut vertically and horizontally, swayed to the left and rolled to the right. Each movement was beautifully controlled, each pause strong and purposeful.

After fifteen minutes or so, every inch of the Leader's skin glistened with a sheen of sweat. His clothes were beginning to sag a bit, absorbing the moisture, wicking it away from his skin. The material was made of a synthetic fiber that pulled moisture through unilaterally. As the exterior became damp, the fibers expanded and separated, exposing more surface to the air, evaporating quickly and increasing the effectiveness of the absorption.

He paused for a moment and reached down for the sheath. After three long, smooth breaths, he began again, this time with both blade and sheath as accessories, creating piles of imaginary corpses at his feet.

Twenty minutes later, he was soaked. He had overwhelmed his clothing, so much so that the details of his anatomy were exposed through the material. Returning the weapon to the display, the Leader knelt before the display, trying to cool his body and find comfort in his posture and breathing.

All of this had been part of his training, and part of the training he required for his team. Augments were only as strong as the bodies that employed them. While it was true that you could GEaR up a weakling and see improvement, results would be limited at best. A fool was a fool no matter how fast or how open he was, and a well-armed fool was as likely to hurt himself or his team as much as anything else.

Calm and cool, he stood and walked to the closet. He pulled off his clothes, placed them within the closet and closed it. The barely audible cleaning hum began a moment later. The Leader showered and dressed himself for the outside world. He wore a fitted black business suit. His beard was perfectly groomed, as was his raven hair.

The lift down to the Kennel was empty, quiet, and continuous. Leader privilege prevented stops, so from the 127th all the way down to the sub-basement, the Leader was in a pocket of solemn isolation. He took the time to evaluate himself, to review his plans.

It was a big risk to call on Mark. The man had carved out a wholly unheard of existence in the modern world. No one pushed on Mark. He had worked for everyone at one point or another, legally or not, and he had never given up a client, never betrayed a trust. Loyal to no one, he had secured the loyalty of everyone, including opposing factions.

He was a priest, so to speak, in a world without religion, and his home was a sanctuary. It was rumored that once a patron had drawn a weapon on Mark and died on the spot. There was no religion in this world, but there was certainly plenty of superstition. Whether fantasy or fiction, Mark operated freely, and survived several changes of government and shifts in power.

The Leader was not a superstitious man, but he would exercise great caution confronting the famous GEaR jockey.

The doors slid open and the Leader stepped out of the lift into the sub-basement. He walked several meters down the hall, several doors and windows on either side. He passed more hallways that were perpendicular to his own, and eventually came to a window larger than the others and looked inside.

The room was almost completely empty. There were a few props that looked like chew toys and baseball bats and a few that looked like tree trunks. A woman stood somewhere near the middle of the room clad in full body armor. The armor was actually a series of interwoven ribbons made of a feather-light force-reactive material. The ribbons were mostly white, but branching fine lines of grey were also apparent even from a distance. The Leader knew from experience that the grey lines were conduits for a photonic response. Punching the armor would cause the molecules to align in direct response to the incoming force. Not only would the weave become stronger, but it would also distribute the force laterally, creating a plate of impenetrable, virtually indestructible material. The only reason it wasn't used in the field was the length of time it took for the weave to become supple again. Depending on the force of impact, it could take more than a minute for the flex to return. Under a heavy rate of fire, an Officer would turn to stone. The armor worked perfectly, though, for the dogs.

The woman held up her hand holding a weapon, a baton that she wielded like a short sword. Suddenly, from across the well-lit room, a burst of charcoal fur flashed toward the woman. She managed to swing the weapon in the general direction of the charging mass of fur, but her reaction was too slow and the two toppled together through space, indistinguishable from one another for a moment.

They hit the concrete floor together with the dog actively thrashing at her arm. A couple of hard, quick convulsions and the weapon went flying across the room. It bounced off one of the side walls, bright blue electricity sparking on contact and arcing to it as it fell to the floor.

The attack dog was a lean, charcoal gray wolf. The two slid along the floor briefly before the woman tried to get to her feet and shake her arm free. The lips pulled back from the jaws of the dark beast, revealing glistening steel-blue fangs and molars. Thrashing again, the dog shook the woman back to the ground. She would not give up. She tried desperately to get her feet beneath her and punched at the wolf with her free hand. Two full-strength blows into the dog's ribs, and the Leader thought surely the beast would relinquish its grip, but it only grew fiercer. With all four feet on the floor, the wolf pulled back hard on the woman's arm. Concrete dust shot up from beneath its paws as its claws punched into the floor. The added leverage gave a huge advantage to the animal, and it embarked on an epileptic display of full-bodied thrashing. The armor stiffened in response, creating a sprawling, uncomfortable-looking statue.

The Leader thought to himself that it was odd they still used live human targets for the training, but he'd seen the analyses. Dogs that had been trained exclusively on target dummies were often surprised by human movements, responses, and smells. The dummy-dogs were slow and unpredictable in the field. So at some point, every dog had his day, an opportunity to maul the master. This particular dog certainly seemed to take pride in the attack.

Suddenly, the wolf released its prey. It retracted its claws from the floor and paced around the fallen woman, ears back and down. After circling twice, it began to fade into the background, the grey of its fur growing whiter and lighter to match the surroundings. A moment before the wolf would have been completely invisible, it snapped back to full color and vividness, ears perked up and rotated, nose pointed to a door opening in the side wall.

A trainer entered the area through the door and the dog bound over to greet her, suddenly full of hope and happiness. The woman was tall and skinny and wore only a flowing linen dress. Her skin was unusually pale, which, by virtue of contrast, highlighted her translucent, dark merlot, earlobe length hair. The glassy strands flowed silky and smooth from her head, and appeared almost dark brown, or black even, until the light passed through them and showed the deep, rich red within.

Preoccupied with the Glass she held in her hands, the trainer took readings and notes, and ignored the excitement of her pet. Without looking up from the Glass, she held out one hand and pointed one finger rigidly down. The wolf responded immediately and sat quickly at attention before her.

The Leader opened the door on his side and walked toward the downed target. "Impressive work," he tossed over his shoulder as he knelt down over the woman. She was just then starting to move again.

"Thank you, Leader," the trainer spoke from across the room as she finished with her Glass. She looked up from her work and smiled at the statuesque wolf, slipped the Glass into an almost imperceptible pocket in her dress, and pulled out a small brown morsel. She knelt down and held out the treat on a flat palm, directly below the snout of the beast. The dog made no movement and simply remained at attention. The trainer hesitated an extra moment, then while maintaining eye contact with the dog, nodded down toward the treat. It snapped up the morsel in an instant and received an enthusiastic pet from the trainer.

"Good boy, Feyd. Good boy!" a last pet, she stood and walked toward the Leader, who was busy helping the armored woman to her feet. "Leader, I'm happy to see you."

"The pleasure is mine, Scinter, as always," he acknowledged the weave-armored woman, "You know how much I enjoy seeing your results."

"Forgive me, Leader, allow me to introduce, Cala," Scinter gestured to the armored woman. Then addressing Cala directly, "Meet 127, my favorite Leader." Smiling, Scinter put her hand through her agate hair and it streamed dark and red as it slid through her fingers.

The Leader nodded at Cala who had full mobility once again. She pulled off the hood and mask portion of her armor, revealing her youthful features. She nodded back, "Leader."

"As usual, I'm here for business rather than pleasure, Scinter," he segued to the matter at hand, "How is Meghan?"

Scinter's eyes lit up, "Meghan? Yes, yes, wonderful!" She slid out her Glass again and executed a few quick strokes. "She'll be brought right out. I'm so glad she'll finally get some field testing. The most responsive animal we've had in the Kennel." She turned excitedly to Cala, "Will you please bring me one of the Ties from the back? Oh, and slip that armor off and submit it for testing. Feyd actually did some damage and I want all of the details."

"Yes, ma'am," Cala nodded toward Scinter and then toward the Leader, "Leader." She walked rigidly toward the door, still ajar from the Scinter's entrance.

"Do I LOOK like a MA'AM to you?" Scinter was smiling as she stared after Cala's departing body, particularly at her ass, cupped neatly by the woven armor. "Well, maybe I am a ma'am by comparison with that ass," pitched to the Leader more than to Cala.

"Like your animals," raising his eyebrows toward the agate-haired vixen, "You will chase almost any tail indiscriminately." The Leader was almost asexual, so consumed with his work, but he enjoyed the banter regardless. Carnal pleasures simply never crossed his mind. His life was blood and strategy, not skin and games. However, Scinter always managed to help him imagine he was someone else, living a different life. *But that was a fantasy.*

Scinter stepped right up into the Leader's personal space and put a hand on his chest. "Oh no, not indiscriminately, my friend," she leaned into him and flexed the fingers against his chest like a claw. Her fingernails grew long and turned from light blue to sanguine, "My taste is highly discriminating, I only go for the alphas."

He had frequented the Kennels often enough to expect nothing but aggressive behavior from the pets and the trainers, so the Leader remained unflappable, "Alphas? I always imagine you preying on the weak and nubile." A rare moment, the Leader looked deeply into the woman's eyes, a flirtatious smile on his bearded face, and challenged her to bite back. Putting the final touch on his tongue, "Cala for instance? I imagine you'll have her well trained before her first year is done."

Scinter narrowed her eyes at the hulking man and licked her teeth behind her lips, "The way you always put me off, I'm beginning to think you don't like me as much as I thought you did, 127." She took a less aggressive posture and allowed her hand to return to her side, nails retracting and turning back to liquid, light blue. "On the other hand, you might be right about me."

A young man stepped through the door. A lean, but imposingly large, shiny black Labrador followed close on the heels of the unremarkable boy. He did, however, seem a little jittery.

"Who released Meghan under *your* care?"

"I... I...," the young man, now a boy in the Leader's eyes, stammered out a useless non-answer, "They... I was told to escort Meghan to Testing Room 1?"

Scinter gestured to Meghan with a point, a fist, and a dismissive wave toward the apprentice. Meghan leapt around to stand between Scinter and the boy, lowered her head, peeled back her lips, and swayed side to side. A low rumble began, thick and powerful from the chest of the dog. Then she stopped and hunched back into her strong legs. She opened her jaws in a single flashing bark and displayed an impressive set of impossibly sharp, silver teeth. Mouth still half open and rigid, the growl continued as saliva began to pool around her gums and teeth.

The stammering boy jerked a step away from Meghan, the blood completely gone from his face. The dog responded immediately with three louder and sharper barks, snapping at the air, demonstrating the quick and deadly action of her jaws. That was it for the boy. Frightened beyond any composure, he turned and ran for his life.

"Hahaha!" Scinter was laughing so hard, tears began welling up in her eyes. The Leader simply stood and smiled and waited for the laughter to subside. Meghan, meanwhile, began to explore the room, walking playfully around, smelling everything.

Scinter laughed even harder for a moment, folded over gently, giving completely over to the feeling. She leaned on the Leader a little and after a moment, regained her composure.

"Well, I have to formally reprimand the foolish handler that released Meghan to that even bigger fool… but I'll probably work a thank you in there, too." She gave another short chuckle and wiped a tear from her eye.

"Is Meghan ready then?"

"Eh," she flashed the Leader a disapproving, almost reproachful look, "spoiling my mood again already? Yes, of course she is ready. You aren't." Scinter looked at her Glass and whispered harshly to herself, "Where the hell is…"

Cala walked into the room and quickly up to Scinter, "The Tie you requested."

"Took you long enough," but the reprimand was half-hearted. "You are dismissed. Thank you, Cala."

Cala nodded at both, then walked out the door, this time sliding a finger down the side and closing it as she left.

"Okay, 127, here it is," she handed the Leader a small, bone-shaped treat. "Wait until I leave the room, feed this to Meghan, and play with her for fifteen minutes. The Tie is a quick-acting psychotropic… in fifteen minutes she'll bond with you as though she's lived with you for fifteen years."

Scinter began walking out of the room, "Be nice to her, Leader. Everything you do will be greatly exaggerated, so go out of your way to show some love… you know," she opened the door and turned to look at him, "The opposite of how you treat me. Subtlety and sarcasm will be lost on her." She stepped backwards out of the room and closed the door.

The Leader sat cross-legged on the floor, "Meghan."

The dog perked up from sniffing in the corner across the room and looked across at the man, a mountain even when sitting.

"Meghan."

Black and shiny, she moved more like a panther than a Labrador as she padded her way softly over.

"Good girl," his voice was low and confident. He had never Tied a dog before, but he had read about it and ordered it done for two of his elite soldiers. He had always been interested, visiting the Kennels regularly, which was why Scinter knew him so well.

He sat there, petting and praising the dog for several moments. He had achieved some clarity during his Kata, but he was not pressed for time, so he gave over to introspection. Self-sufficiency he had mastered, and he understood squad-based tactics better than anyone, but he had never adapted himself to working an assignment with another soldier. In fact, he kept his Squads completely separate from his Solos and considered them non-interchangeable. Today though, required something new. Eve was out there, and she knew him better than anyone else. If he wanted an edge over her, he required a new and unlikely asset. In order to get the best of Eve, he would have to rewrite himself on the fly. She would never suspect his presence in the field and that alone was one gigantic advantage. He could not underestimate her though because she would recover quickly, and she was better than the Leader, more creative in combat… and she had clearly been operating off the grid for some time… he did not know his enemy as he should.

Yes. It was time for a dramatic shift in the paradigm of his rules and tactics. "Here girl," he held his hand out, palm flat, bone in the middle, and she casually sniffed at it, then licked and bit it out of his hand. If the bond was going to work, he would have to let himself go, awkward as it was for him.

He rolled around on the ground.

She rolled and pounced.

He laughed and played.

She licked and bounded.

He ran and chased.

She circled and danced.

What the heck? Scinter pulled up the Training Room 1 monitor on her Glass, "He knew the Tie was for the dog, right?"

SPIRE

Last Exit

Twenty-Three

Sara burst onto the street, yanking Joshua with her. She looked right and left, trying to get her bearings. She wasn't sure how Ezechial would find them, or if she even wanted him to find them… in the meantime though, she wanted out.

Her eyes flashing wet with fear and adrenaline, "Joshua, I'm out. You can come with me if you want, but I'm getting as far away from this as I can. I don't know who is after you and I don't care anymore."

Joshua grinned, "I'm going with you and your beautiful lavender petals." He stared into her eyes as though they were alone on the planet, as though his bridge to reality was completely broken.

She hesitated, but the overwhelming, uncontrollable need to be close to him kept her from guessing twice, "Okay. Okay, fine." Glancing around quickly, "We're going to my Exit. I only paid for one but I can probably get you through…" A Collective Vehicle whirred around the corner, lights flashing. Sara threw Joshua up against the outside of the building and pressed her body into him. *It worked in the movies.*

It's okay, Sara. I can handle this. The words floated through her mind as though they were her own. Her voice was strange though, mimicking Joshua's. It was as though she was having a conversation with Joshua that they'd never had. It felt like she was making it up. Luckily, she didn't have to worry about the origin of the voice in her head for very long as Joshua picked her up by the shoulders and moved her aside as though she were feather light.

He was grinning widely, eyes swirly marbles again, two cracked black slits staring down at her. As he moved Sara to the side, they seemed to spin together through space, like they were holding hands in the center of a playground toy.

Her back was against the wall now. Joshua slid his hands down her shoulders gently, *Stay here.*

. . .

Gorgeous. Her eyes jubilant, energetically searching for answers, eventually settled on mine. I could see fear in the excitement, fueling it. There were sharp flashes of light cascading through her skin and hair, tension and stress. I wished I had time to stare at her, to capture her looking just like that and digest every emotion radiating from her, but the moment was curling in on itself, withering away to make room for the next.

My moment. I turned away from Sara and stared out into the larger world. Heady and giddy, I felt the concrete and asphalt rubbing against the skin of my hands. I knew that I was standing, that I was human. I was of human proportions and limitations, but my awareness extended beyond my form.

The cars, enamel and plastic, felt smooth and cool against my skin. I reached out to touch a tire and the friction burned at my fingertips. But I was still standing, hands by my sides, several feet away. Staring down at my hands, I turned them over and back again, and there was no indication of burning.

People flowed by, sharing currents with one another, jumping from one to another, with no understanding of the co-mingling of their lives. They were vacant and shapeless, phantoms of humanity. I felt like I was staring out over a long river, watching leaves and twigs floating by, bumping into one another, spinning off into various tributaries, and escaping down other smaller branches of the river.

At the extent of my vision, I imagined this river of disconnected souls pouring over a cliff, all of the people disappearing into the foam at the bottom of the fall.

Some of the detritus did have a purpose, though I didn't notice them at first. Some had come looking for me, looking for Sara. They were armed and armored. They were connected to a greater organism, trails of electric dust following them, their awareness exchanged with others far away. The split presence of the Collective, part of each member was always a part of the whole.

Anger began deep in my stomach. It grew and swelled, and flooded my chest. I took a long breath through my nose, and my nostrils burned from the speed and volume of the air I pulled through. My heart was pounding, and I was growing, pushing the rest of the world away to focus on the Collective's soldiers.

I heard and saw a scream, distant and muffled, damp. It was the sound of a person screaming under water. People moved away from me, slowly at first, followed by a few startled jumps, and then they ran. They were all running, stumbling over one another, unable to run fast enough… away from me.

The Collective Officers were staring wide-eyed at me, and I smelled their sweat leaking through their armor, pungent and super-heated. I saw them struggle, consciousness flowing from where they stood to somewhere far away, asking permission, seeking guidance. Meanwhile their instincts, like a banshee's wail, demanded their full attention. Because I was here and now. I was an immediate threat to their lives. The hive, well, the hive was far away. Far away and later.

The lights from the Collective car were flashing, asking for my attention. I was all too happy to oblige. The tiny vehicle had extra-wide, smooth tires, and sat low to the surface of the street. It had a posture like an animal poised to attack, on its haunches, showing its colors, whooping out a threatening bark. Its doors opened out in a bluff, attempting to appear larger than it was. I reached one powerful hand out to challenge the tiny monster.

The roof of the car fit plumb into the palm of my hand. I tested its integrity a bit with a couple of gentle squeezes. Then, I applied real pressure. The satisfying sound of the crunching metal scratched my inner ear. The glass of each window shattered as my fingers pushed through them and then the windshield popped out, a sheet of webbed glass, onto the street. The collapsing frame felt more like balsa wood than steel, more like an empty aluminum can than an automobile.

I weighed the vehicle in my hand and it felt like a child's toy. I couldn't stifle my laughter as I tossed the fragile, broken toy across the street. It hit the side of a building in full flight, punching a hole in the wall, breaking out several bricks and throwing up a shower of granite and dust. The sounds of the destruction were music to my ears—satisfying, remarkably loud, and beautifully melodic.

The Collective Officers had other toys and they tried a few of them on me. They pointed their streamlined assault weapons at me and fired off round after round. The projectiles moved in slow motion. I avoided some, but not all. A few exploded on my skin with sparkling blue electricity that burned. My muscles twitched and convulsed in response, but the result was more irritation than pain. The C.O.s were simultaneously backing away, yelling at each other, yelling at their hive-mind, and shooting at me with each retreating step.

The bullets fired at me changed, the officers switching ammunition, throwing everything at me. Some embedded themselves in my skin, others exploded on impact, and still others burned through me. Those last ones moved fast—energetic enough to pass through every layer of my skin—on the way in and on the way out. No one bullet hurt me more than the others, but the combination of all of those different and simultaneous irritations, was unbearable. I was overwhelmed and I needed them to stop, or to get away, or both.

Trying to put my hands down on the ground, to be down on all fours, I discovered there was no room in the street. There was no empty space for me to fit my hands. I had to knock vehicles and objects aside just to take a step. I felt frustrated and claustrophobic. Suddenly, my anger was not full, but pinching. The strength was flowing out of me instead of into me, and the two little monsters continued to shoot at me, an unending barrage of mass and force. I hated them.

Stop it!

The echo of my voice in my own head shook me inside out. My vision quaked for a moment, violently from side to side, and remained blurry for several seconds. I weaved my head and neck back and forth trying to clear away the residual vibration. Looking down, I saw the small soldiers had been knocked to the ground. They were rolling around trying to find their weapons, which had landed far away from their bodies. One tried to stagger to his feet, but immediately slipped and fell back to the street.

I closed my eyes tightly, squeezed and unsqueezed the lids several times. The pressure felt good. When I opened them again, my perspective was different, lower to the ground, more from the side than from above. The tight frustration was gone, but it had been replaced with fatigue. My chest was shaky and my legs were jelly. Sweat trickled down my spine between my shoulders. I felt diminished. I tried to reach out to touch the asphalt, but I could only see it with my eyes, I couldn't taste it like before.

A sudden wave of nausea crashed against me and knocked me to the concrete. *Well, I feel the asphalt now.* It was different though than it was a moment ago, rougher and colder against my soft skin. Dry heaving, once then twice, then gripped by a third hard and maintained convulsion, I finally came completely back to my body.

I collected myself and stood up slowly. The Officers were still down and disoriented. They seemed so far away, more than fifty meters from me. I hugged myself, slouching and trying to stay warm. *Where is Sara?*

"Sara!" I turned, yelling.

"I'm right here." She was right where I left her, back against the wall. Only now, she was no longer in an excited state. Her petals drifted around her, quietly and softly. She was completely with me, attention directed entirely at me. Sara's voice was a whisper, "You... are you okay?"

235

I could not decide if she was asking if I was hurt, or whether or not it was okay for her to come close to me. "Sure, I uh...," another moment of assessing myself, "I'm a little shaky, but I feel better now. My stomach really hurts from dry-hacking, but I think I'll be fine."

The Collective Officers were starting to make noises, grunts, and some chatter but I couldn't understand any words from where I was standing. I tried to take a step toward Sara, but I felt woozy and my legs were slow to respond to my shifting weight. It was as though I was drunk.

"I think I'm in trouble," looking down at my hands, flipping them over and over again. They looked so strange to me.

A silky lavender petal fell into my palm. I couldn't resist the urge to slide my thumb into the curve of it, rubbing it around and gently pushing the petal into my skin. It turned into a creamy liquid and I massaged it around until it was completely absorbed into my hand. From the center of my palm, a cool and soothing sensation began, echoed in my chest and the soles of my feet. Smiling, I looked up to see if Sara saw it. Suddenly, she was standing right next to me. I hadn't noticed that she'd moved.

Sara put her hands around my hands, "We have to go. Those guys are going to call for back up. After what you did to them, I'd expect the entire Spire to show up any minute."

My brain was muddy, thick and slow. I knew she was expressing an urgent need, but I could not comprehend the specifics.

Thwap-crack! Thwap-crraaaack!

We both turned to a whipping sound echoing off the walls of the buildings around us. It was Winter, or Ezechial I suppose, near the C.O.s. He looked like a dancer, arms and legs moving in coordinated grace. The whips, extending out several feet from each hand, licked at the air like serpent's tongues, and the C.O.s were swiftly silenced, and then forever still.

I reached out to Ezechial, butterflies flying fast from my body out to the rugged man, but as they began to land on him, he slipped forward oily-quick, his shadow-trick. The butterflies burst away from him, bodies to fluttering wings, to dust. It hurt a little to feel that murderous force, even from a distance.

And then he stood beside us.

"I told you to move and keep moving. What the hell is this?"

"It was Joshua," Sara looked around befuddled, "He... they were..."

Ezechial had no shadow. People cast lingering shadows, shadows that stayed even after they'd passed. People, not Ezechial. I could not look away from his scruffy, hard face. I could almost... almost... see his connection to my world, but I needed help understanding, "Why are you here, Ezechial?"

"Eve sent me." He looked at me evenly, confidence trimmed with melancholy. "I'm sure you figured that. What you really want to know is if you can trust me," his eyebrows raised, putting a question mark on the end of his statement.

"I don't have the time to earn your trust, and even if I did, how long would it be before you started questioning it again? I'm not trying to kill you... that's all I can offer, really." He shrugged, "I think it is better than your other options."

I could think of nothing to say in response. My thoughts were like stepping through slough muck. I wasn't really sure what I was asking the shadowy man standing before me.

"I have an Exit," Sara interjected with a mix of excitement and trepidation, "Joshua and I can disappear..."

A mini-copter approached, its distinctive sound announcing its imminent arrival. It wasn't the bassy, heavy sound of an assault helicopter, but the higher pitched buzzing of a vehicle closer in size to a motorcycle. An average pilot could maneuver the mini-copter into an alleyway, into a subway tunnel even. There was no way we could outrun it if it caught sight of us.

Ezechial shadow-stepped to the building across the street and waved us over. Sara and I didn't even look at each other, we just started running. When we reached Ezechial, he began to run with us. We ran together, the three of us, down the street and into an alley.

Without stopping, "If you have a reliable way to disappear, you should use it, Sara. You might be able escape all of this, but Joshua," running hard and breathing harder, "Joshua, is top priority for the Collective…"

The mini-copter was near, but in the alley it was impossible to tell from which direction it was coming, the rapid loud beating rebounding from every wall.

Ezechial stopped fast in front of an old door. His thumb turned greasy and black and he slid it down the reading edge of the door. I heard a soft *thud-click* of the lock mechanism and the door was opened.

Sara glared at Ezechial suspiciously.

"Come on!" he ushered us inside.

Sara hesitated so I grabbed her and pulled her inside with me. Ezechial closed the door immediately behind us, a moment before the mini-copter turned down the alley.

We were standing together at the bottom of a large stair well. The pungent smell of human urine and feces soured the air.

"There isn't much time," with soft and controlled breathing. He recovered from the run quickly for someone with grey in his beard. Sara and I were still panting.

He continued, "The Collective wants what Joshua has. They want to dissect it, reproduce it, control it. They will not stop coming for him." He examined the room as though devising a strategy for taking it apart brick by brick.

"What he has!? What the hell is that supposed to mean?" Sara was at the end of her patience, "He turned into a fucking dragon back there! Are you trying to tell me that's just some new GEaR?! Or what? That he's *talented*?!"

"I don't know. Neither does anyone else," Ezechial allowed a good-natured, almost apologetic glance to slip out. "I'm not sure

I can help you understand. I can tell you that he is no dragon," he shrugged.

As the mini-copter sounds subsided, I noticed again that Ezechial was shrouded from me. He left no impression. I could not touch him the way I touched others. He hid himself from me.

"Looked like a big fucking dragon to me," Sara folded her arms across her chest and hiked up her hip, as dramatic and sensual a pose as I had come to expect.

"I'm not a religious man, but there is more power in the human soul than most will ever understand and fewer will imagine," Ezechial listened by the door. Apparently, he'd decided to go back out the way we came in.

He looked back to Sara, "And… I've mastered some pretty handy tricks myself over the years," a charismatic smile.

Ezechial held up his hand seeing that Sara was about to interrupt and he leaned closer to the door again. Nothing. Not a sound.

"Soul, spirit, chi… I don't care what you call it, there is a strength in each of us that is born of creativity and driven by our imaginations, our passions. It is open and beautiful when set free… deadly when focused. The Collective would like to define it and control it." He shrugged his shoulders and cocked his head to the side, "My best guess? Our boy here is capable of complete manifestation. No limits."

Sara's lips parted as if to protest, but she thought better of it and just stood there. Her posture reminded me of a teacher whose students had just defeated her with an argument so irrational that it could not be contested. Under her breath, "I saw a fucking dragon."

Suddenly, I realized that some part of the conversation had been about me, but I wasn't sure which parts. Ezechial and Sara seemed done with each other, resigned to agree to disagree or some such nonsense.

"We need to split up."

"Huh?"

"I'm going to run out this door and get some attention from our Collective friends out there," Ezechial was neither excited nor frightened by the prospect of confronting numerous assault rifles. "You two will go, get as far away from here as you can."

"Really?" she was nonplussed, but lacked the energy to pursue an understanding.

"You said you have an Exit? Are you meeting a hack for that or...?"

"I've got a locker, Cuff and Creds inside. Usual instructions. Got it all from a guy I've used a few times before. He's no hack."

Ezechial reached out for Sara's wrist. She reacted a second or two after he already had her held in a vice grip, staring at her arm, soft-side up.

It wasn't that his movement was fast, or that she was slow, it was more like an illusion, that he'd been moving the whole time, but neither of us was able to focus on what he was doing. His motivations were hidden.

Sara jerked and pulled, but Ezechial held her effortlessly and examined her forearm, "Hmmm, artfully done. Mark?"

Sara stopped pulling long enough to cast another suspicious glare at the man, "I guess someone like you would also have need of a specialist?" She yanked hard at her arm, but Ezechial released her in the same moment and she almost fell from losing her balance.

I noticed that I was dripping with sweat. I confused the rank smell of the surroundings with the smell of my body, my heat and moisture capturing and carrying the scents to my nose and mouth. Sickeningly sweet, the aroma pushed me around the stairwell, causing vertigo.

"Okay, well if you're in good standing with Mark, it might be a good plan to go to him with Joshua," he thought it over aloud. "Yes. Do you think you could get in touch with him?"

"I don't know!" her frustration screeched out, "I bought stuff from him. It's not like we're old friends!" She stood with a mix of defiance and fear.

In the dimly lit service stairwell, I saw the smoky impressions walking around us, the remains of the sick and decaying spirits that wallowed here. The smoky impressions were faint even though they were definitely fresh… fresh as the steaming pile in the corner.

"Well, we're out of time for discussion. Try to get a message to Mark if you can, Eve has done quite a bit of business with him. He'll know what to do." He paused a moment, "When you hear an explosion, run."

The door opened and he silently slid out. The man was dream-memory slippery. The harder I tried to place him, to remember him, the more doubtful and fuzzy the memory became. I scrutinized the last few moments with him, and I honestly couldn't say if he was just in my imagination or not.

Sara leaned into Joshua, "You'd better be worth all of this."

SPIRE

Little Red Riding Hood
Twenty-Four

Eve had thought to steal another motorcycle then thought better of it. The Collective was certainly casting for her at this point. Casting implied a lot more than her description and recent photos linked and searched through multiple media. It meant that every stream in the city was being checked for anyone approximating her size and shape. It meant that anything matching greater than sixty-five percent was going to be reviewed by a Watcher. It meant that her life depended on stealth.

So, instead of larcenously borrowing another Italian, two-wheeled work of art, she went for grand theft Beemer. It had been harder lifting her Glass from the evidence box at the Local Collective than circumnavigating the security system of the beautiful vehicle. She spun her Glass around in her hand triumphantly.

It was a larger vehicle than most, able to fit two passengers easily. The seat was a custom-fit electro-gel that molded perfectly to her curves, then turned solid under low current. She could even adjust the stiffness and temperature of the material. It was one of the rare luxuries that hadn't made it to the masses yet. An ounce of the highly sensitive electro-gel was expensive, a human-sized chair-full was ludicrously so. Attempts to mass produce the gel with lesser quality synthesizers had resulted in many cement buckets, and a few expensive water balloons.

She drove over the bridge and the Spire loomed over her. Eve felt no fear, but that dark obelisk, standing off the shore, staring down at her, made her feel unsure. Would Joshua be able to stand against the dark tower? So much power was contained within the walls of that stronghold, it seemed an impossible task. The first task though, was simply not to die. She would worry about the Spire later, if they survived long enough for it to matter.

The car drove on, silent as a coffin. Eve touched her Glass mounted in the dash and disabled the noise cancelling feature. The soft whir of the tires and engine were comforting after the silence. Sounds of urban life increased in volume and variation as she came down off the ramp from the bridge and entered the city proper.

Eve had been to every major city in the unified world, but this city, her city, had never lost its hold on the claim of greatest. It was only a little more than 20 square miles, but it was home to the greatest towers of production and commerce in the world. The island was covered with scrapers that reached to the sky, and at the nucleus of it all were some of the most impressive works of architecture ever created.

There was an interesting shape to the city. The heart had grown strong over the years and eventually overtook the entire island. When the buildings couldn't be made any taller, but the growth continued, enormous arteries of bridgework were built to sustain it and even expand it. The massive city pumped life into the body of the state and beyond. It was truly awe-inspiring.

The car drove on, deeper into the complex system of the city. Left here, right there, taller and taller buildings isolating the interior from the world outside. Finally, after several minutes, Eve no longer saw the Spire. It was lost behind the wall of buildings. It didn't matter that she couldn't see it, she knew it was there. It had been her home for so long that imagining a world without it was impossible.

The car stopped and docked itself near the Park. Eve took a moment before opening the door. She wanted to hold on to this relaxed space for a few seconds longer. She felt safe and anonymous which, she knew, would change dramatically as soon as she stepped out of the car. Checking her StatDiag, she found that she was well on her way back to full functionality, fully recovered, even without new scrubs. All of the GEaRless training the Leader had insisted on was worth something after all.

She focused on her IOD, which activated it, making it slightly more opaque, and she tested all of her systems. All of her spikes and augmentations were clean. Closing and opening her eyes, she looked at various spectrums and magnifications. Everything seemed in order. Her muscles still ached somewhat, but the throbbing was more a pleasant reminder of her humanity than a debilitating condition. No more delays. Putting off the inevitable was futile. She tapped a panel and the door opened with a barely audible vacuum.

Out in the open air the park was cold, but not unbearable, even in her running clothes. The clothes were dry now anyway, though maybe not as clean as she would like. There were several pedestrians—some walking, some jogging, others sitting and reading, still others simply people watching.

A man drinking coffee with a friend looked up from his cup and made eye contact with Eve. He was younger than Eve, but not by much, and handsome. He smiled that careful smile that invited a smile in return, but managed to put no pressure on it. It was a smile that spoke of confidence, desire without need, prowess without pride. Eve glared back a mixture of malice, hate, and distrust, which were easy to manufacture because she was feeling all of those emotions at that very moment. The man did not flinch, rather, he smiled broader, nodded, and continued his conversation with his friend without skipping a beat.

I'm losing my touch. Dating had never really been one of her fortes, but the men and women she'd been with had at least been bright enough to run when she gave that look.

She was becoming distracted. Her skin was crawling. The scene was making her jittery. No obvious chokes or channels, she needed eyes in the back of her head, not distractions. Slipping right now would only end in a fatal fall.

Taking in her surroundings, she fired up a focus spike and mapped her vision to a bird's eye display on her inter-ocular display. She casually looked around the park, taking in the full 360-degree view. The resulting top-down map showed no demonstrable meaning or pattern in the positions of the civilians. She marked all of the people in her vision and cross-referenced their positions with what her IOD showed. The display was based on the Global Positions Monitor Server and overlaid with her visual map. The dots all matched up. There were no unregistered people, at least not that she could detect. Eve still had high-level access to GPMS through some Creds she jacked several months ago, so she felt confident there was no real Collective presence on the scene. She wanted to access all of the Creds in the area, but that would ping a Watcher, which wouldn't stop her immediately but her Cred-jacking would fail under review. Too risky.

The Leader had resources. In fact, the entire lower Spire was in the purview of his command and should not be underestimated. She had to assume that he knew all of her accomplices. However, Mark was certainly one who he would have difficulty confronting or pursuing. Despite her need to treat Mark as compromised, she still thought him beyond the reach of The Leader.

She walked the path for several hundred yards. The interior of the park was such a different place at the end of autumn. The foliage was almost completely shed now, leaving nothing but the leafless browns and greys of bare branches. The ground was pale too, most of the grass having lost the lively green color, turning instead to shades of yellow and tan. Some fallen leaves littered the ground, but the bulk of the autumn shed had already been removed.

Turning down another path, Eve made it farther into the park, into the less-frequented and less-populated spaces. Eventually she saw the man she was looking for.

Mark was down in a slight depression, in an area of grass ringed with small, smooth stones. He was barefoot, practicing Tai Chi. His movements were graceful, obviously the result of years of discipline and dedication. He was tall, six feet and a few inches, with natural dark brown hair. The clothes he wore were loose and soft in appearance—not totally unlike those worn within the Spire—but there were some important differences. The pants and shirt had seams in them, as though they were sewn. It was a fad that had come and gone, to mimic the old methods of manufacturing apparel, but his clothes looked handmade, truly rare. There were buttons and ties as well, adding another dimension of authenticity to the look.

Eve turned off the path and walked toward Mark who appeared too deep in his slow-motion dance to notice her approaching. His eyes were closed as he turned in her direction. She almost thought he looked at her but then his movement took him away from her again and she thought better of it.

Not knowing the best way to interrupt him, she stood there for several minutes watching. It was an interesting display for the runners going past, a juxtaposition of ancient and modern forms. Eve was lithe, tall, and lean. Her well-developed muscles were obvious beneath her smooth, skin-tight athletic wear. Mark, on the other hand, was tall and broad, and his strength was hidden by his loose-fitting garb. The spikes of her short, thick hair stuck up and out in small, azure pyramidal twists. His medium-length, brown hair was somewhat disheveled but otherwise flat against his head, untreated. She was perfectly motionless, her relentless will augmented but the finest GEaRS controlling every organ, the tension of each fiber of every muscle to produce a veritable statue. He continued his practice, a constant flow of motion. They made quite the pair.

"I do this all day, you know," he continued, his eyes closed, standing on one bent leg, arms wind-milling at millimeters per second.

"I would have interrupted you eventually," she responded flatly.

"You still haven't interrupted me," smirking. He gradually placed his hanging foot on the ground toward her.

"Well, I'm glad that my presence hasn't inconvenienced you," dropping her guarded pose somewhat, she relaxed her stance and shifted to a somewhat perturbed slant.

One arm eventually met the other and his feet came together at the same time. It was slow, but he was standing fully facing Eve by the end of his motion, with his hands pressed together at the center of his chest. He bowed slightly, then fully erect, he relaxed his arms to his side and opened his eyes.

Two soft maple irises looked at her, "Hello, Eve."

"Mark," she respected him deeply even if she didn't really want to show it.

"The Collective is casting for you. Highest priority. Processing resources are diverted to scanning every stream in the city for you whenever they are available. It's pretty intense," casually.

"Yes," she straightened up, serious, "I think my time there is probably up. But that's why I'm here of course."

"Of course."

"What are my options?"

"Well, first of all, you shouldn't steal BMWs from wealthy, eclectic types. That guy? He hopes people will steal from him. He likes to play the hunter... and the things he's done to his prey... you don't want to know. On the other hand, what you would do to him...?" laughing softly more or less to himself, he stopped short. "Anyway, you are damn lucky my monitors are superior to those of the Collective. I capped and dumped it already."

"You're already running blockers for me?" her gratitude is surprising even to herself.

"Well, don't get the wrong idea," admonishingly, "It's not a permanent solution. I cannot cover up your existence and exploits from now until you die or anything. As it is, I'm taxing all available unused processes to keep up." Mark fills with pride, "You'd be impressed, actually. My interference is a mimic of the Collective's cast, so they *think* all that work to find you is theirs."

"Thanks, Mark," a genuine moment of admiration passes between them. "*Is* there a permanent solution?"

"Well, they can't run this hot forever either." He was focusing on something a few feet in front of him, clearly accessing elements of his IOD. "I might be able to subtly muddy your Creds enough that the Cast has trouble matching you, but it isn't as though I can erase you from the Collective. They *know* you in ways that I can't control or change."

"So... wait it out? Hide? Find a nice quiet jungle somewhere?"

"We knew this was a risk," grave and unyielding, "I'm going to do everything I can for you, but short of dissolving the Collective, you're in a bad way."

"Well," she wasn't giving up, "I can hide pretty well. I'll figure it out." With renewed interest, "Have you seen anything of Joshua?"

Mark was still staring into the middle distance, a playful expression on his face, "Oh, yes. Yes, I have."

An alert appeared for Eve and she accessed it. The stream was oddly distorted, but not so much so that she couldn't see what was happening. Joshua had woken up from his fevered sleep with newfound power, and he was trying it out. He wrecked a car and threw it across a street and into a building. The damage implied a terrific and terrifying amount of force. Through the blurred images, Eve could barely make out a form in the rippling energies flowing out from Joshua: large reptilian legs, claws, and wings. The energy wasn't constant or opaque, but if Eve had to call it something, "Fuck, a dragon?"

"Wait for it..."

The C.O.s were firing their rifles continuously into the form projected from Joshua. Wispy tendrils of green and purple trailed from his body out to the extents of the dragon. Each bullet caused ripples and shakes to appear where they penetrated or exploded on the ghostly monster, causing a reactive force to be sent down through the tendrils and into Joshua. He looked like he was standing up to the assault pretty well at first, but then his standing posture began to weaken as though he was becoming exhausted. Then, just when Eve thought he was going to fall, he stood fiercely, defiantly upright. The ghostly dragon's head and neck became vivid and distinct and recoiled angrily from the Officers. The next moment it snapped sinuously forward, its mouth open wide, releasing a wave of destruction, more visible from its effect than anything else. Cars wrinkled and slid away. Glass exploded out from the vehicles caught in the cone of the blast. At the farthest extent of the wave, it hit both C.O.s, lifting them off their feet and sending them several meters through the air.

"Holy shit."

"Holy, indeed."

"Did those Officers live through that?"

"They lived through the dragon, yes… but not through the Ezechial that followed," Mark tilted his head, brows raised questioningly.

"Well, I didn't expect that…," Eve, stunned, watched the last several seconds of the stream over and over again.

"I wish I was closer to understanding it," disappointment obvious in his tone, "Gabriel has lost his connection completely. The man might have single-handedly been responsible for discovering and expediting the evolution of humankind, and now he's practically speaking in tongues. Not sure what I'm going to do with…"

Mark was suddenly shoved forward toward Eve, tiny red projectiles bursting out around him, bending around his body, deflected by some unseen protective measure. Eve lunged to the side, barely avoiding his sprawling body.

In a split second, Eve activated her combat GEaRS, and her cloak. She tore her clothes from her body and rolled to the side just as flash of movement appeared in her peripheral vision. She felt the wind of it as it passed by and snatched part of her shirt out of the air, carrying it several feet before letting it drop. A quick glance at Mark revealed that he was alive and conscious, although he had hit the ground pretty hard. Nothing could be done for him right now though, because she couldn't find her enemy. She needed distance and time.

Her legs felt amazingly agile, sensitive and powerful as they propelled her up an oak tree. Halfway up, she hooked her arm around the trunk and sank her nails in. Scanning furtively for any movement, she waited and watched. Mark was writhing around on the ground. Something had gotten through his protection. She knew very little about his personal GEaRS, but imagined they defined the bleeding edge of technology.

Who the fuck was out there?

A single cold claw of emotional defeat dug into the base of her spine and traced its way all the way up to her neck as a man shimmered into existence, crouching next to the fallen Mark. It was a huge man with raven-colored hair and close-cut beard. His muscles bulged from beneath his clothing. Crouched down as he was, it seemed that his enormous legs might explode through his charcoal slacks if he flexed them only slightly more. He stood up, a mountain of a man, solid and confident, and looked around the park.

Leader 127.

"Still using your custom-built dermal cloak, I see," his voice resonated deep and almost soulful, in her ears. "So talented, my prized pupil… a master technician."

He's baiting me. Eve felt an overwhelming sense of defeat. The Leader had fought all of his personal soldiers numerous times—it was part of the training—and to her knowledge he'd never been bested. He was inevitably one step ahead.

"I honestly do not understand the deception," he managed to sound slightly hurt, "I consider myself, unreservedly, your father. I would have been supportive, and interested in this… this endeavor of yours."

Frantically, she scoured the area with every passive scan available to her. Desperate, she tried cycling through spectrums and filters, but found nothing. Mark continued to lie there, conscious but unmoving. Certainly, he wasn't fooling the Leader. *What tricks does Mark have up his sleeve?*

Nothing but question marks, again she felt the sick feeling of losing the battle.

"Eve, you know me—better than most, anyway. You understand that I will never give up a target. Tragically, you are my target. My greatest success… you will not become my greatest failure." He looked around, the bass of his voice shaking her will. "You also know that I have no cause to make this painful if you give me answers."

There is a dog. Mark's words appeared in an alert. The Leader's response to the transmission was swift, emotionless. With a full-bodied lunge, he stomped the back of Mark's head into the ground. The bone-snapping sound was sickeningly dampened.

Eve catapulted herself back, away from the trunk, and allowed herself to fall to the ground as the Leader changed focus. In a blur, he charged the tree and leapt toward it. As he landed, perching more gracefully than his mass would ever imply, his hand smashed into the trunk. The strike sent splinters of wood flying in all directions, followed by a thunderous *crraaaack* as the trunk split down the center.

She waited, motionless, breathless.

The Leader jumped down from the tree and landed several meters from her, between her and Mark's corpse. He looked around curiously, confidently.

A dog? Eve thought for a moment about the Kennel, and without deeper consideration, she sniffed quietly at the air. She sampled it once, twice, three times, all while tracking the Leader's every movement. Her sense of smell had been augmented several times over the years, and more than that, she had trained herself to use it well. Eve sifted through the enormous amount of chemical information hanging in the air. Trees, decaying leaves, various droppings, last night's alcohol, bread crumbs, the Leader's adrenalized sweat, a dead pigeon, and…

… and there she was. Eve could not see the animal, but she knew that the dog was hovering around her clothes, improving her recognition of Eve's scent. It was a female dog, a couple of days from heat. She carried the smell of other dogs from the Kennel, so many that Eve could not distinguish among them. Trying several different kinds of filters, staring in the direction of the dog, Eve could find nothing that would give her a visual. Heat shielding, noise cancelling, no detectable light distortions, the damn mutt had been outfitted with higher quality stealth than Eve, at least before she had gone off on her own.

"Eve, I'm not leaving without your willing…" she tuned out his voice. She knew his tactics well. There was no negotiation taking place, no explanation forthcoming. He was talking because he felt he could gain some advantage from it. She knew better than to try to outwit the practiced verbal tactician with words. It was not in her skill set. Silence was her best response.

Eve surveyed the scene and couldn't help feeling that she needed to press her advantage, now that she knew the location of both of her adversaries. As she stood, nose slightly up, ears back, studying her enemies, she felt an odd kinship with the dog. A sad recognition, a realization, surfaced. She, too, had been his pet, his weapon, his to command. And now she felt a kind of guilt for biting the hand that fed her. *Shit. I've been right there before… sniffing out our targets.* Then she thought better of it, *Actually, no, I wasn't even as good as this dog,* sarcastically, *That fucker never took me to the park. He never went out with me.*

She was an adult, aware and intelligent, and still she felt a pang of jealousy and hate for the animal she'd never even met. A kind of laughing madness filled Eve as she realized she could even smell the dog on the Leader. *It's official, if I survive this, I'm going to therapy.*

The Leader's voice droned on. He wasn't stalling, but she could not conceivably escape and he knew it, so he took his time, until Eve took it from him.

She dug in and dashed forward toward her pile of rent clothing. The feeling of so many augments and spikes activating at once, euphoric. Eve even had a short burst inertial dampener that could easily cover the distance, so the chemical high was pushed by a dreamy, flying lightness.

Meghan was the most beautiful animal Eve had ever seen. The blur of black fur slowed to an image of an immense, jet black Labrador as Eve entered the pocket of high-velocity combat. The dog's legs catapulted it forward toward Eve with masterful coordination. Its ears were laid back as it leapt to meet Eve's attack, but Eve grabbed the earth with all four of her limbs and shifted, turning to the side. As the fangs came out, mouth wide and menacing, Meghan flexed her body trying to reach Eve even as she passed. Eve's shoulder curled around the mouth and it snapped shut on the air as Eve's hands knifed out. The enhanced nails, like stilettos at the end of each finger, shredded Meghan's flank and allowed Eve's hands to pass right into her belly. Eve closed her hands and the dogs hips, from the inside, slammed into her forearms and they spun each other 180 degrees.

As Eve stood up, she eviscerated Meghan. There were no thoughts, only actions. She threw everything she held in her hands toward the last position of the Leader. The entrails hit him square in the chest, blood and guts splashing and revealing him, despite his cloak.

The Leader drove forward at her regardless and put his full weight behind an elbow thrust. He managed to catch her in the right shoulder as she tried to fade to the left. The man's elbow was like a baseball bat, only worse because it penetrated the muscle instead flattening it. The violating force struck through to the bone and exploded the nerves down her arm.

The hit turned her around, and she continued the motion, redirecting his energy. She spun herself the rest of the way and as she came fully around again, her head at the Leader's knees, she attacked his calf. His pants were armored, designed for close combat. They could easily withstand thrusts and slices from the sharpest melee weapons. Eve though, slipped her left hand beneath the cuff of his pants. If they'd been in the park under other circumstances, if they'd been different people, the deftness of the move could easily have been mistaken for seduction. They were no lovers though, and her claws cut twice. Up shallowly and down deeply, she dug through as much flesh and tendon as she could before dashing around him.

Instinctively, she used all limbs to try to put instead between them. Instead of support and propulsion, though, her right arm offered only excruciating pain. She pushed forward awkwardly, going for the trees again, running upright. Holding her right arm with her left, close to her body, she did her best to maintain speed and balance.

Her HUD was lighting up with information as she cut through the first copse. She was hurt badly.

The Leader was worse off than she was. She could hear him following, but not closing the distance. An absolute win to trade an arm for a leg, she pushed herself harder to increase the gap between them. Looking down at herself, all Eve saw was blood floating and sliding up against the implied surface of her breasts and arms.

Quickly changing course, not caring that the Leader would intuit her intention, Eve headed for the river. She quit trying to avoid branches from trees and bushes, taking several cuts and scratches to put a few more meters between her and the Leader. He was having difficulty navigating the rougher terrain. Cresting a small hill, she spotted the river. She crossed over a path, heedless of two older runners, passing closely and aggressively enough to trigger one of their proximity alarms. She only got hit with a tingling sensation.

Stupid! That was careless. Any closer and she could have been done, right there, knocked cold by a random pedestrian. But she had neither time nor energy to chastise herself more.

The Leader stopped chasing her, but she didn't look back. She dove into the river. The water was icy cold, but nothing her GEaRS couldn't stave off. The current was fast and it was extremely difficult to swim with one arm, but she wasn't planning on swimming. She floated down the river, nothing more than a strange eddy, an odd depression on the surface.

...

He watched her dive in from the top of the hill. Or watched what he saw of her anyway, the edges of red coming around her sides and the shifting, bending light of her dermal cloak trying to keep up with her speed.

Not leaning, not swaying or giving the slightest impression of a man creating a pool of blood at his feet, the Leader stood and looked out for several moments at the river, at the park. He was visible, but somehow people didn't really notice his presence, bloody chest and leg or not. Such an imposing and well-known figure in the Spire, he elicited acknowledgement from everyone, but here he was no one.

He took his time getting back to Mark's body, dragging his useless leg behind him and grabbing at trees for help along the way. Snapping a thick branch from a tree, he created a makeshift crutch, but it wasn't a great help, the ground not yet frozen for the coming winter.

Not sure if he would find anything useful when he finally arrived at the scene, he just observed without touching anything for a while. He thought about what worked and what didn't. It wasn't at all what he had predicted; his understanding of Eve was wrong. He need not have feared her knowledge of him; it was her knowledge of his weapons that made her impossible to kill or capture. The dog was effectively no surprise at all… she was as intimately familiar with Meghan on sight as she was with her own body and mind.

The bleeding continued and Leader 127 was beginning to feel weakness despite his GEaRS. But he wasn't done here. He saw the blood trail—not his own—and followed it to Meghan. The dog was dead, entrails spilled out from beneath its body. He looked over Meghan affectionately and felt a deep and genuine sadness. The animal had pulled itself along the ground with its front legs for several meters in a clear attempt to follow the Leader. He wished this were just a children's game, training, practice… but it wasn't.

Enough.

"Jacobs. I need a pick up."

"Sir. Also, I'll alert medical," with some concern, "You really should stay connected when you are afield, sir."

"Noted."

SPIRE

Mark One

Twenty-Five

Mark sat at his Desk. By all accounts, it was an average Desk. It had the typical surface interface, a comfortable but unremarkable chair, and it output to a seemingly generic Wall. He sat and silently worked the controls of this Desk.

Mark's skin was fair and freckled, and his short-cropped hair was reddish brown, which was somewhat exotic considering it was naturally colored that way. There was a soft downward curve drawn by his eyes and cheeks that made him not only attractive, but also, approachable. Regardless of his striking looks, he could easily blend into a crowd and disappear, but anyone paying attention—anyone else that was in the crowd, but not part of the crowd—could see that the population treated him differently. People would intuitively respond to his confidence and give him the berth of a man twice his size. Others would stop and look at him for just a moment too long; perhaps unconsciously registering his strength, or recognizing something familiar in him. But then he would slip by, out of sight, and the world would get back on track.

He didn't spend much time in public.

The green of Mark's eyes was highlighted by the light of the Wall and clearly held no additional lenses or enhancements. He wore a shirt and pants typical of a university student's, although he had never attended school. The poem on the shirt was not unusual, but it wasn't common either:

The cycle began as a lady bug came crawling over one shoulder, then flew down to his chest where it tore a hole into the shirt and disappeared into it. From the tattered hole a vine sprouted and grew out, then it branched and branched again. Each branch wound round his torso and connected back onto itself. Then the vines tightened, tighter and tighter for a couple of seconds, before beginning to pulse. The vines throbbed randomly at first, but eventually mimicked a heartbeat. Petals sprouted from several places all over the vines all around the shirt. When they unrolled, they revealed baby ladybugs of vibrant colors. Each baby insect moved slowly at first, waking up. After a few seconds though, they began eating the petals that gave birth to them. They grew as they ate and eventually began eating the vine itself, which led them to each other. Some made love when they met, others violently attacked each other. Eventually, there was one large ladybug left alone on the back of the shirt. It crawled up and over his other shoulder and the cycle began again.

If Mark had attended a university and spent an average amount of time obtaining a degree, he would have graduated from college more than two decades ago. In truth though, he'd never even considered a formal education beyond high school, which he'd barely completed as it was. The academic life wasn't his style. Mark was an artist.

GEaRS were so much more than technological feats to him and they were his art. He studied nature, uncovered its secrets. He studied the human body, unlocked its potential. Each day, human beings as his canvas, he painted. His world was the realization of magic and fantasy, the manifestation of his imagination.

Mark worked the controls of his Desk with one hand while sipping his espresso with his opposite. The beans, well, he roasted them himself. It was his ceremony. A slow cultivation of beans, roasting them dark and darker, he did it all himself in small batches. He ground the beans per cup, adjusting the grind for ambient humidity. A test pull. Check the crema. Sniff the shot glass. Sip. Not quite right. Adjust the grind. *Tamp tamp.* Another pull. *Ahhhh. Perfect.* It was the only activity that he ever gave his full attention, undivided. Mark made an unfucking-believable shot of espresso.

The apartment was a typical studio. There wasn't much space, but it suited Mark's well enough. The Desk was the primary focus, the kitchenette was empty save for the heavy antique espresso machine, and the bed was tucked neatly away. The bathroom was a typical multipurpose single stall that provided for all of the necessary personal hygiene rituals.

All in all, if a person walked into this apartment and never read the writing on the Wall, never watched what Mark was actually doing, that person would not think twice about the resident. That person would fail to notice the multiple overlaid threads of data. There were numerous streams playing on top of each other displaying an overwhelming and seemingly incoherent amount of information on the Wall continuously. But that was Mark One. The original Mark. He digested the data easily, and could have taken even more.

His organization of Marks worked all over the Unified Republic of Earth and he kept live, uninterrupted connections running with all of them. In many ways, he had defeated the ancient adage about being in more than one place at one time. If he had ever thought to think about it, he might consider himself omnipresent. Certainly, some of his clients over the years had considered him omniscient or even omnipotent, but he had dismissed those remarks immediately as wholly inaccurate. He saw too much to ever believe such ridiculous observations. Omnipresent though? He was close. But because no one had ever said it to him—or anything similar—he had never contemplated it, dismissed it, or affirmed it. He was the only person on the planet capable of judging such a claim, so until someone brought it up, the world will never know.

He had been careful to always protect his Marks. He was aware that powerful people would want to pressure one, to control one, to hurt one. So, in an effort to prevent such things, he'd employed many defensive tactics. Rumors of deadly consequences were effective, but even more than that, impartially and objectively helping everyone— no matter their factional associations—created a balance that few wanted to upset. It was a great threat deterrent to be valuable to all powerful people, to treat them all equally. He was neutral territory. Mark was sanctuary.

But today, the world had changed. A Mark was dead. It was his fault. He could have stopped the progression of the Apple experiment, but instead, he'd catalyzed it. When other forces had tried to stop it, he'd continued. He wasn't entirely sure why he had pushed. The Collective was pushing, so that had certainly been a factor. Curiosity too, had contributed. Mark had seen the development of the Compound and its early effects. What was it? How did it work? As a man who had devoted his life to improving, augmenting, and adapting the human form, how could he resist this new inexplicable force?

Somewhere in the midst of all of his work, all of his behind-the-scenes efforts, he had lost his focus. The individuals he augmented had grown numb to their increased sensitivities and abilities and Mark struggled to give them even more, to have an impact. People came to expect the advantages to be handed to them, and used the advantages for trivial tasks. He removed the physical roadblocks and limitations of the body, believing that the soul would grow, but people stopped challenging themselves and their capacity for understanding withered. Instead of growing the understanding of the human condition for everyone, he had diminished it for most. Mark had painted his subjects into complacence.

There were still people in the world that sought beauty, but they were fewer and fewer. Though, Mark was not alone. He was a designer and observer, but he was not the sole distributer and creator of GEaRS. Someone had been working on something spectacular and new, but it was still unrefined and random. The Compound was some kind of chemical key that unlocked a latent potential in some individuals, and Mark believed it could be perfected. He had put the world to sleep with his work, maybe with the Compound he could wake them up?

So Mark had put money into the right hands and pressure on the right minds. He'd watched the Collective carefully to stay ahead of them and to learn from them, but there were dark places in that tower that even he could not see into. But their motivations were clear by their actions, overtly turning from passing interest into the lust of necessity. There was a threat in the Collective's persistence to understand the Compound, to yoke its strength. It was a threat that Mark had misjudged. Now, one of his own was dead. Mark was dead.

He finished his espresso.

He purchased a ticket.

He sent the signal.

Mark wasn't sure what would happen next, but he knew he was done observing. He was ready to participate directly and he needed some help to do that. He knew just the man for the job.

SPIRE

Disconnected

Twenty-Six

Sara was standing with her chest slightly lifted, leaning into Joshua, but not touching him when the explosion shook the building. Startled, she fell into his body. He barely budged. Rigidly staring through the door, through the wall, he seemed to be watching a movie only he could see. She pushed herself away from him, both hands into his chest, but again he did not seem to notice. Surprised, she stared at him, trying to see into his thoughts...

I saw the man. Out in the alley, just around the corner from us, he was tangled up with several Collective. His movements, like his whips, were precise, fast, and deadly. He disarmed a woman. Severed at the elbow, her stump sprayed blood into the air and as the hand fell with the rifle it continued to squeeze the trigger, aiming at nothing. As she fell to her knees, Ezechial slid into the shadows and disappeared from view entirely.

He also faded from my memory. Whenever I tried to look for him, I found I couldn't remember where he was the last time that I saw him, or even which way he was facing. Attempting to place him, I saw him everywhere. I had momentary impression of knowing exactly where he was—*right next to that garbage can*—but then that image was replaced with an equally strong sense of him being near the light post.

Then out of a darkly shaded area, his whips lashed out like long demonic tongues. They flicked out, one after the other, opening up the backs of two C.O.'s necks. Each officer slumped to the ground in turn, alive but unable to move. Ezechial faded back into the darkness. It was like the shadow was cast over him like everything else, but as the light left his body, even more details disappeared until he was indistinguishable from the background.

The throbbing sound of propellers beating the air was calling out the location of the mini-copter. It swooped in and out of the alley from the sides and from above, trying to find Ezechial. But Ezechial found it first. He was up on a fire escape, three flights up, when the mini-copter made a low pass of the alley.

It was moving slowly, kicking up dust and debris as it went. A bright xenon spotlight was shining from its tail, swinging into any potential hiding spot in the stacks of recycling canisters, the delivery crates, and the industrial waste bins. The pilot was blind to the threat from above.

He dropped. Free-falling, he dove down the side of the building. Then he began flashing his legs up and down to match the speed of his fall, running down without pushing himself away from the wall. He deflected himself in a slight arc along the wall, defying gravity, and launched himself toward the copter.

The Devil's Tails lashed out from him in mid-flight. The ends looped around the pilot's neck and hands, and Ezechial pulled hard. The result was a rapid swap. The pilot was yanked from the open side of the copter and Ezechial was thrust up and through the tiny cockpit. On his way through, Ezechial ripped at the control stick and as he exited out the other side, his whips followed him like contrails.

The pilot was limp, already dead as he fell, and Ezechiel faded out before he landed. I lost him.

The mini-copter spun wildly out of control and the torque of the engine sheared its own tail off in seconds. The tail, propeller still spinning, flew off wildly, along with other pieces of the vehicle, as they broke apart under the centrifugal force. The main mass was flung haphazardly into the building across from where Ezechial might have landed, or…

The building I'm in?

I could feel the impact like a small earthquake, but I couldn't stop watching. The Collective Officers scattered. I could hear them talking to their headquarters, asking for help, calling for reinforcements. They were scared. *Why can't we see him?* They had faith in their instruments, but nothing was helping them find the man who was dismantling them.

They didn't understand that Ezechial wasn't trying to fool their radar and clock-detection, he was fooling them. If they saw his outline in sonar, they looked over it, missed it. It didn't matter what spectrum of analysis they used because he was that thing, right in front of them; the harder they looked the more they could not see him.

Ouch. My face was stinging, the skin of my cheek humming as though I'd been slapped.

A flash of light followed by a wash of black, I winced at the pain and saw nothing. I held one hand to my cheek and the other up in front of my face to defend myself…

"Joshua! Wake the fuck up! We gotta go!" Sara prepared to punch him again. At least he was moving.

Gradually opening one eye, Joshua looked out at Sara. It took a second but eventually he recognized her. Then he slowly lowered his guard and faced her, "Why did you hit me?"

"We have to go," she opened the door, "That was our distraction. Ezechial said we should make a run for it when we hear the explosion. I'm pretty sure now is the time." She stared out at the alley, smelled burning things she could not identify, and looked back over her shoulder at Joshua, "I'm leaving."

Joshua came up next to her quickly, not wanting to be left behind, but not really sure where they should be going. He felt like he was moving in thick liquid and his breathing was labored.

Looking back at him, she seemed pleased he'd decided to step up behind her. She took a deep breath and bolted. He was slow to react, but he followed after closely enough. He heard the door close and lock automatically behind him as he ran after Sara.

They ran in the opposite direction of the flames and smoke. Joshua stole a quick glance at the wreckage of the mini-copter as they exited the alley. He had seen it all happen but it was hard to put it all together. There was a different light out here. It was more vibrant than he remembered and the edges of objects were sharper than when he saw them before. It might have been a different scene entirely, but he knew instinctively that it was the same. Now it was tangible.

Joshua ran hard to catch up with Sara even though she lagged at points to give him a chance. They only ran about five blocks at that pace before slowing down to a brisk walk. Collective cars and cycles passed them, their sirens and lights in full effect, but the pair carried on as casually as possible.

"We're almost there," she spoke out of the side of her mouth, eyes still fixed ahead of her. She dodged a woman who was clearly watching something on her internal HUD, smiling and laughing about it. Sara just rolled her eyes and continued, "What are you going to do if I can't get ahold of Mark?"

His breath was still coming in harsh breaks after the run, "I really, really have to exercise more," then he reached out to Sara, touched her arm to get her to stop, "Wait, what do you mean? What am I going to do?"

"I mean, I still plan on swapping my Creds and cutting free of this whole mess, even if you can't," she flushed, but Joshua wasn't sure if it was embarrassment, shame, or just the run in the cold. "Mark might be able to help you out, but Ezechial made it sound like new Creds wouldn't help you." She started walking again, "I'm taking the first Javelin out of here."

Joshua started after her again, "Well, you'll try Mark again when we get to your Exit, right?" He felt like there really was nothing for him to do. There was something new inside of him, aching to get out, but also tired. It was like coming down. The fascination had faded and left behind haunting impressions, but no tangible way to return to them. "Your petals are gone," looking at her with disappointment plain on his face.

"What?" the look was one of annoyance, "You've been staring at me all day like you're in love with me. While I admit that this whole thing began with an agenda to get you into bed, I'm certainly not in love with you."

She nodded toward the other side of the street, "There it is." Sara was indicating a post office building and as she noticed there was still time to cross, she ran over to the crosswalk. He followed her over and both of them stopped short of the entrance.

"I'll try Mark again," it was a perfunctory statement, "*After* I've swapped Creds inside, "It shouldn't take long." She refused to make eye contact with him, looking at people on the street, cars driving by, anything and anyone save Joshua.

"You don't have to feel guilty," he was genuinely absolving her, "I'm starting to understand... well, I'm starting to get it." He reached out with one hand, placed it on her shoulder. Her eyes, her brilliant lavender eyes focused on his. "I can *feel* you. For a while, I had the inside line to your soul... something like that anyway. It was all real and true, you know? But sometimes what you feel and what you want aren't the same."

He felt his heartbeat hasten, and his breath quicken. It was happening again. The taste of her sensuous lips on his tongue and on his fingertips was pure velvet. The world around her faded and became lilac and lavender again. But he caught himself. He shut his eyes. He shook his head. He broke off the connection with her.

"It's like I have all of this extra emotional... I don't know," Joshua shuffled uncomfortably.

Sara looked down then back to him, "You have something, something new. Something I've never seen before. GEaRS, maybe? Some newly architected chemical power? I'm *sure* I don't understand it."

269

She took a deep breath and absorbed the crisp autumn coolness of it. The sunlight was just beginning to wan. It felt way too early for sunset, the way it always does this time of year.

"I don't understand it, but I like you," she touched his cheek where she punched him earlier, he looked up at her, his eyes wholly human albeit a little wet. "And… you're right, I did feel caught up in this and in you, under your spell," smiling honestly, "But I'm fully awake now, and I don't want this. I want my small anonymous life back."

He felt a warmth growing inside of him, an earnest awareness of all of the crazy emotions that had been coursing through him around the idea of "Sara." A new enthusiasm rushed into him, it felt good to be so alive, so plugged in. He felt himself stretching out again, but calmed himself enough to say, "I know… Goodbye, Sara."

It was a little abrupt for her, but it felt right. She had that *close* feeling again with Joshua. His eyes were filling up with blue, but not full-on eerie the way she was used to seeing them. Standing here in the street, looking into those bright blue oceans of light and confidence, she felt lucky and special.

Pulling her hand away from his face, "I'll… I'll still try…"

Cutting her off gently, "No. It's okay. Mark might be able to help me disappear, but I think I want to be here." He looked down at his hands and rubbed his thumbs into his palms, savoring the feeling.

"Go on," he nodded toward the Post Office entrance, "Change your life." The sarcasm was more playful than anything else, but he wasn't able to fully mask his disappointment. She was going to keep running.

Her face shrugged. Cheeks, lips, eyebrows, and eyes went up for a brief moment. She tilted her head slightly, then straightened up and relaxed her face. The expression was apologizing for her choice, but only half-heartedly. It was also knowing and accepting, *This is who I am.* Sara wasn't ready for a real change. She was still escaping a past Joshua could only imagine.

Without any more words, she turned and walked inside. From where he stood on the other side of the glass doors, he could see her working a kiosk, gaining access to her lock box. She disappeared for a while. He knew she was getting her Creds installed, probably using some kind of surgical device in a bathroom or somewhere private, but he was still nervous while she was out of sight.

Suddenly, surprising Joshua, a Collective vehicle pulled up and projected two whining, dying notes into the air. He tucked his head and shuffled along down the street. It was easy for him to join the flow of people, to match their speed and blend in.

He moved away from the building, but listened closely. The Officers opened their doors and stepped out heavily, boots and armor distinctive against the sounds of the street. But they moved slowly and not toward him. He tried to concentrate, to reach out and see from above, but he couldn't. There was nothing to do but turn around if he wanted to see what was happening. Even if Sara was done, she might need a distraction to avoid the Officers. New Credentials were good for starting over, but they weren't a cloak of invisibility. They could still recognize her, straight up.

Shifting quickly and smoothly, he switched lanes and started back. The foot traffic split and spread a bit to allow the Officers to pass through unimpeded, so Joshua could see them easily as they entered the post office.

Shit. It was stupid to let her enter a government building, of course they had her current Creds flagged.

Walking up to the glass wall beside the doors he peered in at the risk of being seen. The window was alive with flowing text and pictures, but the advertising was done tactfully, allowing people to look through without difficulty.

The Officers were talking to a manager of some kind. One of them was staring straight ahead, focused on something unseen, probably reviewing the stream of the security cameras. The other maintained a conversation with the manager while watching the patrons closely. Then the conversation ended abruptly and the Officers moved together to a hallway of lock boxes, the row that Sara had disappeared down.

Joshua felt time slowing as he watched them wait. They were careful to watch the exit periodically, and took turns watching all the rows of boxes that emptied out into the main lobby, which was open save for all of the people coming and going. There were few people standing around and never for very long, so the Officers stood out strongly. It occurred to Joshua that he probably looked strange, standing still for so long, peering through the glass.

He started moving, started walking, tried to think. Officers were trained to notice exactly the behavior he was exhibiting; he was sure to draw their attention. He'd purchased drugs practically in front of the Collective and kept his cool better than he was now. Circling back, he thought maybe if he just went in that he would send off another alert and pull the C.O.s off Sara.

Stopping next to the post office entrance again, he looked in and saw nothing had changed. Then he held up his left hand and looked at his wrist, his Credentials. He began breathing hard, his heart thudding against his chest in slow powerful beats. His veins swelled as he grabbed his left wrist with his right hand and squeezed.

Staring into the sub-dermal capsule, the world faded away and he saw only the micro-placement burs and the identifying proteins suspended in gel. It was a signature—unique and unmistakable—and it was a key. Scans would accept that key and gain access to his profile. Depending on the security level of the accessor, he or she could see pictures and hear music or find out how many days he attended classes in high school, or see how much debt he'd accrued. The information was out there, and the tiny capsule with microscopic strands of proteins all lined up and configured was the key to getting at it. As long as it stayed inside him, all that data was tied to him; he was on the grid.

He squeezed harder, stared deeper, and his skin began to prick and itch. The world, the people, the post office, and the cars, faded even further into the background. The area of skin around the capsule heated up, and the itching and pricking grew more intense. He felt himself snarling at it, wanting to bite it out of his wrist. Then the heat turned into burning and a sharp spike of pain shot up his arm to his shoulder. Squeezing even harder, he saw jagged blue electric branches arc from inside the capsule out to the small beads of sweat forming on the surface of his skin. He could smell the burning silicon, skin, and hair and he deeply inhaled it.

It was like smelling salts. Joshua came to, holding his wrist realizing that several people were staring at him coldly, and suspiciously. Pedestrians passing by activated any germ neutralization fields if they had them or covered their mouths and noses, stepping aside if they didn't.

He swallowed hard and relaxed his grip on his wrist. The Credits were not visible anymore, hidden beneath blackened, singed skin. Running his finger along the wound, it felt numb and leathery.

Then he felt the eyes on him. He turned and looked into the lobby and noticed that both Officers were staring back out at him. They looked like two hollow shells of armor, hardened and emotionless. Their uniforms were black and their eyes glowed dull yellow. Joshua saw their whisper trails as he had before with the other Officers; they weren't altogether *here*, divided between their bodies and somewhere else.

Trying to act like he just hurt himself, he massaged his forearm and started walking again. He pushed his hands deeply into his pockets and pinned his arms against his sides trying to hide his blackening veins. *Why am I trying to control this or hide this?*

Joshua was confused. Where was the euphoria and power that accompanied all of these feelings before? Why was he scared of a couple of husks with guns? They couldn't stop him.

He stopped and grinned, feeling the energy course through his veins. People began giving him a wide berth, but he didn't notice or even really see them at all. They were hollow—bodies that neglected their imaginations and contentedly allowed their souls to wither and die. They were inconsequential. They were in his way.

The cool air of winter twilight began to gather around him. It pulled the heat from the skin of his arms and neck and face. It gathered speed, spinning and whirling around him. The breeze pushed under his shirt and swirled around his back. Where it touched the skin around his spine, it began a slow shiver that eventually shook his whole body. He closed his eyes, lost to the feeling of the wind dancing with him. He borrowed the vigor of the brisk air, and allowed the energy of the accelerating wind to penetrate him. An enormous inhale.

A gigantic exhale.

Joshua opened his eyes and saw a liquid world. The wind swirled around him, eddies and whirlpools forming at his fingertips. He tilted his head back, opened his mouth, and held his chest open, his shoulders wide and back. Making a sudden and tight turn toward the post office, he sent ripples from his body and the world moved. It wasn't much, but it was feedback, and Joshua was in the loop. He scooped handfuls, armfuls of the cool air forward with feral arm swings.

The tunnel of ripples that formed first pushed vehicles, and then people, away from the center of it. Then, in the wake of the wave, bodies and cars were pulled back in powerfully. Cars crashed into each other in the street. The people who were still standing ran. There might have been screams but Joshua could not hear them.

The Collective vehicle was spun around, more by the car that ran into it than by the tunnel of force released by Joshua. Nevertheless, the disturbance was enough to get the Officers out of the building. They tumbled out aggressively, training and instinct kicking in.

They saw Joshua and raised alarms and weapons against him. Every movement was thick and slow in Joshua's mind. It would be easy for him to take them apart because there was nothing holding them together. There was no fabric. Their souls were threadbare, thin and wasted.

He swept his arms back, narrowed his gaze to focus on his targets, and lowered his head. Joshua was ready to attack them, to remove them, when he smelled her.

Lavender and Lilac.

She came out of the building in a rush and one of the Officers barked a command to her. Obeying, she covered her head and got down on the ground. But she passed Joshua a look before kissing the pavement.

He had time to look at it all, to understand it, even to reflect on it. There was a better way to ensure her escape. There was a better way for him to handle all of this.

Joshua slowly fell to his knees and wove his fingers together behind his head. He felt the moment closing, the pocket of his awareness collapsing. Then, with sudden speed, the world snapped back to full speed, open and airy.

The Officers moved forward. One stood before him, assault rifle at the ready, aimed at his head. The other Officer roughly pulled Joshua's hands behind his back and held them together for a moment before slapping a long piece of thin, stiff plastic against his wrists. The plastic snapped, bending against his wrists, and wrapping itself around them. It tightened up quickly and secured his hands. That Officer then stood Joshua up and patted him down.

Joshua was silent. He watched Sara stand. She was careful, moving slowly but not suspiciously. She affected some concern for her health—for her safety—but again, nothing too dramatic. As the Officer tried to scan Joshua's Creds and realized he couldn't, Joshua smiled. There was some humor in it, watching the Officer try several times to read his wrist, but that wasn't what made him smile. He smiled because Sara gave him a meaningful look of gratitude before she turned and walked the other way.

Her hair was white now, and the eyes, tangerine. Sara wasn't Lily anymore. She wore a warm-looking, long furry jacket. It was dark blue with a low collar at the top and skirt-like flare at the hips. She fingered her Glass as she walked away, deeply absorbed in whatever its contents.

The Officers escorted him over to their car and realized that the damage was too significant to drive it. Backup was already on the way, as were ambulance services. The drivers of the vehicles that collided appeared fine and were busily and loudly discussing the circumstances of the accident.

Joshua took a deep breath and felt an overwhelming sense of humanity flowing through him. These people weren't soulless, after all. They were just people trying to make sense of things. Maybe their perspectives were all fucked up, but they were trying to live their lives.

He watched Sara as she rounded the corner and disappeared, and then he stepped into his new world. His clothes fell to the ground along with the suspect-band. The Officer who held Joshua's arm suddenly held nothing at all and awkwardly closed his hand, trying desperately to make sense of the body that wasn't there. They looked around feverishly, pointing rifles, whispering to each other and to their Watchers, but they saw nothing.

Joshua stood naked in the shadows growing long across the street. His eyes were blue, swirling liquid marbles with deep black cracks for pupils, his veins thick and dark. There was a smile on his lips, serene and beautiful as he watched the Officers look for him.

This moment, this precious moment, was his. Tears welled up in his eyes, filling up until the tension was shimmering and shaking and threatening to burst. He closed his lids and a single drop began down each cheek. He was overwhelmed with so many new and inexplicable feelings. It was wonderful and frightening. He couldn't say that he really understood it, or that he even wanted to understand it right now, but he felt it was real, like he could change the world. He believed it.

The First Angel

Twenty-Seven

His view from the Wall of the Spire was dark. He had failed. He had not recovered Eve or Joshua. He had no new information about the Apple project. He was uncomfortable in his defeat.

His ankle had been sewn up fastidiously and multiple pain-reducing chems had been administered. Coupled with his own medicinal spikes and hormone regulation systems, his body's complaints were subdued. The ankle-assist wrapped around his right foot and calf allowed him a close semblance of normal mobility. Bioclamps held his connective tissue together, nourishing and rebuilding the structures as they dissolved. The Leader had actually run over a mile on that ankle. Reviewing the damage now, it was hard to believe, even for him; that his ankle was limply dangling off his leg when he came in.

The lights in his office were dimmed to almost nothing. He did not sit behind his Desk, but rather, he stood looking out over the ocean. It looked so cold out there tonight, cold and vacant. It seemed to the Leader that there were fewer ships, less movement, less life than his previous viewings. Maybe the truth was that he had not looked in a long time, not really *looked* anyway.

He was lost. When he returned to the Spire, he had reviewed his team's positions, and all of the accumulated data; there was nothing he could use. Eve was alive, but somehow continued to avoid detection. The Watchers had found nothing of her, which was impossible unless SENTRy's recognition system had been defeated. He had redirected several of the Watchers to discovering what was wrong with the system, but so far they had uncovered no explanation. The rest of the Watchers had set about a search for Joshua. With the system obviously compromised, though, the Leader had little faith they would uncover anything. Well, except for the open confrontation earlier that day. That was clearly Joshua, even if SENTRy disagreed.

Several Collective Officers were dead or severely injured. Joshua had apparently survived, and more than that... he was projecting images and energy in ways unlike anything the Leader had ever seen, in person or otherwise. It was an unsettling display of raw power and the Leader analyzed the stream thoroughly. There were weaknesses though. Joshua could be brought under control.

There were other items of interest, too, like, *what the hell was a Laterali doing in the mix?* He had reviewed the streams many times and could say very little about it. The man with the Devil's Tails had taken out more than a dozen of his men and received, as far as the Leader could tell, not a scratch. He had notified the Laterali that one of their brethren had gone off the deep end. The Leader wasn't worried about retaliating against the Shadow, which he could do with impunity, but so far they hadn't even touched the bastard. Although there was no provision for it, he hoped to put some pressure on the Laterali to have them to take care of it.

The most recent administrations of the Compound had turned up nothing. Several candidates were brought in, but nothing new or promising resulted. The Leader approved the next round of testing without hesitation. The Collective's scientists had made some adjustments to their method of choosing, based on Joshua's survival. Maybe they didn't have Joshua but they owned most of his life, through streams and medical records.

So really, the Leader had nothing. That was how he concluded his report. Since his submission, he'd been standing at the Wall, watching the light fall. He'd had minor setbacks before—even called those setbacks *failures*, he wasn't one to candy-coat it—but there had always been a way to come back, to snatch a final victory from his adversaries.

He shook the feeling of defeat from his body, stepped forward and slid his finger down the Wall. The image faded away quickly and the ambient lights came up slightly to compensate for the loss. The Leader needed rest. He was seeing his future through a weak lens and he knew it. The weight of Eve's defection was more than he had expected. And he thought maybe he *had* pulled punches if he was honest with himself. All of these uncharacteristic feelings and outcomes… he would sleep and tomorrow, he would put everything back in its right place.

Stepping to his inner-chamber door, he slid his finger along the side and it opened for him. It was a hushed movement, familiar and welcome. Going from a darkened office to an even darker bedroom, at first he saw nothing out of the ordinary. As he walked through the doorway though, the light-level automatically followed him— the room adjusting to his setting from the office—and as the door hushed closed behind him, he saw that the Wakazashi was absent from the center table.

The Leader's heart pounded in his huge chest. He activated all of his combat systems, felt the rush as several GEaRS were activated in sequence. Warmth flowed through his body as his muscles were made ready for action. He gained a nuanced, integrated understanding of his body's capabilities and strengths. The feeling was animalistic, a low growl vibrating his bones, tightening his skin, heightening his awareness. His pupils grew wide and he blinked to his low-light vision augmentation. The IOL flipped to a crystalline, light-gathering material, which made his huge pupils glow golden in the darkness. Activating his entire sensory array, he surveyed the room.

But there was darkness there and nothing more.

The door to his bathroom suddenly slid open and the Leader recoiled, poised to strike. He identified the Secretary and had to catch himself mid-lunge to prevent striking him. As it was, it took him a moment to compose himself because he was so hot with anticipation and augmentation.

Deliah, seemingly oblivious, "Oh, you're here?" He walked into the room, hands clasped behind his back; inspection mode again.

"Full bright," the Leader spoke clearly into the empty space of the room and the lights came up quickly. His eyes adjusted automatically to prevent over-exposure and harm to his retinas. Stepping down some of his more aggressive combat measures, he reduced his adrenaline and serotonin levels. An insane rage was sometimes valuable in battle, but probably would not serve him bandying words with the Secretary.

"Oh, I rather liked the moody lighting. It suited your sulking." Deliah's smooth, thick voice would have served a therapist well. It was confident and soothing, or would have been if it wasn't coming from a man who had stolen into the Leader's inner-chamber undetected. He must have been in here for hours while the Leader was working.

"What do you want, Deliah?" the Leader saw no reason to hide his ire toward the intrusion, or distaste for the man.

"Deliah, is it? Not Secretary? Pretty presumptuous. I assure you, this is not a social call," his eyebrows were somewhat hidden against his chocolate skin, but they were obviously raised in affected surprise and disappointment.

"In my private chambers, you are nothing to me," aggressively closing the distance between them, "*What do you want?!*" The Leader did not raise his voice, but the words were laced with venom to compensate for the lack of volume.

"Your soul," plainly.

Exhausted from the day, the Leader did not see fit to play games with this errand-runner for the Upper Spire, "You were not sent here to kill me, Deliah. You might be an assassin, but the politics involved in removing a Leader? Far too complex for even a well-trained dog like you." Then, growling, "I have to assume you are here on your own foolish behalf, or that this is a pathetic attempt at a threat from the Upper Spire to *manage* me! Neither of which do I have much care for!"

Standing chest to chest, but not touching, the Leader was twice the size of the Secretary. It seemed clear who was threatening whom. The Leader stared down into the amber-eyed Deliah and waited for the gravity of his anger to pull the intruder down off his high horse. Satisfied, he pressed on, "Now, let's have the truth of it, Deliah... or you can get out. Either way, that sword isn't yours, and you should put it back."

Deliah smiled, his lips peeling slowly back away from his teeth, gradually revealing long upper and lower fangs. His amber eyes were intensely shimmering; smiling and laughing. As his jaws parted, his fangs seemed to grow and swell, becoming glassy and shiny from his hunger-watered mouth. Then, with his insidious grin fully in effect, Deliah's skin darkened until it was as black as obsidian.

The Leader was fascinated, mesmerized, and uncharacteristically slow to react as Deliah's hands flashed from behind his back. The Wakazashi in his left hand, he thrust it and twisted it hilt-first into the Leader's stomach. In the same moment, he struck with his right hand, palm first into the Leader's sternum. The head of the hilt pushed all the way through to the Leader's spine before the force of both strikes threw his body across the room.

The Leader's back hit the wall then his head snapped back with a nerve-tingling, hollow thud. His legs were limp and lifeless as he slouched to the floor. Chest caved-in and aching for air, he finally took a gasping breath. Deliah's jet-black skin seemed to ripple as he walked across the room. Heat gradients rolled up and trailed from his body in whisps. He stopped a few feet short of the Leader, crumpled against the wall.

His IOD was lighting up with red flashes, demanding attention. He tried to reach out, to communicate, to send signals to the room, to Jacobs, to anyone in the Spire for help, but his systems were all quiet and unresponsive. The Leader could not feel anything below his waist. He felt anger and frustration, but still no fear.

Deliah's voice was strange—alien and salival, coming through the menacing teeth. "Who do you think is there to give *me* orders?" He flipped the blade around in his hands, from one to the other, spinning it carelessly. "I *am* the Upper Spire, Adam."

Choking, gasping for air, "What? What the fuck are you talking about, you piece of shit errand boy." The last was dampened to a pathetic whisper, entirely removing the edge from the insult.

"You really don't know? I am the first survivor!" His laugh echoed eerily in the small chamber. The resonance and reverberation made no logical sense in the room that was actually designed to dampen sound.

"Huh? You've gone mad, Deliah," a kind of hysterical laughter shook the Leader.

"I was the first experiment… then I began experimenting on them." He shrugged, which looked oddly hypnotic, like a cobra expanding its hood, "I've been working my way down the Spire ever since, and I told you already, you were next on my list."

"Why would…," another choking gasp interrupted him, followed by a bloody, sputtering cough. He gathered himself by pressing his hands into the floor and pushing himself back toward the wall. His legs felt normal enough, but when he asked them to move, they silently remained motionless. "Why would we experiment on you? Your name wasn't on any list." The Leader's eyes were fiercely focused on the Secretary.

"Not as bright as everyone thought, I guess," he looked down at Adam reproachfully, "I am the reason that the project exists." Then full of pride, to himself more or less, "I'm the proof of concept."

The Leader maintained the intensity of his stare. Still no open connections. Deliah must be running some kind of interference or… it didn't matter. He was at this lunatic's whim.

"You aren't getting it are you? You think you are somehow going to survive this moment, that you are going to pay me back… for what I've done to you?" the last was nothing but venomous disbelief as though the Leader's refusal to grasp reality was hurting him personally.

Deliah folded neatly at his hips, bending down toward the broken man, heated air curling up off his back. "I really, *really* want you to try."

The Leader focused and punched. A hollow and thunderous wave rolled over the room. It shattered the table and the wooden fork that used to display his sword was thrown up into the air and carried to the far wall. He had aimed his fist for the face of the amber-eyed freak, but connected with nothing.

Eyes and head darting around the room, flicking from one corner to another, Adam tried to find the Secretary. He was holding himself steady with both hands on the floor when he felt a tremendous amount of heat on his left, as though someone had opened up a vent beside him.

He looked up to the left, and there, flat against the wall, was Deliah beaming down at him. The smiling golden irises had eaten up the whole of both of his eyes, leaving the Secretary pupil-less and almost blind-looking.

In a smooth arc, Deliah swung his arm down and drove the blade of the Wakazashi through the Leader's left shoulder up to the hilt. Adam was anchored to the wall behind him.

Not a sound or harsh breath passed the war hero's lips. There was no new pain yet. He couldn't yet feel the shoulder, but his lower back began to feel cool. At first he felt nothing from below his waist, but then a floating, slow spinning sensation began. He was trying to find out where his legs were in space by attempting to move them, but there was no feedback, and so they seemed weightless. He put both hands strongly to the ground to hold himself up, suddenly unsure of his balance, and the warmth began. It began in his left shoulder, spreading like a glass of hot water down his back. It was only a second, maybe two, then he was ejected from the fuzzy-state.

Searing pain tore through his shoulder. Adam let his left arm go totally limp, hoping for some relief. He groaned and spit. Snarling, with bloody drool running thick in his mouth and down one corner of his lips, "I'm going to *fuck* you into *oblivion*, Deliah." The words were sharp enough to cut diamonds. They were laced with absolute certainty and conviction—the kind of words that cultivate hope in allies and mortal fear in enemies. Tonight, however, in the Leader's private chambers, used against Secretary Deliah, the words only fell weakly from his lips, punctuated by an abrupt silence.

The Secretary stepped away from the wall and Adam's eyes followed him. None of his wounds were fatal... yet. The Leader was wet with sweat and blood. He sat there wondering about the truth of Deliah's claims. He quickly came to the conclusion that it didn't really matter whether or not he believed the assassin. If he was going to die, he preferred that it be to the man that took down the entire Spire alone.

Conducting his own experiments, eh? Picturing Deliah's descent from the Upper Spire, a cold prickle washed over the Leader's skin.

Standing before Adam, the Secretary turned and faced his victim again. The heat radiating from his body seemed to come in thicker and faster waves. The sickly sweat of fear and pain on the Leader's brow was mixed with plain perspiration.

"I killed them all," emotionless, "I sense your doubts and I'd like to put them to rest." Deliah paused then nodded, "You are curious about the details, but it was easier than you'd think. They isolated themselves after all. Security barriers exist at every entrance for their *protection*." He shrugged, which put an extra fold and curl in the gradients rising from his body, "Security systems that trust *me*."

The strength was leaking from Adam. If he moved at all it only sharpened the pain in his shoulder and back, and what could he do to this monster anyway? Then he noticed that the Wakazashi was getting hot. His exposed flesh and nerves were conveying the heat dully at first, but then the pain hit. It was like running his hands under hot water that quickly turned to boiling, realizing that it was too much even after removing his hands... but he couldn't pull his hands out.

"Hmmm," a satisfied, fanged grin, "I'm starting to get to you. Good." Deliah leaned in, waves of hot air following him, "Scream for me, Adam. *Scream*."

The Leader grabbed the hilt with his right hand. His palm sang with horrible pain—the hilt already hot enough to burn his skin—but he redoubled his effort instead of letting go. He pulled and gripped tighter and his hand ached with the bone-deep pain of the hot metal. He could smell the stink of his flesh cooking, both his hand and his shoulder.

The deep aching message from his body was primitive and irresistible. There was no Leader, only heat-pain and need, need to get away. His lips curled back and he gritted his teeth as he gripped the hilt with all his strength and embraced the pain of it. Pulling and leaning, the hilt came up against his clothes and melted the cloth against the skin of his chest.

He screamed. Loud and pure, it was the echoing scream of a great predator in his death throes. Dangerous, trapped, and in pain, it was the terrifying scream of an animal you did not mean to catch. You are too afraid to approach to release it, but if you leave the beast and it escapes anyway? Well, it's too frightening to consider.

The Secretary was completely satisfied and apparently not at all afraid of his prey.

He stepped forward and put his hand against Adam's chest, "Hurts like hell does it not?"

No breath left in his lungs, and no strength left in his body, the Leader slumped forward and became silent. His head hung down in the crook of his right elbow, his right hand held fast, melted to the hilt of his only possession.

The room was returning to its normal temperature as Deliah stood up and looked at his work. He was proud of the neat tableau that he'd created. For several minutes he admired his work, not moving, not even breathing.

With a long deep inhale, Deliah took it all in. He tasted the air and breathed in the smell of burning flesh, hair, and fabric. It was exactly as he had envisioned it. Perfect.

His eyes returned to simple irises, pupils within and whites without. The blackness of his skin was replaced with the previous rich cocoa. No heat radiated from him as he left the Leader's personal chamber. He looked calm and casual as ever.

Sunrise

Twenty-Eight

Eve never expected to survive. She didn't. And there was certainly no expectation of success, even though she strove for it above all else. Now she was here, alive and without a plan.

The ocean was beautiful. It broke hard against the shore in places and gently lapped at others. She could smell it though, the salt hanging on the air. And she could see the waves crashing against a wall of rocks on the shore of the island in the distance, the foamy spray exploding up and over them. But she couldn't hear any of it over the bow of the ferry crashing through the water.

Under the shadow of the Spire, the city was waking up behind her. Eve was glad to be out from under that shadow. The Spire looked different from here. It was magnificent, even awe-inspiring. She zoomed in on it and imagined she was looking at the 127th floor, wondering if the Leader was staring back out at her.

It was too bad that she had to leave him there like that, but what other choice was there? He was working for the wrong side, and she had no doubts of his conviction; she could not have told him. She'd tried the drug.

That was nine months ago.

Eve was one of the few who were completely unaffected. Well, unaffected by the Compound anyway. But trying it and failing—at least that was how she saw it then—changed the way she looked at herself. She wasn't special. She wasn't chosen. She was average.

Eve had dived in head first to determine why she'd had no reaction. She tried to discover what was different about those who died and those who became something more. The results seemed so random...

"Eve?" the voice was clear in her ear as her noise cancelling kicked in.

"Ezechial. I'm glad to hear from you. How's our boy?"

"He's getting the change under control. I think you were right about him."

She felt some satisfaction. Maybe the Compound had changed her for the better? An overwhelming sense of accomplishment and righteousness came over her. Staring into the breeze as the ferry moved over the water, she allowed the salt to sting at her eyes.

"I did a lot of damage securing them and he still showed himself outright to a couple C.O.s. I guess he was just playing with them though, because he..." There was a long pause, "... he escaped. It wasn't a trick of light or hypnosis... he simply let himself go."

"Good. So where is he now?"

"I don't know."

"Huh?" she suddenly felt worried.

"Eve, he's beyond me now. Easily beyond me. I can't track him anymore."

"The highest tier Laterali alive, and you can't find him?"

"My discipline teaches me many things, Eve. Most importantly, it reminds me that there are things outside of my control, outside of my comprehension. Joshua has ascended. In the terms of my order, he has obtained the unobtainable."

"I'm not one of your brethren, Ezechiel... what does that mean?"

"It means the war has begun. *The souls of mortals will fight for Heaven and Hell here on Earth.* He is the first…"

"But… this is happening too fast. I just want out. I'm tired! But if the war starts… well, I don't want to be a spectator for Armageddon! Fuck that!"

"You are the one who found him. You brought him out and set him free. He is able to choose his own side now. Not an insignificant role."

"Well, I know too much to sit this one out. What can we do now?"

"You tell me. You found the first, right? Help me find the second."

"But, I'm not one of you. I'm a soldier, built with GEaRS and training, not with any kind of spirituality. I'm not a priest of the shadows. And I tried Apple! Remember? I learned nothing! I'm not the one." She took a deep breath of sea air and controlled herself. "Ezechial, I can't help you."

Eve disconnected and refused further connections.

SPIRE

The Beginning

Twenty-Nine

The Javelin was pretty full. It was the right time of year for people to head to warmer climates if they were into that sort of thing. Jasper made himself comfortable in his seat, and was glad for the vacancy on his left.

The trip was short, only about twenty minutes once they were airborne. Still, he found small talk—even a small amount of small talk—to be infinitely tiresome. He sat in a business-class seat, befitting his successful entrepreneurial status, so he had extra room. Somehow, as many technological advancements that had been made in his lifetime, space was still a premium. More efficient use of space was always important; but inevitably, human beings were people-sized. There was no way around it.

Maybe he could have some people killed? No, that was his old life. As Jasper he needed to simply sit and enjoy his life, and sometimes share it with others. Again, he felt lucky that the seat beside him was vacant and he looked at it affectionately.

That was when he saw the red-haired man staring down at him from the aisle.

"May I?" he was polite. His goatee matched the hair on his head and he was an attractive fellow, except for the fact that he was asking for that seat.

"Really?" Jasper filled the two short syllables with as much contempt as they could hold.

"Thanks!" the freckled man was not to be put off—either that or he was completely oblivious. Jasper hoped it was the former and not the latter, because he could handle a hard-ass, but a mindless twit would probably run-on at the mouth irrationally for the duration of the trip.

"Excuse me, your shirt?" Jasper pointed to the animated poem playing on the gentleman's shirt, "It's somewhat distracting for me. Do you think you could turn it off for the trip? I mean, unless you'd rather sit elsewhere?" He tested the water.

The man laughed a strange laugh. It spiked and jumped irregularly, a nervous laugh maybe? Oddly familiar. He slid his finger along the neck of the shirt, which looked like a signal to cut someone's throat, and the shirt animation ceased. It was just a lady bug on the front now, without movement.

"Better?"

"Thank you," Jasper managed to leave out any sense of gratitude from the statement.

"It's the least I can do," the average looking man gave Jasper a look of total domination, "considering all that you are going to do for me, Marius."

His face went pale, "You must…," but he was unable to finish.

"Come come, Marius, no need to play around," disarmingly, "You'll be fine. Or, at least, I'm not going to hurt you."

The red-haired man ordered drinks with a few gestures on the seat panel in front of him. "We need Gabriel. He's the key."

The drinks arrived and the man handed Marius his favorite, a vodka tonic on the rocks with extra lime zest. The bright green flakes sparkled on the surface of the drink and Marius poked the ice down with his finger to make the zest fall like snow down through the liquid.

Marius took a sip and finally spoke. "Gabriel has gone mad. He took the Apple himself. Actually, I doubt he's alive."

Mark—the one and only now—took his absinthe over a cube of ice. He spun the glass around and around, watching the tendrils form and fall off the ice. "He's fine. He just hasn't accepted his lot yet. He'll need convincing."

Marius sipped his drink and was surprised at the flavor. Much better than he expected for a Javelin ride. "And that's where I come in?" Marius knew he was at the mercy of this man. Best laid escapes and all that rubbish…

"Maybe. We have to find him first," he sipped his wormwood, "And then we need to find others. When the Spires fall, well, we're going to need more Joshua's." He leaned back in his chair and closed his eyes. Absentmindedly, he reached to his collar and turned his poem back on.

Marius faced forward and wondered how he'd gotten involved, already missing the life he was about to start as Jasper, but only for a moment. The strange truth was that he was glad. Glad for the entire situation. Retirement would have been boring anyway. He wanted to be down in the dirt, digging in the dark. Opportunity was knocking and he wouldn't shy away from it.

"More? I haven't seen the boy do much that well-GEaRed C.O. couldn't do."

"You haven't seen anything, yet."

ABOUT THE AUTHOR

Aaron Safronoff was born and raised in Michigan where he wrote his first novella, *Evening Breezes*. In his early twenties, he moved to California to attend culinary school. He fell in love with the Bay Area and has never considered leaving, although he did eventually leave the school.

During his ten years in the games industry, he worked at various levels and for several disciplines including quality assurance, production, and design. All the while he was writing a novel, short stories, plays, and poetry. His career in design introduced him to amazingly intelligent, fun, and creative people, many of whom he considers family today.

Safronoff self-published, *Spire*, in 2011, and won the Science Fiction Discovery Award for the same in the summer of 2012. By the end of that year he decided to drop everything and free fall into fiction. In the following three months he completed work on the sequel to *Spire*, *Fallen Spire*, edited *Evening Breezes*, and published both.

Today, Safronoff is co-founder and Chief Storyteller of Neoglyphic Entertainment and working on his fifth novel, the second book of the *Sunborn Rising* series. In his spare time, Safronoff enjoys reading a variety of authors, Philip K. Dick, Cormac McCarthy, and Joe Abercrombie among them. He enjoys living near the ocean, playing and watching hockey, and video games. He has a deep love of music and comedy.

DON'T MISS THE CONCLUSION...

TO LEARN MORE ABOUT THE SPIRE SERIES & AARON SAFRONOFF VISIT:

www.SPIRESERIES.COM
www.AARONSAFRONOFF.COM

NEOGLYPHIC
Entertainment

Neoglyphic Entertainment believes story is the heart of the human experience. Story inspires creativity, shapes minds, and catalyzes social change. Story connects us to one another, celebrating our greatest triumphs and exposing our deepest fears, establishing a common ground to learn, to understand, to be.

Stories are shared through written word, visual art, film, music, video games and more. Neoglyphic develops technology to cultivate story across all these art forms, and reduces the traditional risk and cost associated with entertainment production. We offer a storytelling platform to connect with fans, derive meaningful insights, and deliver immersive experiences.

Whether you're an author writing your first novel, or a studio creating a feature film, Neoglyphic will be your trusted partner to untether your imagination.

www.neoglyphic.com